SOMEONE
WE KNOW

SOMEONE
WE KNOW

SHARI LAPENA

DOUBLEDAY
CANADA

Doubleday Canada and colophon are registered trademarks of
Penguin Random House Canada Limited

Library and Archives Canada Cataloguing in Publication

Title: Someone we know / Shari Lapena.
Names: Lapeña, Shari, 1960- author.
Identifiers: Canadiana (print) 20190077883 | Canadiana (ebook) 20190077891 | ISBN 9780385690829
(softcover) | ISBN 9780385690836 (EPUB)
Classification: LCC PS8623.A724 S66 2019 | DDC C813/.6—dc23

This book is a work of fiction. Names, characters, places and incidents are products of
the author's imagination or are used fictitiously. Any resemblance to actual events
or locales or persons, living or dead, is entirely coincidental.

Based on a jacket design by: Ervin Serrano
Cover images: Devon Opdendries/Getty Images; (torso)
Laura Kate Bradley/Arcangel; (head) whiteisthecolor,
(legs) fotoduets, both iStock/Getty Images

Printed and bound in the USA

Published in Canada by Doubleday Canada,
a division of Penguin Random House Canada Limited

www.penguinrandomhouse.ca

10 9 8 7 6 5 4 3 2 1

Penguin
Random House
DOUBLEDAY CANADA

To Manuel

ACKNOWLEDGMENTS

I know I wouldn't be where I am today if it weren't for the following people, to whom I owe my deepest gratitude: My publishers in the UK—Larry Finlay, Bill Scott-Kerr, Frankie Gray, Tom Hill, and the phenomenal team at Transworld UK; my publishers in the US—Brian Tart, Pamela Dorman, Jeramie Orton, Ben Petrone, and the rest of the fantastic team at Viking Penguin; and my publishers in Canada—Kristin Cochrane, Amy Black, Bhavna Chauhan, Emma Ingram, and the superb team at Doubleday Canada. Thank you all, once again, for everything. I know there's an element of luck in publishing and I feel tremendously lucky to be working with all of you! You're among the very best in the business, and the nicest, hardest-working, and most fun bunch of people to boot. Thank you, each and every one.

Helen Heller—what can I say? You've changed my life. And I enjoy and appreciate you more than I can ever express. Thank you also to everyone at the Marsh Agency for continuing to do such an excellent job representing me worldwide.

ACKNOWLEDGMENTS

Special thanks, again, to Jane Cavolina for being the best copyeditor an overly busy author could ever have.

In addition, I want to thank Mike Illes, M.Sc., of the Forensic Science Program at Trent University, for his invaluable help answering my forensic questions, which he did with speed and good humor. Thanks, Mike!

I would also like to thank Jeannette Bauroth, whose charitable donation to the Writers' Police Academy earned her name a spot in this book!

I'd like to point out that any mistakes in the manuscript are entirely mine. I don't think there are any, but you never know.

Finally, thank you to Manuel and the kids. I could not do this without you. And Poppy—you're the best cat, and the best company, day after day, that any writer could hope for.

SOMEONE
WE KNOW

PROLOGUE

FRIDAY, SEPTEMBER 29

She's standing in the kitchen, looking out the large back windows. She turns toward me—there's a swing of thick, brown hair— and I see the confusion and then the sudden fear in her wide brown eyes. She has registered the situation, the danger. Our eyes lock. She looks like a beautiful, frightened animal. But I don't care. I feel a rush of emotion—pure, uncontrolled rage; I don't feel any pity for her at all.

We're both aware of the hammer in my hand. Time seems to slow down. It must be happening quickly, but it doesn't feel that way. Her mouth opens, about to form words. But I'm not interested in what she has to say. Or maybe she was going to scream.

I lunge toward her. My arm moves fast, and the hammer connects hard with her forehead. There's a grisly sound and a shocking spurt of blood. Nothing comes out of her mouth but a gasp of air. She starts to drop even as she raises her hands up toward me, as if she's pleading for mercy. Or maybe she's reaching for the hammer. She staggers, like a bull about to go down. I bring the hammer down again, this time on the top of her head, and there's extra force this time because her head is lower. I have more momentum in my swing, and I want to finish her off. She's on her knees now, crumpling, and I can't see her face. She falls forward, face down, and lies still.

I stand above her, breathing heavily, the hammer in my hand dripping blood onto the floor.

I need to be sure she's dead, so I hit her a few more times. My arm is tired now, and my breathing labored. The hammer is covered in gore, and my clothes are streaked with blood. I reach down and turn her over. One eye is smashed. The other is still open, but there's no life in it.

MONDAY, OCTOBER 2

Aylesford, a city in New York's Hudson Valley, is a place of many charms—chief among them the historic downtown along the Hudson River and two majestic bridges that draw the eye. The Hudson Valley is renowned for its natural beauty, and across the river, an hour's drive on mostly good highways can get you deep into the Catskill Mountains, which are dotted with little towns. The Aylesford train station has ample parking and frequent trains into New York City; you can be in Manhattan in under two hours. In short, it's a congenial place to live. There are problems, of course, as there are anywhere.

Robert Pierce enters the Aylesford police station—a new, modern building of brick and glass—and approaches the front desk. The uniformed officer at the desk is typing something into a computer and glances at him, holding up a hand to indicate he'll just be a second.

What would a normal husband say? Robert clears his throat.

The officer looks up at him. "Okay, just give me a minute." He finishes entering something into the computer while Robert waits. Finally, the officer turns to him. "How can I help?" he asks.

"I'd like to report a missing person."

The officer now gives Robert his full attention. "Who's missing?"

"My wife. Amanda Pierce."

"Your name?"

"Robert Pierce."

"When was the last time you saw your wife?"

"Friday morning, when she left for work." He clears his throat again. "She was going to leave directly from the office to go away with a girlfriend for the weekend. She left work as planned, but she didn't come back home last night. Now it's Monday morning, and she's still not home."

The officer looks at him searchingly. Robert feels himself flush under the man's gaze. He knows how it looks. But he must not let that bother him. He needs to do this. He needs to report his wife missing.

"Have you tried calling her?"

Robert looks at him in disbelief. He wants to say, *Do you think I'm stupid?* But he doesn't. Instead he says, sounding frustrated, "Of course I've tried calling her. Numerous times. But her cell just goes to voice mail, and she's not calling me back. She must have turned it off."

"What about the girlfriend?"

"Well, that's why I'm worried," Robert admits. He pauses awkwardly. The officer waits for him to continue. "I called her friend, Caroline Lu, and—she says they didn't have plans this weekend. She doesn't know where Amanda is."

There's a silence, and the officer says, "I see." He looks at Robert warily, or as if he feels sorry for him. Robert doesn't like it.

"What did she take with her?" the officer asks. "A suitcase? Her passport?"

"She was packed for the weekend, yes. She had an overnight case. And her purse. I—I don't know if she took her passport." He adds,

"She said she was going to park at the station and take the train into Manhattan for a shopping weekend with Caroline. But I went through the parking lot first thing this morning, and I didn't see her car there."

"I don't mean to be insensitive," the officer says, "but . . . are you sure she's not seeing someone else? And lying to you about it?" He adds gently, "I mean, if she lied to you about going off with her friend . . . maybe she's not really missing."

Robert says, "I don't think she would do that. She would tell me. She wouldn't just leave me hanging." He knows he sounds stubborn. "I want to report her missing," he insists.

"Were there problems at home? Was your marriage okay?" the officer asks.

"It was fine."

"Any kids?"

"No."

"All right. Let me take down your particulars, and a description, and we'll see what we can do," the officer says reluctantly. "But honestly, it sounds like she left of her own accord. She'll probably turn up. People take off all the time. You'd be surprised."

Robert looks at the officer coldly. "Are you not even going to look for her?"

"Can I have your address, please?"

ONE

SATURDAY, OCTOBER 14

Olivia Sharpe sits in her kitchen drinking a cup of coffee, gazing blankly out the glass sliding doors to the backyard. It's mid-October, and the maple tree near the back fence is looking splendid in its reds and oranges and yellows. The grass is still green, but the rest of the garden has been prepared for winter; it won't be long before the first frost, she thinks. But for now, she enjoys the yellow sunlight filtering through her backyard and slanting across her spotless kitchen. Or she tries to. It's hard to enjoy anything when she is coming to a slow boil inside.

Her son, Raleigh, still isn't up. Yes, it's Saturday, and he's been in school all week, but it's two o'clock in the afternoon, and it drives her crazy that he's still asleep.

She puts down her coffee and trudges once again up the carpeted stairs to the second floor. She hesitates outside her son's bedroom door, reminds herself not to yell, and then knocks lightly and opens it. As she expected, he's sound asleep. His blanket is still over his head—he pulled it over his head the last time she came in, a half hour ago. She knows he hates it when she tells him to get up, but he doesn't do it on his own, and what is she supposed to do, let him sleep all day? On the weekends she likes to let him relax a little, but for Christ's sake, it's midafternoon.

"Raleigh, get up. It's after two o'clock." She hates the edge she hears in her voice, but she expends so much energy trying to get this boy out of bed every day, it's hard not to resent it.

He doesn't so much as twitch. She stands there looking down at him, feeling a complicated mix of love and frustration. He's a good boy. A smart but unmotivated student. Completely lovable. He's just lazy—not only will he not get out of bed on his own, but he doesn't do his homework, and he doesn't help with chores around the house without endless nagging. He tells her he hates her nagging. Well, she hates it, too. She tells him that if he did what she asked the first time, she wouldn't have to repeat herself, but he doesn't seem to get it. She puts it down to his being sixteen. Sixteen-year-old boys are murder. She hopes that by the time he's eighteen or nineteen, his prefrontal cortex will be more developed, and he will have better executive function and start being more responsible.

"Raleigh! Come on, get up." He still doesn't move, doesn't acknowledge her existence, not even with a grunt. She sees his cell phone lying faceup on his bedside table. If he won't get up, fine, she'll confiscate his cell phone. She imagines his hand flailing around, reaching for it before he even takes the covers off his head. She snatches the phone and leaves the room, slamming the door behind her. He'll be furious, but so is she.

She returns to the kitchen and puts his phone down on the counter. It pings. A text message has popped up. She has never snooped in her son's phone or computer. She doesn't know his passwords. And she completely trusts him. But this message is right there in front of her, and she looks at it.

Did you break in last night?

She freezes. What the hell does that mean?

Another ping. **Get anything good?**

Her stomach flips.

Text me when ur up

She picks up the phone and stares at it, waiting for another message, but nothing comes. She tries to open his phone, but, of course, it's password protected.

Her son was out last night. He said he'd gone to a movie. With a friend. He didn't say who.

She asks herself what she should do. Should she wait for his father to get back from the hardware store? Or should she confront her son first? She feels terribly uneasy. Is it possible Raleigh could be up to no good? She can't believe it. He's lazy, but he's not the kind of kid to get into trouble. He's never been in any trouble before. He has a good home, a comfortable life, and two parents who love him. He can't possibly . . .

If this is what it looks like, his father will be furious, too. Maybe she'd better talk to Raleigh first.

She climbs the stairs, the earlier love and frustration shoved abruptly aside by an even more complicated mix of rage and fear. She barges into his room with his phone in her fist and yanks the covers off his head. He opens his eyes blearily; he looks angry, like a wakened bear. But she's angry, too. She holds his cell phone in front of him.

"What were you up to last night, Raleigh? And don't say you were at the movies, because I'm not buying it. You'd better tell me everything before your father gets home." Her heart is pounding with anxiety. *What has he done?*

Raleigh looks up at his mom. She's standing over him with his cell phone in her hand. What the hell is she doing with his cell phone? What is she blathering on about? He's annoyed, but he's still half asleep. He doesn't wake up just like that; it's an adjustment.

"What?" he manages to say. He's pissed off at her for barging in here when he's asleep. She's always trying to wake him up. She always wants everyone on her schedule. Everyone knows his mom's a bit of a control freak. She should learn to chill. But now she looks really mad. She's glaring at him in a way he's never seen before. He suddenly wonders what time it is. He turns to look at his clock radio. It's two fifteen. Big deal. Nobody died.

"What the hell have you been up to?" she demands, holding his phone out like an accusation.

His heart seems to skip a beat, and he holds his breath. What does she know? Has she gotten into his phone? But then he remembers that she doesn't know the passcode, and he starts to breathe again.

"I just happened to be glancing at your phone when a text came in," his mom says.

Raleigh struggles to sit up, his mind going blank. Shit. What did she see?

"Have a look," she says, and tosses the phone at him.

He thumbs the phone and sees the damning texts from Mark. He sits there staring at them, wondering how to spin this. He's afraid to look his mother in the face.

"Raleigh, look at me," she says.

She always says that when she's mad. Slowly he looks up at her. He's wide awake now.

"What do those texts mean?"

"What texts?" he says stupidly, playing for time. But he knows he's busted. The texts are pretty fucking clear. How could Mark be so stupid? He looks back down at the phone again; it's easier than looking at his mother's face. **Did you break in last night? Get anything good?**

He starts to panic. His brain can't come up with anything fast enough to satisfy his mother. All he can think of is a desperate, "It's not what it looks like!"

"Oh, that's good to hear," his mom says in her most sarcastic voice. "Because it *looks* like you've been up to a bit of breaking and entering!"

He sees an opening. "It's not like that. I wasn't *stealing*."

She gives him an enraged look and says, "You'd better tell me everything, Raleigh. No bullshit."

He knows he can't get out of this by denying it. He's caught like a rat in a trap, and now all he can do is damage control. "I did sneak into somebody's house, but I wasn't *stealing*. It was more like—just looking around," he mutters.

"You actually broke into someone's house last night?" his mother says, aghast. "I can't believe this! Raleigh, what were you thinking?" She throws her hands up. "Why on earth would you even do that?"

He sits there on his bed, speechless, because he doesn't know how to explain. He does it because it's a kick, a thrill. He likes to get into other people's houses and hack into their computers. He doesn't dare tell her that. She should be glad he's not doing drugs.

"Whose house was it?" she demands now.

His mind seizes. He can't answer that. If he tells her whose house he was in last night, she'll completely lose it. He can't bear to think of what the consequences of that might be.

"I don't know," he lies.

"Well, where was it?"

"I can't remember. What difference does it make? I didn't take anything! They won't even know I was there."

His mom leans her face in toward him and says, "Oh, they'll know all right."

He looks at her in fear. "What do you mean?"

"You're going to get dressed, and then you're going to show me the house you broke into, and then you're going to knock on the door and apologize."

"I can't," he says desperately.

"You can, and you will," she says. "Whether you want to or not."

He starts to sweat. "Mom, I can't. Please don't make me."

She looks at him shrewdly. "What else aren't you telling me?" she asks.

But at that moment, he hears the front door opening and his dad whistling as he drops his keys on the table in the hall. Raleigh's heart starts to pound, and he feels slightly sick. His mother he can handle, but his dad—he can't bear to think of how his dad's going to react. He didn't anticipate this; he never thought he'd get caught. Fucking Mark.

"Get up, now," his mother commands, ripping the rest of the covers off him. "We're going to talk to your father."

As he makes his way down the stairs in his pajamas, he's sweating. When they enter the kitchen, his dad looks up in surprise. He can obviously tell from their expressions that something's up.

The whistling stops abruptly. "What's going on?" his dad asks.

"Maybe we'd better all sit down," his mother says, pulling out a chair at the kitchen table. "Raleigh has something to tell you, and you're not going to like it."

They all sit. The sound of the chairs scraping against the floor rips at Raleigh's raw nerves like nails on a chalkboard.

He has to confess. He knows that. But he doesn't have to tell them everything. He's more awake now, better able to think. "Dad, I'm really sorry, and I know it was wrong," he begins. His voice is trembling, and he thinks it's a good start. But his dad's brow has darkened already, and Raleigh's afraid. He hesitates.

"What the hell have you done, Raleigh?" his father asks.

He stares back at his dad, but the words don't come. For a moment, he feels completely paralyzed.

"He broke into somebody's house," his mother says finally.

"*What?*"

There's no mistaking the shock and fury in his father's voice. Raleigh quickly averts his eyes and looks at the floor. He says, "I didn't *break* in. I *snuck* in."

"Why the hell did you do that?" his father demands.

Raleigh shrugs his shoulders, but doesn't answer. He's still staring at the floor.

"When?"

His mother prods him with a hand on his shoulder. "Raleigh?"

He finally raises his head and looks at his dad. "Last night."

His father looks back at him, his mouth hanging open. "You mean, while we were here having friends over for dinner, and you were supposed to be at a movie, you were actually out sneaking into someone else's *house?*" His voice has grown in volume until, by the end of the sentence, his father is shouting. For a moment, there's silence. The air vibrates with tension. "Were you alone, or were you with someone else?"

"Alone," he mumbles.

"So we can't even console ourselves with the idea that someone else led you into this *completely unacceptable, criminal, behavior?*"

Raleigh wants to put his hands over his ears to block out his dad's shouting, but he knows this will only incense his dad further. He knows it looks worse that he acted alone.

"Whose house was it?"

"I don't know."

"So what happened?" His dad glances at his mom, and then back at him. "Did you get caught?"

Raleigh shakes his head, and his mom says, "No. I saw a text on his cell phone. Raleigh, show your dad the texts."

Raleigh unlocks and hands over the phone, and his dad looks at the screen in disbelief. "Jesus, Raleigh! How could you? Have you done this before?"

This is the thing about his father—he knows what questions to ask. Things his mother, rattled by shock, didn't think to ask. Raleigh *has* done it before, a few times. "Just one other time," he lies, avoiding his father's eyes.

"So you've broken into two houses."

He nods.

"Does anyone know?"

Raleigh shakes his head. "Of course not."

"*Of course not,*" his dad repeats sarcastically. His dad's sarcasm is worse than his mom's. "Your friend knows. Who's he?"

"Mark. From school."

"Anyone else?"

Raleigh shakes his head reluctantly.

"Is there any way you might get caught? Security cameras?"

Raleigh shakes his head again, and looks up at his dad. "There weren't any security cameras. I checked."

"Jesus. I can't believe you. Is that supposed to make me feel better?"

"They don't even know I was there," Raleigh says defensively. "I was really careful. I told Mom—I never took anything. I didn't do any harm."

"Then what were you doing there?" his dad asks.

"I don't know. Just looking around, I guess."

"Just looking around, I guess," his dad repeats, and it makes Raleigh feel about six years old. "What were you looking at? Ladies' underwear?"

"No!" Raleigh shouts, flushing hotly with embarrassment. He's not some kind of a pervert. He mutters, "I was mostly looking in their computers."

"Dear God," his dad shouts, *"you went into people's computers?"*

Raleigh nods miserably.

His dad slams the table and gets up. He starts pacing around the kitchen, glaring back at Raleigh. "Don't people use passwords?"

"Sometimes I can get past them," he says, his voice quavering.

"And what did you do, when you were *looking around* in people's private computers?"

"Well . . ." and it all comes out in a rush. He feels his mouth twist as he tries not to cry. "All I did was write some prank emails from—from someone's email account." And then, uncharacteristically, he bursts into tears.

TWO

O livia sizes up the situation. Paul is angrier than she's ever seen him. That makes sense. Raleigh has never done anything remotely like this before. She knows a large part of the anger is because of fear. Are they losing control of their sixteen-year-old son? Why did he do this? He wants for nothing. They've brought Raleigh up to know right from wrong. So what is going on?

She watches him, sniffling miserably in his chair, his father staring at him silently as if deciding what to do, what the appropriate punishment should be.

What, she asks herself, is the civil, decent thing to do? What will help Raleigh learn from this? What will assuage her own guilt? She wades in carefully. "I think Raleigh should go to these people and apologize."

Paul turns on her angrily. "What? You want him to *apologize*?"

For a split second she resents that he has turned his anger on her, but she lets it go. "I don't mean that's *all*. Obviously, he will have to face consequences for his behavior. Very serious consequences. At the very least he should be grounded if we can't trust him. And we should take his phone away for a while. And restrict his internet time to homework only."

Raleigh looks at her, alarmed, as if this is far too harsh a penalty. He really doesn't get it, she thinks. He doesn't understand the enormity of what he's done. She feels a chill settle around her heart. How are you supposed to teach kids anything these days, with all the bad behavior they see around them, on the news, all the time, from people in positions of authority? No one seems to behave well or have any appreciation for boundaries anymore. That's not how she was brought up. She was taught to say sorry, and to make amends.

"He can't apologize," Paul says firmly.

"Why not?" she asks.

"He broke into people's houses. He went through their computers. *He broke the law.* If he apologizes, he opens himself up to criminal charges. Do you want that?"

Her heart seizes with fear. "I don't know," she says crossly. "Maybe that's what he deserves." But it's bravado, really. She's terrified at the thought of her son facing criminal charges, and clearly her husband is, too. She realizes suddenly that they'll do anything to protect him.

Paul says, "I think we'd better talk to a lawyer. Just in case."

The next morning, Sunday, Raleigh is sound asleep when his mother comes into his room and shakes him by the shoulder.

"You're getting up, *now*," she says.

And he does. He's on his very best behavior. He wants his phone and internet access back. And he's terrified of going to the lawyer, which his dad is going to make him do. Last night at the dinner table his father was saying maybe it would be best, in the long run, if

Raleigh were to face charges and take the legal consequences. His dad wouldn't really make him do that. He thinks he was just trying to scare him. It worked. Raleigh's shitting bricks.

Once he's dressed and downstairs, his mom tells him, "We're going to get in the car, and you're going to show me the two houses you broke into."

He looks back at her, wary. "Why?"

"Because I said so," she says.

"Where's Dad?" he asks nervously.

"He's gone golfing."

They get in her car. She hasn't even let him have breakfast first. He sits in the passenger seat beside her, his stomach growling and his heart thumping. Maybe his parents talked, after he was in bed, and decided he had to apologize after all.

"Which way?" she says.

His brain freezes. He can feel himself starting to sweat. He's only going to show her a couple of the houses he's broken into to get her off his back. And he certainly won't tell her the truth about where he was last night.

He's tense as his mother reverses out of the driveway and drives down Sparrow Street. The trees are bright gold and orange and red and everything looks like it did when he was little and his parents raked leaves into a big pile on the lawn for him to jump in. At the corner, he directs her to turn left, and then left again onto Finch Street, the long residential street next to, and parallel to, their own.

His mom drives slowly along Finch until he points out a house. Number 32, a handsome two-story house painted pale gray with blue shutters and a red front door. She pulls over to the curb and parks, staring at the house as if memorizing it. It's a sunny day and it's warm in the car. Raleigh's heart is pounding harder now and sweat is forming on his forehead and between his shoulder blades. He's forgotten all about his hunger; now, he just feels sick.

"You're sure it was this house?" she asks.

He nods, shifts his eyes away from hers. She continues to stare at the house. There's a horrible moment when he thinks she's going to get out of the car, but it passes. She just sits there. He begins to feel conspicuous. What if the people come out of the house? Is that what she's waiting for?

"When did you break into this one?" she asks.

"I don't know. A while ago," he mumbles.

She turns away from him and studies the house some more.

"What are we doing here, Mom?" he asks finally.

She doesn't answer. She starts the car again and he feels himself go weak with relief.

"Where's the other one?" she asks.

He directs her to turn left again at the end of the street, and left again, until they are back on their own street.

She looks over at him. "Seriously, you broke into our neighbor's? We didn't need to take the car, did we?"

He doesn't answer. Silently, he points at Number 79, a two-story white house with a bay window in the front, black shutters, and a double garage.

Again, she pulls over and stares at the house uneasily. "Are you sure it was *this* house you broke into last night, Raleigh?"

He looks at her furtively, wondering what she's getting at. What's special about this house?

As if reading his mind, she says, "His wife ran away from him recently."

That's not my fault, Raleigh thinks sulkily, wishing that he'd shown her a different house.

His mom starts the car again and pulls out into the street. "Are you sure you didn't take anything, Raleigh? That it was just a prank?" she says, turning to look at him. "Tell me the truth."

He can see how worried she is, and he feels awful for making her feel that way. "I swear, Mom. I didn't take anything." At least that's the truth. He feels bad for what he's put his parents through, especially his mom.

Yesterday, he promised his parents he would never do it again, and he means it.

Olivia drives the short way home in silence, turning things over in her mind. The houses on these familiar streets were built decades ago. They're set far apart and well back from the road, so they are only dimly lit by the streetlights at night; it would be easy to break into them without being seen. She'd never given a thought to that before. Maybe they should get a security system. She recognizes the irony of it; she's thinking of getting a security system because her own son has been breaking into their neighbors' homes.

Tomorrow is Monday. Paul will call a law firm he knows and make an appointment for them to see someone about this. She'd spent a good part of the previous afternoon searching Raleigh's room as he looked on, miserable. She hadn't found anything that shouldn't be there. She and Paul had discussed it again in bed last night. She hardly slept afterward.

Parenting is so stressful, she thinks, glancing sidelong at her moody son slouched in the seat beside her. You try to do your best, but really, what control do you have over them once they're not little anymore? You have no idea what's going on inside their heads, or what they're up to. What if she'd never seen that text? How long would it have gone on—until he was arrested and the cops showed up at the house? He was breaking into places, snooping through people's lives, and they'd known nothing about it. If anyone had accused her son of such a thing, she would never have believed it. That's how little she knows him these days. But she saw those texts herself. He admitted it. She wonders uneasily if he's keeping any other secrets. She parks the car in their driveway and says, "Raleigh, is there anything else you want to tell me?"

He turns to her, startled. "What?"

"You heard me. Is there anything else I should know?" She looks at him, hesitates, and adds, "I don't necessarily have to tell your father." He's obviously surprised at that, but shakes his head. It makes her wonder if she should have said it. She and Paul are supposed to represent a unified front. She says in a neutral voice—which takes real effort—"Tell me the truth. Are you doing drugs?"

He actually smiles. "No, Mom, I'm not doing drugs. This is it, I swear. And I won't do it again. You can relax."

But she can't relax. Because she's his mother, and she worries that his breaking into people's homes—not out of greed, not to steal, but just to "look around"—might indicate that there's something wrong with him. It isn't normal, is it? And those emails he sent from someone's email account worry her. He wouldn't tell her what they said. She hasn't really pushed it because she's not sure she wants to know. How messed up is he? Should he see someone? Some of the kids she knows are seeing therapists, for all kinds of things—anxiety, depression. When she was growing up, kids didn't see therapists. But it's a different time.

When they get inside, she retreats to the office upstairs and closes the door. She knows Paul won't be home from his golf game for hours. She sits at the computer and types up a letter. A letter of apology, which she will not sign. It is not easy to write. When she's satisfied with it, she prints two copies and puts them into two plain white envelopes, seals them, and then goes downstairs and places them in the bottom of her purse. She will have to wait until after dark to deliver them. She will go out late to run an errand at the corner store. Then she'll slip around and deliver the letters. She won't tell Paul and Raleigh what she's done; she already knows they wouldn't approve. But it makes her feel better.

After a moment's consideration, she goes back to the computer and deletes the document.

THREE

It's early in the morning on Monday, October 16; the light in the sky has been growing steadily stronger. The air is chilly. Detective Webb stands perfectly still, watching the mist rise off the lake, holding a paper cup of coffee that has long since gone cold. The surface of the lake, farther out, is perfectly still. He hears a bird cry in the distance. It reminds him of camping as a boy. It would be a peaceful scene if it weren't for the crew of divers and the various vehicles, equipment, and personnel nearby.

The area outside of Aylesford is a lovely place for a vacation. He's been out here before with his wife. But it's first thing on a Monday morning, and he's not here to enjoy himself.

"You still drinking that?" Detective Moen asks, looking sideways at him.

She's his partner; a head shorter and a decade younger, late twenties to his late thirties, and sharp as a tack. He likes working with her. She has short brown hair and perceptive blue eyes. He looks at her and shakes his head, dumps the cold coffee out on the ground.

A local retired man by the name of Bryan Roth had been along here in his rowboat at dawn, fishing for bass. He thought he saw something beneath his boat, something that looked like a car, not far from shore. He called the police. The County Sheriff's Office Regional Underwater Search and Recovery Team had come out. They could see there was a car down there; now they need to find out what else might be under the water.

The divers have just gone down to take a look. Webb stands and watches the water, Moen beside him, waiting for the divers to surface. He wants to know if there's a body in the car. Or worse, more than one. Odds are, there is. In the meantime, he thinks about the logistics of it. There's a road behind them, a lonely road. A suicide spot, maybe? The car isn't far from shore, but the water in this particular spot gets deep quickly. There's a strip of beach, and then the edge of the lake. He turns and looks back again at the road behind him. The road curves here—if someone was driving too fast, or was drunk or high, could the car have missed the curve and gone down the slight incline into the water? There's no guardrail to prevent it.

He wonders how long the car's been there. It's an out-of-the-way spot. A car that went into the water here might stay unnoticed for a long time.

His attention shifts to the man standing at the edge of the road. The older man waves a nervous hello.

Webb and Moen walk over to him.

"You the one who spotted it?" Webb asks.

The man nods. "Yes. I'm Bryan Roth."

"I'm Detective Webb and this is Detective Moen from Aylesford Police," he says, showing the man his badge. "You fish along here regularly?" Webb asks.

The man shakes his head. "No, I don't generally come down here. Never fished along this bit before. I was just floating along here"—he points out at the water with a finger—"with my line in the water, and I felt it snag. I bent over to have a look and started pulling on it, and I saw a car."

"It's good that you called it in," Moen says.

The man nods, laughs nervously. "It really freaked me out. You don't expect to see a car under the water." He looks at them uneasily. "Do you think there's someone in it?"

"That's what we're here to find out," Webb says.

He turns away from the man and looks back at the lake. At that moment a diver breaks through the surface and looks toward the shore. He shakes his head firmly, no.

Webb says, "There's your answer."

But it's not the answer he was expecting. If there's no body in the car, how did the car get into the water? Who was driving it? Maybe somebody pushed it in.

Moen, beside him, looks just as surprised.

Could be all sorts of reasons there's nobody in that car. Maybe whoever was driving managed to get out and didn't report it because they'd been drinking. Maybe the car had been stolen. They'll get it out of the water and get the license plate and then they'll have somewhere to start.

Moen stands beside him, silently going over the possibilities, just as he is.

"Thanks for your help," Webb says to Roth, and then turns abruptly and walks toward the lake, Moen falling into step beside him. The man stands uncertainly, left behind.

The diver is coming up to the shore now. The marine officers stand by; it's their job to get the car out of the water. They've done this countless times. A second diver is still down there, getting things ready to lift the vehicle out.

The diver lifts up his mask. "It's a four-door sedan. All the windows are wide open." He pauses and adds, "Might have been sunk deliberately."

Webb bites his lower lip. "Any idea how long it's been in the water?"

"I'd guess a couple of weeks, give or take."

"Okay. Thanks. Let's bring her up," he says.

They step back again and let the experts do their work. Webb and Moen stand in silence and watch.

Finally there's a loud swooshing sound and the car breaks through the water. It's raised a few feet above the surface when they see it for the first time. Water streams from the windows and out the cracks in the doors. It hangs there suspended from cables in the air for a minute, resurrected.

The car swings slowly over and onto the shore. It lands on the ground with a bounce and then settles, still leaking fluids. Careful about his shoes, Webb approaches the vehicle. It's a fairly new Toyota Camry, and just as the diver said, all four windows are open. Webb looks in the front seat and sees a woman's purse peeking out from beneath the seat. He looks into the backseat and sees an overnight case on the floor. The car smells of stagnant lake water and rot. He pulls his head out and walks around to the back of the vehicle. New York plates. He turns to Moen. "Call it in," he says. She gives a curt nod and calls in the plate number while the two of them walk around the vehicle. Finally they've come full circle and stop at the back of the car again. It's time to open the trunk. Webb has a bad feeling. He turns and looks back at the man who first saw the car in the water. He doesn't come closer. He looks as apprehensive as Webb feels, but the detective knows better than to show it.

"Let's get this open," he directs.

A member of the team approaches with a crow bar. He's obviously done this before—the trunk pops open. They all look inside.

There's a woman there. She's lying on her back with her legs folded up to one side, fully clothed, in jeans and a sweater. She's white, probably late twenties, long brown hair. Webb notes the wedding ring and the diamond engagement ring on her finger. He can see that she has been savagely beaten. Her skin is pale and waxy and her one remaining eye is wide open. She looks up at him as if she's asking for help. He can tell that she was beautiful.

"Christ," Webb says under his breath.

FOUR

Carmine Torres rises early Monday morning. Sunlight is beginning to filter through the front windows and into the entryway as she makes her way down the stairs, anticipating her first cup of coffee. She's halfway down when she sees it. A white envelope lying all by itself on the dark hardwood floor just inside the front door. How odd. It wasn't there last night when she went up to bed. Must be junk mail, she thinks, in spite of the NO JUNK MAIL sign she has displayed outside. But junk mail doesn't usually get delivered late at night.

She walks over to the envelope and picks it up. There's nothing written on it. She considers tossing it into the recycle bin without opening it, but she's curious, and tears it open casually as she walks into the kitchen.

But as soon as her eyes fall on the letter inside, she stops and stands completely still. She reads:

This is a very difficult letter to write. I hope you will not hate us too much. There is no easy way to say this, so I will just spell it out.

My son broke into your home recently while you were out. Yours was not the only home he snuck into. I know that's not much comfort. He swears he didn't steal anything. I've searched his room very thoroughly and I'm pretty sure he's telling the truth about that. He says he just looked around. He was very careful and didn't break or damage anything. You probably don't even know he was there. But I feel I have to let you know that he snooped in your computer—he's very good with computers—and admits that he wrote some prank emails from someone's account. He wouldn't tell me the content of those emails—I think he is too embarrassed—but I feel that you should know. I would hate for them to cause you any trouble.

I am mortified by his behavior. I'm sorry that he can't apologize to you in person. I can't tell you my name, or his name, because his father is worried that it will leave our son open to criminal charges. But please believe me when I tell you that we are all deeply sorry and ashamed of his behavior. Teenage boys can be a handful.

Please accept this apology and I assure you that it will never happen again. My son has faced serious consequences for his actions at home.

I just wanted you to know that it happened, and that we are deeply sorry.

Carmine lifts her eyes from the page, appalled. Someone broke into her house? What an introduction to the neighborhood. She's only lived here for a couple of months; she's still getting used to the place, trying to make friends.

She's not happy about the letter. It makes her feel unsettled. It's awful to think that someone was inside her house creeping around, going through her things, getting into her computer, without her even knowing. She'll look around and make sure nothing's missing—she's not going to take this woman's word for it. And she'd better check her computer for any sent emails that she didn't write herself. The more she thinks about it the more upset she gets. She feels *invaded*.

Carmine wanders into the kitchen and starts making coffee. As upset as she is, she can't help feeling sorry for the woman who wrote the letter. How awful for her, she thinks. But she'd love to know who it was.

Robert Pierce stops at the bottom of his stairs, staring at the plain white envelope on the floor in his front hall. Someone must have pushed it through the slot while he was upstairs in bed last night.

He steps forward slowly, his bare feet making no sound on the hardwood floor. He reaches down and picks up the envelope, turning it over. There's nothing written on it at all.

He opens the envelope and pulls out the single sheet of paper, then reads the letter in disbelief. It's unsigned. Reaching the end of it, he looks up, seeing nothing. Someone has been inside his house.

Sinking down onto the bottom stair, he reads the letter again. Some teenager, messing about. He can't believe it.

He sits for a long time, thinking he might have a problem.

Raleigh goes to school on Monday morning, relieved to get out of the house.

He's also feeling completely disconnected—he hasn't been online all weekend. He feels almost blind without his cell phone. He has no way to reach anyone, to make plans, to know what's going on. He feels like a bat without radar. Or sonar. Or whatever. He has to hope he runs into Mark in the hall or in the cafeteria, because they don't have any classes together today.

But then he finds Mark waiting for him by his locker. Of course Mark will have figured it out.

"Parents take your phone?" Mark asks, as Raleigh opens his locker.

"Yeah." His anger at his friend's stupidity had subsided as he recalled that he'd probably sent equally stupid texts to him. Plus, he needs a friend right now.

"Why? What'd you do?"

Raleigh leans in closer. "Those texts you sent—my mom saw them. They know."

Mark looks alarmed. "Shit! Sorry."

Raleigh is very sorry now that he ever, in a moment of bravado, told Mark what he was doing. He'd been showing off. But now he wishes he'd kept his mouth shut.

Raleigh glances over his shoulder to see if anyone can hear them. He lowers his voice. "Now they're taking me to see a lawyer to decide what to do. My own parents are considering turning me in!"

"No way. They wouldn't do that. They're your *parents*."

"Yeah, well, they're pretty pissed." Raleigh shrugs off his backpack.

"See you after school?" Mark asks, obviously worried.

"Sure. Meet me here after last class." He grabs his books. "I fucking hate not having a phone."

Olivia has work to do, but she can't focus. She works from home as a copy editor of educational textbooks. She has enough work to keep her moderately busy, but not overly so, so that she can manage the house and family. It's a satisfactory, but not particularly fulfilling, arrangement. Sometimes she daydreams about doing something completely different. Maybe she'll become a real estate agent, or work in a gardening shop. She has no idea, but the thought of change is appealing.

Olivia had been too distracted to work, waiting for Paul to call her about when they're meeting the lawyer. And now that she's learned that it will be today she can't think about anything else. She hesitates, but then picks up her phone and calls Glenda Newell.

Glenda picks up on the second ring. She works from home, too, putting together fancy gift baskets for a local business a few hours a week. She's usually up for coffee if Olivia calls. "Do you want to meet at the Bean for coffee?" Olivia asks. She can hear the tension in her own voice, although she's trying to keep it light. "I could use a talk."

"Sure, I'd love to," Glenda says. "Everything all right?"

Olivia hasn't decided how much she's going to tell Glenda. "Yup. Fifteen minutes?"

"Perfect."

When Olivia arrives at the local coffee shop, Glenda is already there. The Bean is a comfortable place, with an old-fashioned coffee bar and mismatched tables and chairs and walls covered in funky, thrift-shop art. Not a chain, and very popular with the locals, in an area where many people seem to work from home. Glenda has found a table at the back, where they can have some privacy. Olivia orders a decaf Americano at the counter and joins Glenda at the table.

"What's up?" Glenda asks. "You don't look that great."

"I haven't been sleeping well the last couple of nights," Olivia admits, looking at Glenda. She really needs to confide in someone. She and Glenda have been close for sixteen years—they met in a moms' group when Raleigh and Glenda's son, Adam, were infants. Their husbands have become fast friends as well. They socialize together frequently; it was Glenda and her husband, Keith, who had been over for dinner on Friday night when Raleigh was out getting into trouble.

She can tell Glenda. Glenda will understand. Mothers can be awfully competitive these days, but she and Glenda have never been that way. They've always been honest and supportive with each other about the kids. Olivia knows that Adam has had his problems. Twice now, at sixteen, he's come home so drunk that he's spent the night hovering over the toilet or collapsed on the bathroom floor. Glenda has had to stay awake watching over him to make sure he didn't choke on his own vomit. Parenting is hard; Olivia doesn't know what she'd do without Glenda to help her through it. And she knows Glenda is grateful for her, too.

"You're not going to believe this," Olivia says, leaning forward and speaking quietly.

"What?" Glenda asks.

Olivia glances around to make sure they can't be overheard and says, lowering her voice even further, "Raleigh's been breaking into people's houses."

The shock on Glenda's face says it all. Suddenly tears are brimming in Olivia's eyes and she's afraid she's going to have a full-blown meltdown right there in the coffee shop. Glenda leans in and puts a comforting hand on her shoulder while Olivia scrabbles for a paper napkin and holds it to her eyes.

The girl picks that moment to bring Olivia's coffee over, sets it down, and moves swiftly away, pretending not to notice that Olivia is crying.

"Oh, Olivia," Glenda says, her face shifting from shock to sympathy. "What happened? Did he get caught by the police?"

Olivia shakes her head and tries to recover her composure. "It was Friday night, when you guys were over for dinner." She'd thought about asking Raleigh to stay home for the dinner party. He'd already made plans with a friend to go see a movie—or so he'd said. She could have insisted he stay home. He and Adam used to be friends, but had drifted apart that spring, when Adam started drinking. But part of her didn't really want Raleigh around Adam. She was afraid he would be a bad influence; she didn't want Raleigh to start drinking. Of course, she couldn't tell Glenda that. Instead she'd told Glenda that Raleigh had already made plans and Glenda had been fine with it. Adam found something else to do. And now it turns out that her own son had found something else to do, too. Olivia tells Glenda the whole mortifying story. Except for the part about the apology letters; she keeps that to herself.

"Why would Raleigh do something like that?" Glenda asks in genuine bewilderment. "He's always been such a good kid."

"I don't know," Olivia admits. "It seems—" She can't continue. She doesn't want to put it into words, to make her concerns real.

"It seems what?"

"*Odd.* Why would he want to snoop around people's houses like that? It's abnormal! Is he some kind of—voyeur? Do you think I should get him some help?"

Glenda sits back and bites her lip. "I don't think you should get carried away here. He's a teenager. They're stupid. They don't think. They do whatever seems like a good idea at any given moment. Kids do this kind of thing all the time."

"Do they?" Olivia says anxiously. "But don't they usually steal something? He didn't take anything."

"Are you sure? Maybe all he took was a bottle of booze, or maybe he drank some alcohol out of a bottle and then topped it up with water. Kids do that shit. Believe me, I know." Her face goes grim.

"Maybe," Olivia says, thinking about it. Maybe that was all it was. She hadn't checked Raleigh's breath when he was sleeping. She hadn't known anything was wrong until the next day. Maybe she should keep an eye on their liquor cabinet at home. "Anyway," she says, "we're seeing a lawyer this afternoon. We'll see what he says. We're mostly doing it to scare him."

Glenda nods. "Probably not a bad idea." They sip their coffees. Then Glenda changes the subject. "Are you still going to book club tonight?" she asks.

"Yes. I need to get out," Olivia says, looking glum. "Don't tell *anybody* about this, okay? It's strictly between us."

"Of course," Glenda says. "And honestly? It's great that you caught it early. Nip it in the bud now. Get the lawyer to scare him shitless. As long as he never does it again, you're good. No harm done."

Glenda Newell makes her way back home from the Bean, her mind on what Olivia has just told her. Poor Olivia—Raleigh breaking into houses! Still, it's a comfort that other families have their problems, too. It does make her feel just a little bit better about her own situation.

She herself is worried sick about Adam—his impulsiveness, his inability to regulate his behavior. She can hardly sleep at night for worrying about her son. And she's worried that he has the addictive gene. He's taken to drinking with a shocking enthusiasm. What's next? The thought of all the drugs out there makes her panic. God only knows what the next few years will bring; the last one has been harrowing enough. Sometimes she doesn't know if she will survive it.

Keith seems to have his head buried in the sand these days. Either he doesn't want to face things, or he genuinely sees nothing wrong with binge drinking at sixteen. But then Keith isn't a worrier. So handsome, with his bluff self-confidence and easy charm—he always thinks things will turn out just fine. He tells her that she worries too much. Maybe he's right. But she's a mother. It's her job to worry.

FIVE

Robert Pierce is leaving for work when he opens the door and sees a tall, dark-haired man in his late thirties and a shorter, mousy-haired woman about ten years younger. Both are well dressed. His first thought is that they are soliciting for something.

Then the man holds up his badge and says, "Good morning. Robert Pierce?"

"Yes."

"I'm Detective Webb and this is Detective Moen, from Aylesford Police. We're here to talk to you about your wife."

He's never seen these two before. Why are they here now? He hears his heart suddenly drumming in his ears. "Have you found her?" he asks. The words come out sounding choked.

"May we come in, Mr. Pierce?"

He nods and steps back, opening the door wide, and then closes it firmly behind them. Robert leads them into the living room.

"Maybe we should sit down," Detective Webb suggests, when

Robert stands uncertainly in the middle of the living room staring at them.

All at once, Robert finds he needs to sit. He collapses into an armchair; he can feel the blood draining from his head. He stares at the detectives, slightly dizzy. The moment has come. The detectives sit on the sofa, their backs straight, the bay window behind them.

"We found your wife's car this morning."

"Her car," Robert manages to say. "Where?"

"It was in a lake, out near Canning."

"What do you mean, in a lake? Was she in an accident?" He looks back and forth between them, his mouth dry.

"It was submerged just offshore, in about fifteen feet of water. Her purse and an overnight bag were in the car." He adds quietly, "A body was found in the trunk."

Robert slumps back against his chair, as if he's had the breath knocked out of him. He can feel the two detectives watching him carefully. He looks back at them, afraid to ask. "Is it her?"

"We think so."

Robert feels himself go pale. He can't speak. Detective Webb leans forward and Robert notices his eyes for the first time—sharp, intelligent eyes.

"I know this is a shock. But we need you to come down to identify the body."

Robert nods. He gets up, grabs a jacket, and follows them outside to the street and gets into the back of their car.

The County Medical Examiner's Office is a new, low brick building. Robert gets out of the car, expecting to be led into a morgue. He imagines a long, cold, sterile room, with shiny, pale tiles and stainless steel, and harsh light, and the smell of death. His head begins to spin, and he knows they are watching him. But instead of a morgue they conduct him to a large, modern waiting room with a glass viewing panel. He stands in front of the glass and watches as the sheet is turned down to reveal the face of the body on the steel gurney.

"Is that your wife?" Webb asks.

He forces himself to look. "Yes," he says, then closes his eyes.

"I'm sorry," the detective says. "Let's get you home."

Silently, they return to the car. Robert gazes out the window, but he doesn't see the passing streets; what he sees is his wife's face, battered, bloated, and tinged with green. He knows what's going to happen next. They are going to question him.

They arrive at his house. The two detectives get out of the car and accompany him to the door.

Detective Webb says, "I'm sorry, I know this is a difficult time, but we'd like to come in and ask you a few more questions, if that's all right with you."

Robert nods and lets them in. They return to the living room they'd been in just a short time before, take the same seats. He swallows and says, "I don't know anything more than I did when she disappeared a couple of weeks ago. I told the police everything I could then. What have you been doing all this time?" It comes out more confrontationally than it should have. Detective Webb looks back at him without blinking. "You weren't even looking for her," Robert says. His voice is bitter. "That's the impression I got, anyway."

"It's a murder investigation now," the detective says, glancing at his partner. "Obviously there will be an autopsy and we'll be looking at everything very closely." He adds, "We need to go back to the beginning."

Robert nods wearily. "Fine."

"How long were you and your wife married, Mr. Pierce?"

"Two years, last June." He notices that the other detective, Moen, is taking notes.

"Were there any problems in your marriage?"

"No. Nothing out of the ordinary."

"Had your wife ever been unfaithful to you?"

"No."

"Had you ever been unfaithful to her?"

"No."

"Any arguments, any . . . violence or abuse?"

He bristles. "Of course not."

"Did your wife have any enemies?"

"No, not at all."

"Anything different about her in the days or even weeks before she went missing? Did she seem preoccupied at all? Did she mention anyone bothering her?"

He shakes his head. "No, not that I noticed. Everything was fine."

"Any financial problems?"

He shakes his head. "No. We were planning a trip to Europe. Work was good for me. She was a temp, and she liked that, the freedom. Didn't like being tied down to the same job fifty-two weeks a year."

"Tell us about that weekend," the detective says.

Robert looks at both detectives and says, "She'd planned to go away that weekend with a friend of hers, Caroline Lu. They were going into New York City." He pauses. "That's what she told me, anyway."

"Did she do this kind of thing often, go away for the weekend?"

"Sometimes. She liked her little shopping expeditions."

"How would she make her travel arrangements?"

He lifts his head. "She made her own arrangements. She booked things online, on her laptop, put it on her credit card."

"You weren't suspicious when she left?"

"No, not at all. I knew Caroline. I liked her. They've done this sort of thing before." He adds, "I don't enjoy shopping."

"So tell us about Friday morning," Webb says, "September twenty-ninth."

"She'd packed her overnight case the night before. I remember she was humming as she went around the bedroom packing her things. I was lying on the bed, watching her. She seemed . . . happy." He looks earnestly at the two detectives. "We made love that night, everything was fine," he assures them.

But it wasn't like that, he remembers, not at all.

"The next morning," Robert continues, "when she was leaving for work, I kissed her good-bye, told her to have fun. She was going to leave directly from work, leave her car at the station and take the train in. It was her last day of that temp assignment."

"Where was that?" the detective asks.

"I told the police all this already," Robert complains. "It was an accounting firm. The information must be in the file." He feels a flash of irritation.

"Did you talk to her again that day at all?"

"No. I meant to, but I was busy with work. When I got home, I called her cell, but she didn't answer. I didn't think anything of it at the time. But she didn't pick up all weekend—it just went to voice mail. We're not a clingy couple, calling each other all the time. I thought she was busy, having fun. I didn't think much of it."

"When did you start to realize something was wrong?" Webb asks.

"When she didn't return Sunday night as expected, I started to worry. I'd left messages on her cell, but she hadn't called me back. I couldn't remember where they were staying either. That's when I called Caroline. I thought her husband might know something, if they'd been delayed. But Caroline answered the phone." He pauses. "And she told me that she'd never had plans with Amanda that weekend, that she hadn't actually talked to Amanda in a while." He rubs a hand over his face. "I went to the police station on Monday morning and reported her missing."

"What kind of work do you do?" Detective Moen asks. It startles him a bit, and he turns his attention to her.

"I'm an attorney." He adds, "I—I should call the office."

The detective ignores that. "Can you confirm for us where you were that weekend—from Friday, the twenty-ninth of September, to Monday?" she asks.

"What?"

"Can you confirm—"

"Yes, sure," he says. "I was at work all day Friday, left about five. I went directly home. I told the police all of this before, when I reported her missing. I stayed in on Friday night. On Saturday, I was home, caught up on some work; Sunday I went golfing with some friends." He adds, "It must all be in the file."

"Did your wife have any family, besides you?" Detective Moen asks.

"No. She was an only child, and her parents are both dead." He pauses. "Maybe I can ask a question."

"Sure," Detective Webb says.

"Do you have any idea what might have happened? Who might have done this?"

"Not yet," the detective says, "but we won't stop until we find out. Is there anything else that you can tell us?"

"Not that I can think of," Robert says, his face a careful blank.

"Okay," Webb says. He adds, as if it's an afterthought, "We'd like to have a team come in and take a look inside your house, if that's all right with you."

Robert says, his voice sharp, "You ignore my concerns for two weeks, now you want to search my house? You can get a warrant."

"Fine. We'll do that," Webb says. Robert stands up and the two detectives get up and leave.

Once he's watched them drive away, Robert locks the front door and quickly makes his way upstairs to his office. He sits in the chair at the desk and pulls open the bottom drawer. There's a stack of manila envelopes inside. He knows that beneath those envelopes is his wife's burner phone, the one the cops don't know about. He sits for a moment, staring at the envelopes, afraid. He thinks about the letter he got that morning, downstairs in a kitchen drawer. Somebody was in his house. Some teenager was here, snooping through his desk. And he must have seen the phone, because one day when Robert had opened the drawer, the phone had been sitting right on top of those manila envelopes. The shock of it had made him start in his chair. He knew he'd put the phone beneath the envelopes. But now he knows. That kid must have seen the phone, moved it. And now the police are going to search his house. He has to get rid of it.

He has a small window of time before they come back with a warrant. But how much time? He reaches beneath the envelopes for the cell phone, suddenly afraid that it won't be there at all. But he can feel its smooth surface in his hand and he pulls it out. He stares down at it, this phone that has caused him such pain.

He closes the drawer and shoves the phone in his pocket. He looks out the window; the street below is empty. When the news breaks that his wife's body has been found, there will be reporters on his doorstep; he'll never be able to get away then. He must act quickly. He changes into jeans and a T-shirt, hurries downstairs, grabs a jacket and his keys by the front door, and stops suddenly, just short of opening the door. What if someone sees him? And later the detectives find out that he rushed out of the house right after they left?

He stands still for a minute, thinking. They'll search the house. He can't hide the phone in the house. What options does he have? He walks to the back and looks out the door from the kitchen to the backyard. It's a very private yard. Maybe he can bury the phone in the back flower garden. Surely they won't dig up the garden. They already have the body.

He spies Amanda's gardening set on the patio, puts on her gardening gloves, and grabs a trowel. He walks to the flowerbeds at the back of the garden. He looks around—the only house that can see into his yard is Becky's, and he doesn't see her, watching at the windows, or from the back door. He bends down and quickly digs a small, narrow hole, about ten inches deep, underneath a shrub. He wipes the cell phone down with his T-shirt, just in case, thinking that if they do find it, he can tell them she must have put it there—Amanda did all the gardening. Then he pushes the phone deep into the hole and covers it up again. You can't even tell the earth had been disturbed when he's done. He returns the gardening tools to their place and goes back inside.

Problem solved.

SIX

Raleigh slouches in English class. The teacher is droning on and on, but Raleigh can only focus on the mess he's in.

It had started quite innocently last spring, sometime in May. He'd left his backpack at his friend Zack's house after school. It had an assignment in it that was due the next day. Raleigh texted Zack that he needed to come get it. Zack texted that they were all out and wouldn't be back until late. Frustrated, he cycled over to Zack's house. He wasn't even sure why. He knew nobody was home. He didn't have a key. When Raleigh got there, he went around the back and looked in the basement window. His backpack was on the floor by the couch where he'd left it, ignored, while he and Zack played video games. Just for something to do, he tried the window. To his surprise, it opened easily. He checked the opening. He was tall and skinny—he knew he could get through it no problem—and his backpack was right fucking *there*. Raleigh looked around to see if anyone was watching, but to be honest, he wasn't too worried; if anyone saw him, he could explain. And then he went in through the window.

That's when things got a little strange. Because he didn't just grab his backpack, heave it out the window, and climb out after it. He knows he should have. And now, he wishes that he had. Instead, he stood in the basement listening to the silence. The house felt different without anyone else in it—full of possibilities. A little shiver of excitement ran up and down his spine. The empty house was his for the moment. A strange feeling came over him, and he knew he wasn't going to turn around and go right back out the window.

He went directly upstairs to see if there was an office—the most likely place to find a computer. He passed by Zack's room and glanced in. He saw Zack's recent chemistry test flung down on his desk, and the mark was 10 percent lower than he'd claimed. Raleigh wondered what else Zack had lied about. Then he made his way to the office and set about trying to hack into Zack's dad's computer. He didn't get in, but the challenge of it gave him a curious thrill.

When Zack asked him about the backpack the next day, Raleigh sheepishly admitted he'd snuck in the window to grab it—he hoped that was okay. Zack had obviously thought nothing of it.

The next time, a few weeks later, Raleigh was more nervous. He could hardly believe he was there, planning to do it again. He stood in the dark in the backyard of one of his classmates, Ben. He knew they were away for the weekend. He didn't see any obvious security system.

He found a basement window unlocked on the side of the house. It was still the kind of neighborhood where lots of people didn't necessarily lock everything up tight, whether they were home or not. Raleigh had no trouble getting in. Once inside, in the dark, his heartbeat began to settle down. He couldn't exactly turn the lights on. What if they'd told the neighbors they were going to be away, too? But fortunately, the moon was bright that night, and after his eyes adjusted, he could find his way around all right. He took care not to walk in front of the windows—and then went upstairs to the bedrooms. He found a laptop at a desk in the master bedroom. This time he was prepared. He used his USB boot stick and got in quite easily, snooped around the computer, and then left the house, going out the same way he got in.

If he hadn't gotten such a charge out of the hacking, he wouldn't have kept doing it. But after that house, there had been others. He became pretty good at getting into people's computers. He saw their private information, but he never took anything or changed anything. He never did any harm. He never left any sign that he'd been there.

It had been a mistake to tell Mark what he was doing. If only Mark hadn't sent that stupid text—

Raleigh is startled by the sound of his name being called over the PA system. All eyes turn to him automatically, then shift away. He packs up his books and saunters casually to the door. But he's painfully self-conscious. He can feel his face flush slightly.

He makes his way down three flights of stairs to the office, the sweat blooming on his skin. He never gets called down to the office. He's afraid that this has something to do with the break-ins. Are the police here? Were there cameras somewhere and he missed them? Maybe someone saw him coming out of the house and recognized him. He fights the urge to grab his things from his locker and avoid everything by just going home and hiding in his bedroom.

When he gets to the office he's swept with relief when he sees his mom there waiting for him. No police in sight.

"We have an appointment," she says. "Get your things. I'll wait in the car out front."

His anxiety spikes again.

As they drive downtown to the lawyer's office, it is painfully silent in the car. His dad works downtown in the central business district and will meet them there. Raleigh spends the time worrying about what the lawyer will say.

The law office is intimidating. He's never been in one before. It's on the top floor of an office building, all glass doors and sleek furnishings. One look and he knows that this must be costing his parents a lot of money.

His dad is already in the reception area and will barely meet his eyes. Raleigh sits miserably, waiting with his parents. They're obviously embarrassed to be here, pretending to read copies of *The New Yorker*. Raleigh doesn't even pick up a magazine; he just stares at his feet, missing his phone.

It's not long before they're ushered down a quiet, carpeted hall into a spacious office with an impressive view of the river. The lawyer behind the large desk gets up and shakes hands with each of them. Raleigh knows his hands are clammy with nerves; the lawyer's hands are cool. Raleigh takes an instant dislike to Emilio Gallo, a heavyset man who stares at him, sizing him up.

"So. Tell me what this is all about, Raleigh," Gallo says.

Raleigh glances at his mom; he doesn't dare look at his dad. He thought his parents would do all the talking and that he would just sit here and look sorry and do whatever he's told. But his mom refuses to catch his eye. So he tells the lawyer the same story he told his parents, terrified that Gallo will be able to see through him. He doesn't want the lawyer to know how many houses he's broken into, or the extent of his computer expertise, what he's capable of doing. All he actually *did* was hack in and look around and get out. That's the truth. He could have done a lot more.

"I see," the attorney says when he's finished. He smooths his tie with his fingers. "So you haven't been caught."

"No," Raleigh says.

"That's breaking and entering and trespassing," the attorney says. "And the computer stuff is even worse. The state of New York takes these kinds of crimes very seriously. Are you aware of New York Penal Code Section 156?"

Raleigh shakes his head, terrified.

"I didn't think so. Let me educate you." He leans forward and pins Raleigh with his eyes. "Under section 156, 'unauthorized use of a computer'—that's a crime. That's when you gain access to or use a computer without the permission of the rightful owner. That's a Class A misdemeanor. People get fines and even a bit of jail time for that. It goes up from there. Are you absolutely sure you haven't taken or copied anyone's data, or deleted or changed anything on their computers? Because that's tampering, and you could go to jail for up to fifteen years for that."

Raleigh swallows. "No, I just looked. That's all."

"And sent those emails. That's identity theft."

"Identity theft?" his father says sharply.

"He wrote emails from someone else's account," the lawyer reminds them, "pretending to be that person."

"Surely a prank email doesn't constitute identity theft," his father says, looking appalled.

"Well, you wouldn't want to risk it, would you? People don't take kindly to having their privacy invaded." The lawyer focuses his sharp eyes on Raleigh, who feels himself shrink further down into his chair. "And there's always the possibility of a civil suit. This is America, and people are very litigious. And that can get very expensive."

There's a long, horrified pause. Clearly his parents hadn't thought of that. Raleigh certainly hadn't.

Finally, his mother says, "I thought he should apologize to these people, maybe make reparations, but my husband was against it."

"No, your husband is right," Gallo says, looking astonished. "He definitely should not apologize. That would be tantamount to confession to a crime, or crimes."

Then she says, "What if he sent them a letter, anonymously, to apologize?"

"Why the hell would he do that?" his dad says.

The lawyer says, shaking his head, "I'm sorry, that's a lovely gesture, and I'm just a cynical criminal lawyer, but that would be very foolish. Far better that these people don't know that he was ever there at all."

Raleigh notices his mom flush a bit at the rebuke.

"Tell me more about this other boy, Mark," Gallo says. "Who's he?"

"He's a friend at school."

"How much does he know?"

"Just that I broke into a couple of houses. And that I snooped in the computers."

"Is he likely to rat you out?"

"No way," Raleigh says firmly.

"How can you be so sure?" the lawyer asks.

Raleigh suddenly isn't sure. But he says, "I just know."

"Anything on any social media we need to worry about?"

Raleigh reddens and shakes his head. "I'm not a complete idiot."

The lawyer sits back in his chair and looks as if he disagrees. Then he glances at both of Raleigh's parents. "My advice is to sit tight and do nothing. If no one's come forward and the police haven't knocked at your door, consider yourselves lucky. But let me remind you, young man," and here he leans forward and pins Raleigh again with his sharp, shrewd eyes, "luck always runs out. So I strongly advise you to leave off your life of crime right now, because if you're caught, you're definitely looking at juvie."

Raleigh swallows nervously, and on that note, they get up to leave.

Olivia doesn't say a word on the way home. Her thoughts are in turmoil. She's furious at Raleigh, and furious at the situation. She regrets, now, those two anonymous letters. She's not going to tell anyone about them, but now she's worried that they may come back to haunt her somehow. She hears the lawyer's voice in her mind, saying, *that would be very foolish.*

Why didn't she leave well enough alone? That's what comes from trying to live ethically, from trying to do what's right in a crazy, cynical world that doesn't give a shit about doing the right thing. What's wrong with apologizing? Instead it seems to be all about not getting caught, about getting away with it. She didn't like that lawyer much, but she's afraid that he knows what he's doing; she's so naive next to him.

She can't help worrying about what all this is teaching their son. He might be scared straight at the thought of jail—and that's a good thing, she'll take it. Although he's probably not as frightened of it as she is. But she wishes he understood why what he's done is wrong instead of just being afraid of what might happen to him. How, she fumes, are you supposed to teach a kid right and wrong when so many people in positions of authority regularly behave so badly? *What the hell is wrong with America these days?*

Carmine has had her lonely supper of a single chicken breast and a salad, eaten at the kitchen table, the television resolutely off. She has standards. She maintains the routine of cooking an evening meal for herself, even though some days she wonders why she bothers. She has cookbooks that celebrate the joys of cooking for one, but it doesn't feel joyful to her. She loved cooking for her husband and kids. But her husband is dead and her kids have all moved on to their own busy lives.

She has established another routine—her evening walk around the neighborhood. Routines give structure to empty days. This nightly walk is both for exercise and to satisfy her natural curiosity about her neighbors. It takes her down Finch and around to Sparrow, then back to her own street. It's a long block and a pretty walk. She will keep it up as long as the weather allows, admiring the well-kept homes, glancing in the warmly lit windows. Tonight as she walks along she thinks about the break-in and the letter. So far she has only spoken to her next-door neighbor, Zoe Putillo, about it. Zoe is the only one she's become friendly with so far. Carmine hasn't completely decided whether to let it go or try to find out who broke into her house. Part of her feels a natural sympathy for the mother who wrote the letter. But part of her feels slightly outraged, and wants to do something about it.

As she turns back down her own street she nears a house that is brightly lit. She can see across the front lawn and through the large windows into the living room, where a small group of women are gathered. They are talking and laughing animatedly, wineglasses in hand. Just then Carmine notices another woman hurriedly approaching. She turns up the driveway of the house, a book in her hand, and rings the bell. Carmine hears the muffled sound of voices briefly, while the door is open and the newcomer is admitted, and then the sound is abruptly cut off again.

It's a book club, Carmine realizes with a pang of longing, stopping for a moment. The longing is mixed with a touch of resentment. People haven't been particularly friendly here.

SEVEN

Olivia, in a rush to leave for book club, almost forgets the book, but grabs it as she heads out the door. She usually looks forward to book club, but tonight she suspects she's too upset about Raleigh to enjoy anything. Supper was strained after the visit to the attorney.

She walks to Suzanne Halpern's house on Finch Street. The book club started years ago, a collection of women from the neighborhood who know each other through school, sports, and other neighborhood events. There are several regular members. They all take turns hosting.

Suzanne loves to host book club: She's a bit of a show-off. She always makes a fuss, preparing elaborate snacks and ostentatiously pairing them with just the right wines. When it's Olivia's turn she usually defaults to a good, solid red and an uninspired white that will go with everything, and grabs a bunch of things from Costco. She doesn't particularly like hosting. For her, book club is about getting out.

Glenda is already there when Olivia arrives. The women stand around the living room chatting, with their glasses of wine and their little plates of food, leaving their books at their seats. Tonight's book is the new Tana French. Of course, they never start with the book. They catch up on small talk first, usually about the kids—they all have kids—which is what they're doing when Jeannette's phone pings. Olivia sees Jeannette give her phone a casual glance—and then Jeannette's face freezes. At the same time Olivia hears two or three other pings from other phones and wonders what's going on.

"Oh, my God," Jeannette blurts out.

"What is it?" Olivia asks.

"Remember how Amanda Pierce went missing a couple of weeks ago?" Jeannette says.

Of course they remember, Olivia thinks. Amanda Pierce had left her husband rather abruptly without telling him. Olivia didn't know Amanda, except by sight. She'd only actually met her once, at a neighborhood party held at the little park between Sparrow and Finch just over a year ago, in September, shortly after the Pierces had moved in. Amanda Pierce was a striking woman, and all the husbands had watched her, practically drooling, stumbling over one another to hand her things—ketchup for her hot dog, a napkin, a drink, while the wives tried not to look pissed off. She looked like a model, or an actress—she was that perfect. That sexy. That confident. Always wearing smart clothes and fashionable sunglasses. The husband—she can't remember his name—but he was ridiculously good-looking, too. He had the same movie-star quality, but was more reserved. A watcher. They lived on Olivia's street, but farther down. They were both in their late twenties, considerably younger than Olivia and her friends, and had no kids, so they didn't have much reason to cross paths.

"She didn't really go missing," Suzanne says. "She left her husband."

"There's a news alert," Jeannette says. "They found her car, in a lake up near Canning. Her body was in the trunk."

There's a stunned silence as the room fills with shock.

"I can't believe it," Becky says, looking up from her phone, her face suddenly pale.

Olivia recalls with a jolt that Raleigh had been inside the Pierces' house.

"Poor Robert," Becky whispers. Becky Harris lives next door to the Pierces. "He did report her missing. He told me that himself."

Becky is a good friend of Olivia's, and had told her all about it. Olivia has a sudden picture of Becky, who is still quite attractive, but perhaps not as attractive as she thinks, talking to the handsome, abandoned husband over the back fence.

"I remember hearing that," Glenda says, sounding shaken. "But if I remember correctly, the story was the police didn't take it seriously because she'd lied to him about going away for the weekend with a friend. They figured she left him, that it wasn't a proper disappearance."

"Well, it's obviously a murder now," Jeannette says.

"What else does it say?" Olivia asks.

"That's it. No details."

"Do you think her husband did it?" Suzanne asks after a moment, looking around at all of them. "Do you think he might have killed her?"

"I wouldn't be surprised," Jeannette says quietly.

Becky turns on her suddenly. "You don't know anything about it!"

There's a strained silence for a moment at Becky's outburst. Then Suzanne says, her voice tinged with something like awe, "It's too creepy."

"The husband could be perfectly innocent," Zoe suggests.

"But isn't it usually the husband?" Suzanne says.

"If he killed her," Becky says, "then why would he tell the police to look for her?" Becky obviously doesn't want to believe that the handsome, lonely man next door may be a murderer.

"Well," Olivia says, "he would have to report her missing, wouldn't he? He couldn't just ignore it. He has to play the part of the worried husband, even if he killed her."

"God, you're morbid!" says Glenda.

"Think about it, though," Olivia says thoughtfully. "It could be the perfect murder. He kills her, reports her missing, and tells the police she said she was going off with a friend for the weekend when she wasn't. Then when she doesn't turn up, the police will think she just left him and won't actually look that hard. It's brilliant, really." They all stare back at her. She adds, "Especially if they'd never found her car in the lake. He'd probably have gotten away with murder."

"I'm not sure I like the way your mind works," Suzanne says.

Becky gives Olivia an annoyed glance and says, "For the record, I don't think her husband did it."

Suzanne stands up and starts refilling everyone's wineglasses. She shudders visibly. "God, remember how gorgeous she was? Remember the party last year? That was the first time any of us really got a look at her. She had all the men wrapped around her little finger."

"I remember," Becky says. "She was too busy being fascinating to help clean up."

"Maybe she had a stalker or something," Glenda says. "A woman like that—"

"She was such a flirt. I don't know how her husband put up with it," Zoe says. Zoe had been at the party, too, Olivia remembers, looking around the room. They'd all been there.

"Maybe that was the problem. Maybe he was jealous, and he killed her," Jeannette says.

They all glance at one another, uncomfortable.

Zoe abruptly changes the subject. "Have any of you heard about the break-ins and the anonymous letters?"

Olivia feels her stomach clench and deliberately avoids looking at Glenda. *Shit.* She really never should have written those letters. She reaches for her wineglass on the coffee table.

"What break-ins? What anonymous letters?" Suzanne says.

"I heard it from Carmine Torres," Zoe says. "She's my new next-door neighbor. She told me she got an anonymous letter this morning from someone saying that her son had broken into her house and that they were sorry." She adds, "It was slipped through her mail slot over-night."

"Seriously?" Jeannette says. "I haven't heard anything about this."

Zoe nods. "She knocked on my door to ask me if I'd gotten one, too, but I hadn't," Zoe says.

"Was anything taken?" Suzanne asks.

"She didn't think so. She said she'd had a good look around but nothing seemed to be missing."

Olivia dares to take a quick look at Glenda and a flash of under-standing passes between them. She'll have to talk to her after book club. She hadn't told Glenda about the letters.

"Who else got broken into?" Suzanne asks. "I haven't heard any-thing."

"I don't know," Zoe says. "The letter says that there were others. Carmine showed it to me—I read it."

Olivia feels slightly nauseated, and puts her glass of wine down. This is not what she meant to happen, not at all. She'd only wanted to apologize. She didn't want other people reading the letter! She didn't want someone trying to find out who had written it! She certainly didn't want people *gossiping* about it. She should have left well enough alone. How could she have been so stupid? The lawyer was right—all she'd done was stir things up.

"You should have seen this letter!" Zoe exclaims. "The poor woman who wrote it. Apparently the kid went through people's computers and get this—he even sent prank emails from their email accounts!"

"No!" Suzanne says, aghast.

"What did they say?" Jeannette asks, appalled and entertained in equal measure.

"I don't know," Zoe says. "Carmine says she didn't find any on her computer. That must have been at somebody else's house."

Glenda says, in a no-nonsense voice, "Sounds like some teenage stupidity to me, and the mother's doing the decent thing, apologizing. It's the sort of thing that could happen to any of us with kids. You know what teenagers are like."

Olivia notices a few rueful, sympathetic nods from some of the other women. She feels intensely grateful to Glenda at that moment but is careful not to show it.

Suzanne says, "I guess I should be more careful about locking the doors and windows. I don't always check them at night."

"It's so creepy to think of somebody going through your house and getting into your computers when you're not there," Jeannette says in a hushed voice. "And to think—if this woman Carmine hadn't got that letter, she would never even have known."

There's silence as they all seem to contemplate that for a minute.

"Maybe some of *us* have been broken into," Zoe says.

"But then we would have gotten a letter," Suzanne says.

"Not necessarily," Zoe says. "What if the kid only admitted to some of the houses, didn't tell his mother the full extent of what he was up to? That's what Carmine thinks. There could be lots of houses this kid's broken into, and people wouldn't necessarily know. Maybe we should all be worried."

Olivia looks around at the women in the circle, all of whom appear to be genuinely alarmed at the idea of having been broken into without being aware of it. Could Raleigh have lied to her about how often he'd done this? Her stomach feels queasy and she wants to go home.

"I guess we should talk about the book," Suzanne says at last.

EIGHT

Olivia follows Glenda out the door. It's chilly now, and she's glad it's dark as the other women slip away. Glenda waits for her and they talk quietly at the end of the driveway, pulling their jackets closed.

Olivia waits until the others are out of earshot and says miserably, "Thanks for not saying anything."

"Why would I say anything?" Glenda replies. "Your secret is safe with me." She snorts. "Awfully smug of Zoe, if you ask me. She's got two girls, she doesn't have any boys. She has no idea." Then she asks, "How did it go with the lawyer?"

They turn down the sidewalk toward Glenda's house. Olivia tells her about the visit to the lawyer. Then she adds anxiously, "I shouldn't have written those letters."

"You didn't tell me about that."

"I know." She glances at Glenda. "I haven't told Paul or Raleigh either. Promise me you won't tell. If Paul finds out, he'll be furious. I never should have sent them. Now everyone's going to be trying to find out who wrote them."

"How many are there?"

"Just two. Raleigh said he only broke into two houses. I made him show me which ones."

"Whose was the other house?"

Olivia hesitates. "The Pierces'."

"Seriously?"

Olivia nods. She feels sick about it. *What if Robert Pierce is a murderer?*

"Do you believe him?" Glenda asks after a moment.

"I did. To be honest, I don't know anymore. Maybe Zoe's right, and he didn't tell me about all of them. I never would have thought Raleigh capable of such a thing." They're quiet for a moment, walking down the sidewalk in the dark, Olivia imagining Suzanne, Becky, Jeannette, and Zoe all getting on to their computers as soon as they can and checking their sent messages looking for emails they hadn't written. After a while Glenda asks, "Do you think Robert Pierce murdered his wife?"

Olivia glances at her uneasily. "I don't know," she says. "What do you think?"

"I don't know either."

"I didn't even know her," Olivia says, "but she was a neighbor— she was one of *us*. It seems awfully close."

Carmine Torres has decided to go door-to-door on her street, telling her neighbors that she'd been broken into and showing them the letter. This morning, she'd spoken again briefly to Zoe next door, who told her that no one in her book club the night before had heard anything about it. Then of course they'd started talking about what had been on the news: a woman from this supposedly quiet neighborhood—just one street over—had been found brutally murdered.

Carmine also plans to go up and down Sparrow Street, the street the murdered woman lived on, and see what she can learn about this woman in the trunk. Carmine loves a good gossip.

Before she goes, she wanders around the house uneasily, touching things, studying them, straightening pictures. She looks inside her medicine cabinet. Has anything been moved? She can't tell for sure. She feels a bit creeped out now, alone in her own house, which she never was before. She hates being a widow; it's lonely. And she hates the idea of someone—even if only a teenage boy—riffling through her things. Reading what's on her computer. Not that there's anything on there that shouldn't be. What kind of kid would do something like that? There must be something wrong with him.

Raleigh finds himself avoiding Mark at school on Tuesday morning. He doesn't want to talk to him about the meeting with the lawyer. He's decided this is it—he's not going to break into any more houses. Ever.

Webb and Moen are back at the medical examiner's office for the autopsy results on Amanda Pierce. The large room is freshly painted, and lots of natural light floods the space from the large windows all along the upper half of the room. The smell is still bad, though. Webb sucks on one of the mints that Moen has brought. His shoes squeak on the spic-and-span tiles. Along the wall beneath the windows is a long counter with sinks and sterilized instruments neatly laid out. Weigh scales hang over the counter—they look just like the scales in the su-permarket where one might weigh a paper bag of mushrooms, Webb thinks.

John Lafferty, a senior forensic pathologist, says, "Cause of death is blunt force trauma. She was struck in the head repeatedly with an object, most likely a hammer, by the looks of it."

Webb focuses on the body lying on the steel table. The sheet has been peeled back. It's a gruesome sight. The decomposing body is bloated and the skin has a hideous, greenish cast. She looks much worse than she did the day before.

"Sorry about the smell, but bodies tend to deteriorate rapidly once they come out of the water," Lafferty says.

Undeterred, Webb moves in closer to study the corpse. The au-topsy has been concluded, the organs studied and weighed, and she has been sewn up again. Her head is a pulpy mess. One of her eyes is mashed out of her face.

"It's almost impossible to estimate time of death under the circum-stances," the pathologist says. "It's very difficult to determine time of death from postmortem changes more than seventy-two hours after death, and the fact that she's been in the water—sorry."

Webb nods. "Understood."

"No obvious evidence of sexual assault or any other injuries," the pathologist continues. "She was definitely dead before she went into the water. No defensive wounds, nothing under her nails. No obvious signs of a struggle, even though it appears she was struck from the front. Perhaps she knew her killer. Most likely the first blow came as a surprise and incapacitated her. She was hit several times, with great force. The first couple of blows probably killed her. The repeated blows indicate uncontrollable fury."

"So it was personal."

"Looks like it." He adds, "She was a healthy woman—no signs of any old fractures that might indicate ongoing domestic abuse."

"Okay," Webb says. "Anything else?"

"She was pregnant. About ten weeks. That's about it."

"Thank you," Webb says, and he and Moen head out. "We know she was alive and at work on Friday, September twenty-ninth," Webb says. "She must have been killed sometime that weekend. She was probably dead by the time her husband reported her missing on Monday."

They walk to the car, both of them inhaling deep breaths of fresh air. Moen says, "Not every man is happy to learn he's going to be a father."

"A bit drastic, isn't it, murder?" Webb counters.

She shrugs. "We've only got Robert Pierce's word for it that she told him she was going away with Caroline," Moen points out. "No one's corroborated it—she didn't mention going away for the weekend to anyone she was working with."

Webb nods. "Maybe she wasn't going anywhere. Maybe he made that up, after he killed her. We haven't found any record of her booking a hotel."

"He could have killed her and packed her bags and sunk her car and hoped she would never be found. So that it looked like she planned to leave him."

"We'd better talk to Caroline Lu," Webb says.

Olivia is having an unproductive week. She blames Raleigh—and the shocking news about Amanda Pierce—for her inability to concentrate. It's early Tuesday afternoon and she's accomplished almost nothing yet today. She turns away from the file open on her screen, gets up, and goes downstairs for a fresh cup of coffee. The house is quiet—Paul is at work and Raleigh is at school. But she can't stop thinking about things other than her current editing project. She's worried about Raleigh.

What if Raleigh isn't telling her everything? She didn't like the way his eyes shifted away from hers when she asked him. He seemed genuine when he said he wasn't taking drugs, but she still feels there's something he is keeping from her.

And Olivia can't put her finger on why, but she can't help feeling that Paul is keeping something from her, too. The last few weeks he's seemed to have something on his mind, something he's not sharing with her. When she'd broached him about it, he'd brushed her off with a comment about being overloaded at work. Of course, now he's upset about Raleigh, too.

Restlessly, she picks up the daily newspaper, the *Aylesford Record*, and carries it over to the easy chair in front of the sliding-glass doors that look out onto the backyard. She's already read it, and followed the story online. But she puts her coffee down on the little side table and opens the paper again. On page 3, there's a picture and a headline. MISSING WOMAN FOUND DEAD. The photograph shows a picture of Amanda Pierce; she's smiling and pretty in the photo, with no hint of the tragedy that will befall her. She looks as lovely as she did at the neighborhood party, everyone eating out of her hand.

Olivia studies the photograph closely, recalling the discussion at the book club the night before. She rereads the article. There are few facts. They pulled her and her car out of a lake early yesterday morning. It says only that her body was found in the trunk. Olivia wonders how she died. The other information is scant. Police are being tight-lipped, saying only that "the investigation is ongoing."

She puts the paper down, decides to go for a walk, and laces up her shoes. Maybe a walk will clear her head and then she can get some work done.

It's awful, Olivia thinks, leaving the house. A woman who lived on their street was murdered. She can't stop thinking about it.

NINE

Robert Pierce glances out at the street from behind one of the blinds in the master bedroom. There's a cluster of people standing outside staring at the house, staring up at him, having caught the movement at the window. He can imagine what they're saying about him.

He turns away from the window and watches the forensics team continue its meticulous search of his bedroom. He watches and thinks. They have nothing on him. The only thing was her unregistered, pay-as-you-go cell phone, and now it's safely buried in the garden.

He thinks about the phone. It had become an issue between Amanda and him. Not one they talked about. That was the thing about them, so much of their marriage went on beneath the surface. They didn't talk about things. They didn't fight. Instead they played games.

He knew she must have had a burner phone. He knew she kept it with her—probably in her purse—and hid it somewhere when she was in the house. Because he'd been through her purses, and her car, and he'd never found it. And then one night not long ago, he surprised her by making her dinner when she got home. Something simple—steak and salad and red wine. And a little something in her wineglass to knock her out.

And while she was sprawled across their bed, oblivious, he'd torn the house apart methodically, much the way this crew is doing right now. And he found her secret hiding place. The box of tampons in the bottom of the bathroom cupboard. The bathroom was the one place in the house she could always count on being alone. Not too creative of her, really. If they look inside her box of tampons now, of course, they won't find anything but tampons.

How much does he really have to worry about?

When she woke up the next morning with a walloping headache, he chided her for drinking too much. He pointed at the empty wine bottle left on the kitchen counter—he'd poured half of it down the sink—and she nodded and smiled uncertainly. Later on, when she was dressed for work, she seemed nervous, out of sorts. She approached him, some unreadable expression on her face. He wondered if she was going to ask him. He wondered if she had the guts. He gazed back at her blandly. "Are you all right, honey? You look upset."

He'd never been violent with her before, but she looked at him as if she were a silky little brown mouse facing a snake.

They stared at one another. He'd taken her secret phone from its secret hiding place. He knew it and she knew it. Would she say anything? He didn't think she'd dare. He waited.

Finally she said, "No, I'm fine," and turned away.

He kept an eye on her to see if she would try to discreetly search the house for her missing phone before she left for work, but she didn't. It was in his bottom desk drawer, beneath some envelopes. Easier to find than where she'd hidden it. But he knew she wouldn't dare go into his desk. Not while he was home. So he stayed home until she left for work.

That was the day she disappeared.

Detective Webb is very much aware of Robert Pierce lurking around the house during their search. Did he kill his wife? And stuff her body in the trunk and sink her car in the lake? He's not coming across particularly well as a bereaved husband. He seems twitchy.

If he killed her here, in the house, they will find something. They know she was beaten to death with a hammer or something similar. There would have been a lot of blood. Even if a surface looks completely clean, if there are traces of blood, they will find them. But Webb doesn't think he killed her here. He's too smart for that.

The team moves slowly over the house. They dust everywhere for fingerprints, look in drawers and under furniture, searching for anything that might shed light on Amanda Pierce's death.

They take her laptop. Her cell phone had been found in her purse; two weeks in the water had rendered it useless, but her cell phone records will be scrutinized. Webb wonders what, if anything, Amanda Pierce might have been hiding. She told her husband that she was going away with a friend. They only have his word for it. But if what he says is true, then Amanda was lying to him about Caroline Lu. If so, who was she meeting? Had her husband found out the truth? Had he killed her in a jealous rage? Or maybe there was some other reason he killed her. Perhaps he was psychologically abusive. Was she trying to escape the marriage and he found out?

Their interview of Caroline Lu had yielded nothing useful. The two women had been friends since college but had seen less of each other in recent months; Caroline hadn't known if Amanda had a lover, and she was unaware of any possible marital problems. She'd been shocked when Robert called saying that Amanda had told him they were together that weekend.

Now, in the master bedroom, Robert looks on silently, coldly observant. A technician approaches Webb and says in a low voice, "Four distinct sets of prints in the house. Downstairs in the living room, the kitchen. Up here, in the office—especially the desk and desk drawers, and in the bedroom on the light switch, the headboard—also in the en suite bath."

That's interesting, Webb thinks, and glances at Moen, who raises an eyebrow at him. He turns to Robert and says, "Have you had friends in lately?"

He shakes his head.

"Did your wife?"

"No, not that I know of."

"A cleaning lady?"

Robert shakes his head. "No."

"Any idea why there would be four different sets of prints in your house rather than two—yours and your wife's?"

"No."

One of these two had a lover, Webb thinks, or maybe they both did. Maybe Amanda had her lover over to the house when her husband wasn't there. That was taking a risk. Maybe it got her killed. They will canvass the neighborhood, ask questions. See if anyone had ever noticed someone else going in or out of the house.

The search yields nothing else. Maybe it wasn't a spontaneous thing, Webb thinks; maybe he planned it, right down to the lie about her telling him she was going away for the weekend. Webb looks over at Robert, standing in a corner, watching everything. They need to lean hard on Robert Pierce. Webb knows that in cases where the wife is murdered, it's usually the husband. But he's not one to leap to conclusions. Things are rarely simple.

As Olivia walks rapidly down the street, she sees something in front of the Pierce house. There's a crowd of people standing around, gazing at the white house with the bay window and black shutters.

The house is unremarkable, like any number of houses on the street. But the usually peaceful scene is quite different now. There are police cars parked along the street, and a white police van. A reporter is interviewing one of the neighbors on the pavement. Olivia doesn't want to be one of those ghoulish people who feast on the pain of others, but she can't deny she's curious. From here, she can't see anything of what's going on inside, except the occasional figure passing in front of one of the windows.

Olivia moves on quickly. She thinks about the people on the street, gossiping, speculating. She knows what they're saying. They're saying that he probably killed her.

Olivia thinks about Robert Pierce, inside his house right now with the police, people outside watching. He has forfeited his right to privacy because his wife has been murdered, and he might not have had anything to do with it.

She finds herself hoping, selfishly, that the renewed interest in Amanda Pierce will make people forget all about the break-ins and anonymous letters.

TEN

Becky Harris looks out her daughter's bedroom window at the side of the house, obscured by the curtain. From here she can see the street below, and the Pierce house next door. She spots Olivia out for a walk, making her way past the little crowd on the street. Becky tears nervously at the skin around her nails, an old habit she'd quit years ago, but that has recently resurfaced. She turns her attention back to the Pierce house.

She wonders what they've found, if anything.

Two people come out of the house. A man and a woman, both in dark suits. She remembers seeing the same two people yesterday, bringing Robert home. Detectives, she thinks. They must be. They stand in front of the house for a moment speaking to one another. She watches as the man's eyes sweep up and down the street. His partner nods in agreement, and they start off down the driveway.

It's obvious they're going to start questioning the neighbors.

———

Jeannette observes the detectives from behind the window. She knows they will be at her house soon. She tries to ignore how anxious she feels. She doesn't want to talk to the police.

When the knock finally comes, she jumps a little, even though she has been expecting it. She walks to the front door. The two detectives loom on her front step—beyond them she has a perfect view of the Pierce house, directly across the street. Her eyes flit nervously away from the detectives.

The man shows his badge. "I'm Detective Webb, and this is Detective Moen. We're investigating the murder of Amanda Pierce, who lived across the street from you. We'd like to ask you a few questions."

"Okay," she says, a little nervously.

"Your name?"

"Jeannette Bauroth."

Webb asks, "How well do you know Robert and Amanda Pierce?"

She shakes her head. "Not at all, really. I only know them to see them," she says. "They just moved in a little over a year ago. They kept to themselves, mostly."

"Did you ever see them arguing, or overhear them arguing?" She shakes her head. "Ever see any bruises on Amanda Pierce, a black eye, perhaps?"

"No, nothing like that," Jeannette says.

"Did you happen to notice Robert Pierce coming or going on the weekend of September twenty-ninth, the weekend his wife disappeared?"

She doesn't remember seeing Robert at all that weekend. "No."

"Did you ever see anyone else coming or going from their house?" Moen asks.

She has to answer. She doesn't want to. She bites her lip nervously and says, "I don't want to cause anyone any trouble."

"You're not causing trouble, Mrs. Bauroth," Detective Webb assures her, his voice quiet but firm. "You're cooperating in a police investigation, and if you know something, you must share it with us."

She sighs and says, "Yes, I saw someone. Their next-door neighbor, Becky Harris. I saw her coming out their front door, in the middle of the night. I'd gotten up to have a glass of milk—sometimes I have trouble sleeping—and happened to look out my window. And I saw her."

"When was this?" Webb asks.

She doesn't want to answer, but she really has no choice. "It was very late Saturday night, the weekend that Amanda disappeared." The detectives share a look.

"Are you absolutely sure of the date?" Webb asks.

"Yes," she says miserably. "I'm certain of it. Because by Tuesday, there was a rumor going around that Amanda hadn't come home and he'd reported her missing." She adds, "Becky's husband is away on business a lot. I think he was away that weekend. The kids are off at college."

"Thank you," Webb says. "You have been very helpful."

She looks back at him, feeling sick at heart. "I never would have said anything, except you're the police. You won't tell her where you heard it from, will you? We're neighbors."

The detective nods good-bye at her as he turns to go, but doesn't answer her question.

Jeannette retreats inside the house, closing the door with an unhappy frown. She hadn't told anyone what she saw. If Becky wants to cheat on her husband, that's her business. But the police, that's different. You have to tell them the truth.

She remembers Amanda at the neighborhood party, her big wide eyes, her perfect skin, the way she flipped her hair back when she laughed, mesmerizing all the men. She remembers Robert, too, just as handsome, but quietly watching his wife. He could have any woman he wanted, if he wanted.

So what does he see in Becky Harris?

Raleigh wrenches his locker open after his last class. He just wants to grab his stuff and go home. He's had a crap day. He screwed up a math test. He smiled at a cute girl and she looked right through him, like he wasn't there. All part of his crap life.

"Hey," Mark says, appearing suddenly behind him.

"Hey," Raleigh says, without enthusiasm.

Mark leans in closer and says, "Where were you after school yesterday?"

Raleigh looks over his shoulder to make sure no one is listening. "My mom picked me up—I had to go see the lawyer."

"That was fast," Mark says, surprised. "So, what did he say?"

Raleigh answers in a low voice, "He said if I ever get caught I'll go to juvie."

"That's it?"

"Pretty much."

Mark snorts. "How much did your parents pay for that?"

"I don't know, and this isn't funny, Mark." He looks him in the eye and says, "I'm done. I'm not going to do it anymore. It was fun for a while, but I'm not going to jail."

"Sure, I get it," Mark says.

"What's that supposed to mean?"

"Nothing."

"I gotta go," Raleigh says.

When the knock comes, Becky jumps out of her skin. She's standing in the kitchen, shoulders tensed, waiting for them.

She opens the door and sees the two detectives. From the window they looked ordinary. Up close they are much more intimidating. She swallows nervously as they introduce themselves.

"Your name?" Detective Webb asks.

"Becky Harris." The detective has an alert, probing look about him; it makes her even more nervous.

He asks, "Did you know Amanda Pierce?"

She shakes her head slowly, frowning. "Not really. I mean, my husband and I had drinks with her and her husband on one or two occasions—just casually. We had them over once, when they first moved in. And they had us over, a few weeks later. But we didn't do it again. We didn't have that much in common, other than the fact that we're neighbors." The detective waits, as if expecting more. She adds, "And I believe Amanda sometimes did temp work at my husband's office. But we barely know them, really. It's just awful what happened to Amanda."

"And you've never spent time with Robert Pierce other than on those two occasions?" the detective asks, looking at her closely.

She hesitates. "I used to see Robert over the fence sometimes, in the summer, sitting in the backyard, reading, drinking a beer. Sometimes we'd chat, very casual. He seems like a nice man." She looks back at the two detectives and says, "He was devastated when his wife went missing."

"So you've spoken to him since his wife disappeared?" Detective Webb asks.

She shifts uneasily. "Not really. Just—across the back fence. When Amanda didn't come home, he told me that he'd reported her missing, but he didn't want to talk. He looked awful."

The detective tilts his head at her, as if considering something. Then he says, "So, you weren't in his house until very late at night on the Saturday of the weekend his wife disappeared?"

She feels herself flush a deep red; they will know she's lying. But she must deny it. "I—No, I don't know what you're talking about. Where did you get that idea?" *Did Robert tell them?*

"Are you sure?"

"Of course I'm sure," she says sharply.

"Okay," the detective says, obviously not convinced. He hands her his card. "But if you'd like to reconsider your story, you can contact us. Thank you for your time."

Robert Pierce watches from the window as the detectives knock on the neighbors' doors, one after another, and question them on their doorsteps. He watches them interview Becky, next door. She's shaking her head. She glances over toward his house. Does she see him, watching from the window? He ducks his head back out of sight.

Olivia has made a penne with pesto and chicken for supper. Paul is eating quietly, his thoughts clearly elsewhere. They'd had a short, stricken conversation about Amanda Pierce when she got home from book club the night before. Then, when he got home from work, he told her that the news about Amanda had been all over the office. She wonders if Raleigh has heard about it, or if he's simply oblivious. Raleigh is wolfing his meal down wordlessly. He's been sullen and quiet since he got home from school, obviously sulking. She feels a spurt of annoyance. Why are they all such hard work? Why is it up to her to inquire how everybody's doing, to make conversation at the dinner table? She wishes Paul would make an effort. He didn't use to be like this—so . . . removed. And Raleigh's recent problems hang over them all like a dark cloud.

"How was school today, Raleigh?" she asks.

"All right," he mumbles, his mouth full, declining to elaborate.

"How did your math test go?"

"I don't know. Fine, I guess."

She says, "The police were searching the Pierce house today." Paul frowns at her. Raleigh looks up. Olivia knows that teenage boys pretty much live in a self-absorbed bubble—Amanda isn't on his radar, even though he'd broken into her house. She turns to him. "The woman who lived down the street from us, Amanda Pierce—she went missing a couple of weeks ago. Everyone thought she'd left her husband."

"Yeah, so," Raleigh says.

"It turns out she was murdered. They found her body yesterday."

Paul puts his cutlery down and goes rather still. "Should we really talk about this at the dinner table?" he says.

"Well, it's all over the news," she says. "They're saying now that she was beaten to death."

"Where did they find her?" Raleigh asks.

"They haven't said exactly. They haven't said much, actually. Somewhere out toward Canning, out in the Catskills," Olivia says.

"Did you know her?" her son asks.

"No," Olivia says, glancing at her husband.

"No, we didn't know her," Paul echoes.

She looks at her husband and notices something pass fleetingly across his face, but it's gone so quickly that she's not sure she saw it at all. She looks away. "It's too close to home," Olivia says, "having someone on your street murdered."

"Do they know who killed her?" Raleigh asks uneasily.

Olivia says, "I think they suspect her husband had something to do with it. Anyway, they were searching the house today." She pushes her pasta around her plate and glances up at her son. He looks disturbed. Suddenly she realizes what might be bothering him. *What if they find Raleigh's fingerprints in the house?*

ELEVEN

B ecky feels shaky as she walks into the police station downtown on Wednesday. She got the telephone call this morning, just after nine o'clock. Even before she picked it up, she just knew. She stared at the phone, watching it ring, but finally answered.

It was that detective, Webb. She recognized his voice before he'd even identified himself; she'd expected it. He'd figured in her dreams the night before, and not in a good way. He'd asked her to come down to the station, at her earliest convenience. He meant as soon as possible.

"Why? What for?" she asked cagily.

"We have a few more questions, if you don't mind," the detective had said.

They know she was in Robert's house that night. Robert must have told them. They'd known she was lying. Her heart is pumping loudly in her ears. If this gets out, it will destroy her marriage, her family.

Of all the shitty luck! How was she to know, when she slept with her handsome next-door neighbor—only twice, as it turns out—that it would all come spilling out because his wife would be murdered and he would become the center of a police investigation? Of course they questioned him, put him under a microscope—he would have to tell.

She'd never been unfaithful before, in over twenty years of marriage.

Now here she is, climbing the steps to the police station, hoping no one who knows her will see her. And then she thinks, what difference does it make, if all of this ends up in the newspapers anyway? She's absolutely mortified; she has children, nineteen-year-old twins—what will they think of her? There's no way they will possibly understand.

The officer at the front desk asks her to wait and picks up a phone. She sits in a plastic chair trying to slow her breathing. Maybe she can persuade them not to use her name. She wonders if she has any rights at all. She wonders if they're going to charge her with anything. Detective Webb approaches her. She stands up hurriedly.

"Thank you for coming in," he says courteously.

She can't even answer; her tongue is stuck in her throat. He leads her to an interview room, where she finds Detective Moen waiting. She's grateful that there's another woman here. She doesn't want to be alone with Webb. He frightens her.

"Please, have a seat," Moen says, and offers her a chair.

Becky sits down and the two detectives sit across from her.

"No need to be nervous," Detective Webb says. "Answering our questions is purely voluntary and you can leave at any time," he tells her.

But she has every reason to be nervous, and he knows it.

"Would you like some water? A cup of coffee?" Moen offers.

"No, I'm fine," Becky says, clearing her throat. She sits with her hands in her lap, beneath the table, where they can't see her picking at the skin around her cuticles, waiting for her life to collapse.

"Were you having a sexual relationship with Robert Pierce?" Webb asks bluntly.

She can't help it; she starts crying. She's sobbing so hard she can't answer the question. Moen pushes the box of tissues on the table toward her. They let her cry it out. Finally she sniffs loudly, wipes her eyes, and looks up at them.

He repeats the question.

"Yes."

"You didn't mention that when we talked to you yesterday," Webb says. "You denied that you were in his house on the night of September thirtieth."

She glances at Moen, who looks at her with what might be sympathy.

"I didn't want anyone to know," she says miserably. "I have a husband, kids. This is going to destroy my family."

Moen leans in toward her and says, "We don't want to destroy your family, Becky. We just need to know the truth."

She looks at the two detectives through swollen eyes. "I didn't tell you because I know he didn't hurt his wife. He wouldn't have hurt her and he certainly wouldn't have killed her. Robert wouldn't hurt a fly." She fidgets with the tissue in her hands. "So I didn't think you had to know. I didn't think it was relevant that we slept together. It only happened twice. I can understand that he had to tell you. I just wish he hadn't."

"It wasn't Robert who told us," Detective Webb says.

Her head shoots up. "What?"

"He denies having had sexual relations with anyone other than his wife during his marriage."

Becky feels like she might faint. Who else knows? And then she realizes that because of her, Robert has been caught in a lie.

"Someone saw you coming out of the Pierce house in the middle of the night, and put two and two together."

"Who?" she demands.

"I don't think it matters who, at this point," Moen says.

She puts her head in her hands and whispers, "Oh, God."

"Unfortunately," Detective Webb says, "this is a murder investigation, and you're collateral damage. The best thing you can do is cooperate with us fully."

Becky nods wearily. She has no choice. But she feels like she is betraying Robert, when he had obviously tried to protect her. She feels warmly toward him for it, which makes what she has to do now all the more painful.

"Tell us about your relationship with Robert Pierce," Moen says.

"There's not that much to tell, really," Becky begins wretchedly, looking down at the shredded tissue in her lap. "My husband is away on business a lot. My twins started college out of town last year and aren't home much. I was lonely, at loose ends. I used to see Robert out in his yard. His wife was away sometimes. We struck up a few conversations, like I told you. But it grew from there. It was stupid, I know. He's much younger than I am." She flushes. "I could tell he was attracted to me— he made it rather obvious—and I couldn't resist. I thought—I thought no one would be hurt. I thought no one would ever know."

Webb listens to her, his expression neutral, but Moen nods at her sympathetically.

She continues. "There was a weekend in August—he said his wife had gone away for the weekend with a friend. He invited me over. No one was home at my house—Larry was traveling for work and my kids were away at friends' places. That was the first time." She hesitates—she doesn't want to tell them the next part. "The second time was at the end of September, the weekend she went missing."

"Yes," Webb says, wanting her to continue.

Becky says unhappily, "You have no idea how hard this has been. And I couldn't talk to anyone about it." She looks back at the two detectives. "I *know* he couldn't have done it. He told me Amanda was away for the weekend with her friend Caroline, and that she wouldn't be back till Sunday night. I stayed there till very late on Saturday night, and went home around two in the morning."

"How do you know he couldn't have done it?" Webb asks.

"Trust me, there's no way he killed his wife." She shifts uneasily in her chair. "We had this unspoken routine—we only talked over the back fence, where no one would see us. I didn't see him again until the following Tuesday. He told me then that Amanda hadn't come home. That he'd reported her missing to the police." She looks at them, anguished. "I was afraid that it might come out then, that we'd been together that weekend."

"And since then, have you spoken to him?" Webb asks.

She shakes her head. "No. He's avoided me. He never goes into the backyard anymore. And I guess I wanted to avoid him, too, after everything. Put it behind me." She adds, "I'm sure he's worried that it will make him look bad, that he slept with me, and his wife—being murdered. But I can tell you, he's a good man. He wouldn't hurt a woman. He's just not the type."

"Maybe he was different with you than he was with his wife," Webb says.

"I don't think so," she says stubbornly.

"We'd like to get your fingerprints, if you don't mind," Detective Moen says.

"Why?" Becky asks, startled. She wonders again if she's going to be charged with something.

"We found some unidentified fingerprints in the Pierces' bedroom and en suite bathroom. We think they might be yours. If not, we need to know who else was in that bedroom."

She feels herself start to tremble. She's never been fingerprinted before. "Are you going to charge me with anything?" she manages to ask.

"No," Detective Webb says, "not at this time."

Becky returns directly home from the police station. She parks the car in the driveway and enters the house through the front door. Then she runs upstairs and throws herself down on her bed.

The kids will be home for Thanksgiving. What will she tell them? More immediately, what is she going to say to her husband when he gets home? Should she tell him everything, or say nothing and hope that it somehow never comes out?

She turns on her side and thinks anxiously about Robert. They can't possibly think he killed his wife. It's impossible. She thinks of his hands running up and down her body. He actually seemed to enjoy her—her company. She thinks of his lean, hard chest, his hair falling over his forehead, his smile that quirks up on one side.

How can she persuade the police that they should be looking elsewhere? Her protests this morning seemed to fall on deaf ears. Robert didn't kill his wife. If they understood that the way she did, they wouldn't be looking at him so closely, and they wouldn't be looking at her. She wants to protect herself, to protect her secret. And she'd like to protect him.

She doesn't want to admit it, but she's a little bit in love with Robert Pierce.

She's pretty sure the fingerprints in the bedroom are hers. When you fall headlong into a fantasy, and break your marriage vows and sleep with another man, you never, ever think that your fingerprints will end up in a murder investigation.

She wants to protect Robert. So she hasn't told the detectives everything.

She hasn't told them that Robert told her that night that he suspected Amanda was having an affair. She's afraid if the police know, they will think he has a motive.

And she hadn't told Robert, when she was lying in bed with him, that she knew who Amanda might be having an affair with.

She won't tell the detectives what she saw. Not unless it becomes absolutely necessary. Because she knows who Amanda's lover is. And there's no way he killed her either.

TWELVE

When Detective Webb looks at Robert Pierce that afternoon, he sees a man who might be perfectly capable of killing his wife. Pierce is very good-looking, clever, a little egotistical, a bit prickly. He must have been quite different with his neighbor, Becky Harris, Webb thinks. We all wear masks. We all have something to hide at one point or another. He wants to know what Robert Pierce might be hiding.

Pierce is in the chair across the interview table, in complete control of himself. He sits comfortably, leaning back in the chair. But his eyes are sharp, missing nothing.

"So, I'm the obvious suspect, is that it?" Pierce says.

"You're not a suspect at this time," Webb replies. "And you're not in custody—you're free to go, if you like." Pierce stays put. Webb studies him carefully and begins. "You say you arrived home right after work about five o'clock Friday, the twenty-ninth. Anybody see you?"

"I don't know. That's your job, isn't it? Isn't that what you've been asking the neighbors?"

Unfortunately for the detectives, the door-to-door had been frustrating. With the exception of Becky Harris, no one seemed to know the Pierces. They kept to themselves. No one remembered seeing Robert Pierce coming or going from his house that weekend. He had a habit of keeping his car in the garage, with the doors closed, so it was hard to say if he was home. Except for Jeannette Bauroth, no one had noticed anyone else going in or out either. There was no one to vouch for him, but he may well have been home Friday and Saturday. Or he might not have been. Records show that his cell phone was at home; that doesn't necessarily mean he was. "What did you do then?" Webb asks.

"Like I told you before, I watched some TV, went to bed early. I'm usually zonked by the end of the week."

"Alone?"

"Yes, alone."

"What about Saturday?"

"I slept in late. Hung around the house. Caught up on some work. Cleaned up a bit."

"Nobody can account for you?"

"No, I guess not."

"What about in the evening?"

He shifts in his chair, folds his arms across his chest, and looks Webb right in the eye. "Look, I wasn't completely honest with you before. In the evening, I had a woman friend in. She spent most of the night."

Webb allows a long pause before he says, "Who was that?"

"My next-door neighbor, Becky Harris. I believe you spoke to her yesterday. I saw you, on her doorstep."

"We have spoken to her."

"I don't know what she's told you. I didn't tell you before because I was trying to protect her. She obviously doesn't want anyone knowing about it. She's married. It was a harmless fling. I'm not proud of it. I shouldn't have cheated on my wife. But I was lonely, and she was there, so—" He shrugs. "It didn't happen again."

Webb studies him through narrowed eyes. "But it happened before, didn't it?"

Pierce looks at him in surprise. "So she told you. You already know all about it." He adds, "Yeah, we slept together one other time, in August. No biggie. Just letting off steam, for both of us."

"So why did you lie to us, Robert?" Moen asks. "You told us you never cheated on your wife."

"Why do you think? It makes me look like a bad husband, and that's what you want, isn't it? And maybe I was. But it doesn't mean I killed my wife." He leans forward and says, "I want you to stop dicking around with me and find out who killed Amanda. I want you to find the bastard who did this."

Webb says, "Oh, we will."

Moen says, "And Sunday?"

Pierce settles back into his chair again. "Sunday I went golfing with some friends all day. I had no idea Amanda wouldn't be coming back that night. All their names and phone numbers must be in the file. They'll confirm it. We had dinner at the clubhouse, and then I went home to wait for Amanda."

"Any idea who those fingerprints in your house belong to?"

"I imagine some of them are Becky's."

"What about the other set?"

He shrugs. "No idea."

"Have you been withholding anything else from us, Pierce?"

He looks back at Webb, his eyes insolent. "Like what?"

"Your wife. Was she having an affair?"

Pierce chews his lip. "I don't know."

"Really?" Webb says conversationally. "Maybe she was having an affair and you found out about it. Maybe you knew it wasn't her friend Caroline who she was going away with that weekend. Maybe you knew and you killed her." Robert doesn't even blink. "Or maybe you just made that up, that she said she was going away with Caroline. Maybe you arranged to meet your wife somewhere, and she had no idea what you had planned for her."

"No," Robert says, shaking his head. "You're way off base. I didn't think Amanda was having an affair then. The idea never even crossed my mind until I spoke to Caroline that Sunday and realized that Amanda had lied to me."

Webb doesn't believe him. "Did you know your wife was pregnant?"

"Yes. She planned to terminate it. We didn't want children." Pierce looks at them as if expecting them to have a problem with that. "Are we done here?" he says.

Pierce is rattled, but doing a good job of trying not to show it, Webb thinks. "Yes, don't let us keep you," he says, and watches as Pierce pushes the chair back loudly and walks out.

"He hasn't got a solid alibi," Moen says, once Robert Pierce has left. "He could have gone anywhere that Friday and Saturday. Left his cell phone at home so it wouldn't give him away."

Webb says, "The more I see him, the more I don't like him. Smug bastard."

"He doesn't seem to be particularly sad about his wife," Moen observes.

"No," Webb agrees. "If Amanda *was* having an affair, then who was she having an affair with?"

"If we knew that, we'd be getting somewhere," Moen mutters.

THIRTEEN

Olivia searched through the newspaper and the online news on Wednesday for any new information on the murder of Amanda Pierce. It's odd how wrapped up in it she's become, so quickly. But there was nothing new, and little in the way of hard facts. It was all simply a rehash of what had been said already. Investigations are continuing.

She'd tried to talk to Paul about it the night before in bed. "What do you think happened to her?" she asked.

"I don't know," Paul mumbled, trying to read his book.

"She must have been having an affair," Olivia said. "Why else would she lie to her husband about who she was with?"

"It's none of our business, Olivia," Paul said.

"I know," she replied, a little surprised at his tone. "But aren't you curious?"

"No, I'm not," he said.

She didn't believe him. And then she'd broached the subject of taking Raleigh to see someone. She didn't expect him to like the idea, but she was unprepared for his reaction.

"Paul," she said. "I'm worried about Raleigh."

"I know."

"I just—I think maybe we should send him to a therapist."

Here he put down his book and glared at her. "A therapist."

"Yes."

"Why the hell would we do that?"

"Because maybe—maybe it would help him to talk to someone."

"Olivia, he does not need a therapist. He needs a good kick in the ass." She glared back at him, annoyed.

Then Paul added, "Don't you think you're overreacting?"

"No, I don't. This is serious, Paul."

"Serious, yes. But he's not mentally ill, Olivia."

"You don't have to be mentally ill to see a therapist," she said in exasperation. Why did he have to be so backward about these things?

"It's just a phase. We'll deal with it. He doesn't need a therapist."

"How do you know? What makes you the expert?"

"I'm not going to discuss it, Olivia," he'd said sharply, and turned out his bedside table light and turned on his side away from her to go to sleep.

She'd lain in bed beside him, fuming, long after he'd begun to snore.

Now, as she drinks an afternoon cup of coffee, she recalls that she'd seen Paul reading the article about Amanda Pierce in the paper last night. He *is* curious. Of course he is. He just doesn't want to admit it. Paul always could be a little sanctimonious.

The preliminary forensics on the car and Amanda's belongings reveal frustratingly little.

"Sorry to disappoint you," Sandra Fisher, a forensic pathologist at the ME's office, says, "but we didn't get much."

Webb nods; he hadn't expected much, with the car having been in the water, but you always hope.

She says, "We didn't find any blood, skin, or hair except for the victim's. Nothing to get a DNA profile from. And we haven't been able to get anything else—no prints, no fibers."

"Anything from the purse or luggage?" Webb asks. They've already looked into her cell phone records and they haven't revealed anything; certainly no sign of any man on the side.

She shakes her head. "Sorry."

Webb nods and glances at Moen. Whoever killed Amanda and pushed the car into the lake didn't leave any trace behind.

Fisher says, "As you know, there was nothing where the car was found to indicate that that was where she was killed. There would have been a lot of blood. Most likely she was murdered somewhere else and the killer drove her car to that spot to sink it."

Webb says, "He probably knew the area, knew that would be a good spot to get rid of a car. Deserted, no guardrail, a decent slope, and the water gets deep quickly."

Moen nods in agreement. "He took a risk that someone might see him, no matter how deserted the road," she says.

"Find anything else in the car? Anything in the glove box?" Webb asks.

"The owner's manual and the service record. A first-aid kit. A tissue packet. She was very tidy." Fisher snorts in apparent disbelief. "You should see the shit in my car."

Webb swallows his disappointment. He'd been hoping for something.

"The fingerprints in the Pierce bedroom are a match for Becky

Harris," Fisher says. "But we don't know who the other set belongs to. Not coming up anywhere. Whoever it was, was in the office and all through the desk, too."

Robert Pierce has taken the week off work. It's only Wednesday. They've told him to take whatever time he needs. He has no interest in returning to the office. He wonders if his fellow attorneys in the small, five-lawyer firm think he's a murderer. They probably do. He wanders around his house and thinks about his interview with the detectives earlier that afternoon, replaying it over and over again in his mind.

He wonders what Becky is doing. He knows she's home. Her car is in the driveway. He's been avoiding her. He used her, rather shamelessly. It doesn't bother him that much. She was awfully easy to seduce. But he's worried about what else she might tell the detectives, now that the cat's out of the bag. She told them that they'd slept together. Did she also tell them that he thought Amanda was having an affair? Will she? He would like to know.

He finds himself in the kitchen, looking out the sliding-glass doors to the patio. It's a mild afternoon, with a tang of fall in the air. He decides to grab a beer and go outside for a bit. Maybe she'll come out, maybe she won't.

Robert saunters toward the back of the yard. If she's watching from inside the house, she will be able to see him there; she can't see him on the patio unless she's outside in her own backyard.

He hears the unmistakable sound behind him of the door sliding open next door, and stops. He knows that no one from the street can see them here; they have all the privacy they need. He turns around and lifts his eyes over the fence at Becky's house. She's standing there, in the doorway, staring at him. He walks slowly back along the fence toward her.

She looks awful. Her usually silky blond hair is lank, and she's not wearing any makeup. He wonders how he ever could have slept with her. She looks as if she's aged over the last couple of weeks.

She stays in the open door, watching him, her posture rigid. He can't read her expression. Perhaps he has misread her all along. For a moment, he feels a stab of annoyance at her. He smiles. And then she gives a tentative smile back, her face dimples, and he remembers why he briefly found her attractive.

"Becky," he says, in that way he knows she likes. Masculine but purring, seductive.

She steps slowly out of the door and toward him as if he is drawing her to him with an invisible string. It's ridiculously easy with her. It always was.

He quirks his mouth up on one side, tilts his head at her. "Come here," he says, and she does. She comes right up to him at the fence, the way she used to.

"Becky," he says, when she's close. There's not twelve inches separating their faces. "I've missed you." She closes her eyes, as if she doesn't want to look at him. Why? Does she think he's a killer? He sees a tear start to form at the corner of one of her eyes.

"Are you okay?" he asks softly.

Her eyes flutter open and she shakes her head. "No," she says, her voice sounding choked.

He waits.

"They think you killed Amanda," she says, her voice a whisper.

He knows that; he wants to know what she thinks. "I know. But I didn't kill her, Becky. You know that, don't you?"

"Of course! I know you didn't kill her!" She's more animated now, almost angry, on his behalf. "You wouldn't be capable of it. I told them that." She frowns. "I don't think they believed me, though."

"Oh, well, you know, they're cops," he says. "They always think the husband did it."

"They know about *us*," she says.

The way she says *us* makes him want to cringe, but he's careful not to show it.

"I know."

"I'm sorry. I had to tell them."

"It's okay. I told them, too. It's okay, Becky."

"I wouldn't have said anything, but they knew already."

"What?"

"Someone saw me coming out of your house in the middle of the night, the weekend Amanda disappeared."

"Who?" His attention is focused more sharply on her now. Who was watching his house in the middle of the night? He'd simply assumed Becky had blurted out the fact that they'd slept together to the police.

"I don't know, the detectives wouldn't tell me." She looks at him, her face blotchy with recent tears and lined by anxiety. "I'm afraid it will get out," she says, her voice trembling. "I think my fingerprints are in your bedroom. They took my prints at the police station. I don't know what to tell my husband."

She looks at him imploringly, as if he can solve this problem for her. He can't help her. He's barely paying attention to her; he's wondering who saw her leaving his place late at night.

"What if the police talk to him?" She looks at him with big, wet eyes.

That's your problem, he thinks. "Becky, what did you tell the detectives, exactly?"

"Just that we had drinks sometimes, that we talked over the fence, that we slept together the one time in August when Amanda was away, and again that Saturday night the weekend she disappeared. And that there was no way you could have hurt her."

He nods reassuringly. "Did you tell them that I suspected that Amanda was having an affair?"

"No, of course not. I'm not stupid."

"Good. Don't tell them that. Because it's not true. I don't know why I said that."

She seems taken aback. "Oh."

He wants to make sure she understands. "I never thought Amanda was seeing someone else. Not until the Sunday night when I talked to Caroline. You've got that, right? You'll remember that?" She might even be a little frightened of him now. Good.

"Sure," she says.

He nods, doesn't give her the quirky smile. "Take care of yourself, Becky."

FOURTEEN

Olivia is working in the upstairs office that afternoon when she hears the doorbell ring. She wonders if it's the detectives, broadening their enquiries. She hastens down the stairs to the front door. But it isn't the two detectives standing there; it's a woman she's never seen before. She's older, maybe close to sixty, with a plump figure. Her wide face is lined, her blond hair is tidy, and she's wearing a pale lipstick. Olivia is about to politely say, "No, thank you," and shut the door, annoyed about the intrusion, when the woman says, "I'm not trying to sell anything," and smiles warmly.

Olivia hesitates.

"My name is Carmine," the woman says in a friendly tone.

The name sounds familiar, but Olivia can't place it. "Yes?"

"I'm sorry to bother you, but I just moved in and my house was broken into recently. I'm going around the neighborhood telling people to keep their eyes open."

Olivia's heart instantly begins to pound. "That's awful," she says, attempting a suitably sympathetic expression. "Did they take much?"

"No, he didn't take anything."

"Oh, that's good," Olivia says. "No harm done then." She wants to slam the door in the woman's face, but she doesn't dare be rude to her.

"I wouldn't say no harm done," the woman answers. "The kid snooped through my house. And not just mine—apparently he broke into other houses as well, and hacked into people's computers."

"Oh, my," Olivia says, taken aback by the woman's abruptness. "Have they caught who did it?" She hopes her face and voice are what this woman would expect in the circumstances. She's so distressed that she can't tell.

"No. But I got an anonymous letter about it. Apparently it was a teenage boy, and his mother wrote this letter of apology. But I don't know who she is."

She holds up the letter. The letter that Olivia wrote and printed and stuck through this woman's mail slot. Has she figured it out? Does she know it was Raleigh? Is that why she's really here? To confront her? Olivia doesn't know how to react, what to say. This woman wouldn't even be here if Olivia hadn't written that letter. The woman looks at her, studying her carefully.

"Are you all right?" she asks.

"Yes, I'm fine," Olivia says, flushing. "I'm sorry, I've been ill recently," she lies, "and I'm still not completely well."

"Oh, then I'm sorry to bother you with this," the woman says, looking at her closely.

"I was resting when you rang the doorbell."

"Sorry," the woman says sympathetically. But she doesn't go away. Instead she says, "I see you've got a basketball hoop in your driveway."

Olivia is rattled and just wants this nosy woman to go away. She really does feel ill and flushed, as if she might faint. But she doesn't want it to seem as if this conversation is upsetting her. In her confusion, she wonders why the woman is mentioning the basketball hoop. And then she realizes.

"Yes." It's all she can think of to say.

"Teenagers?" she asks.

Olivia looks back at her now, her eyes meeting the other woman's. And it's like there is an unspoken communication between them—the woman is asking her if it was her son who broke into her house and whether she is the one who wrote the letter. The bloody awful nerve of this woman, standing on her doorstep! "Yes. There are lots of teenagers around here."

"Teenagers can be so difficult," the woman says.

"Do you have children?" Olivia asks.

The woman nods. "Three. All grown up now and moved away. One of them was a real handful."

Olivia hesitates, on the brink of inviting the woman inside, but then she remembers Paul, and the lawyer, and most of all Raleigh. She can't admit anything to this woman. Olivia must hold her ground.

"I have one, a boy," Olivia says, rallying. "I've been very lucky. I've never had any problems with him," she lies, "at least not so far. I'm very proud of him."

"You're very fortunate," the woman says a little coldly.

This woman must know—or suspect by now—that it's her son who broke into her house, and that she's the mortified woman who wrote the letter. Olivia feels sick to her stomach and wants urgently to be done with this conversation. "Yes, I know," Olivia says. "I really must go. Good-bye." She closes the door and hurries upstairs, where she runs to the bathroom and throws up her lunch into the toilet bowl. Tears come to her eyes, as they always do when she throws up. But as she remains hovering over the bowl, the tears come in earnest. She has really messed things up. She feels fear and anger in equal measure. This woman is onto her. She has to be. What will happen to Raleigh now? That woman can't prove anything, can she? But Olivia doesn't want Paul or Raleigh—especially not Paul—knowing that she sent those letters. So she can't tell them about that woman's visit to their house, obviously, either.

Olivia slowly gets to her feet and rinses her mouth out at the sink. She looks at herself in the mirror—she looks terrible. Unable to deal with this on her own, she calls Glenda and asks her to come over. Glenda arrives about fifteen minutes later, her short auburn hair windblown and her face lined with concern.

"What's the matter?" she asks, as she steps inside.

Olivia knows what she looks like. She looks like she just threw up. She looks distraught. But if there's anyone she can trust with this, it's Glenda. She can tell Glenda, but not her own husband. What does that say about her marriage? Olivia thinks fleetingly. But there's nothing really wrong with her marriage, she tells herself; this is a special circumstance. She normally doesn't keep anything from Paul, and he doesn't keep anything from her—it's just this one thing—that she now wishes she had never done. But she also doesn't want Paul to find out. She wonders if she should simply tell him, or not. That's what Glenda's for—emotional support, and to advise her on what to do next.

"Glenda," she begins, "something terrible has happened."

Glenda's face falls, as if she thinks someone has died. "What is it?"

Olivia leads her into the kitchen and then turns and faces her. "I did such a stupid thing, with those letters," she says.

"Oh," Glenda says, in obvious relief. "I thought there'd been an accident or something."

"No," Olivia says.

"Don't worry so much about the letters," Glenda says. "It'll blow over. Nobody's going to find out it was Raleigh."

"I think someone already has."

They sit down and Olivia tells her about Carmine. "She must be the one who lives next door to Zoe," Olivia says. "Remember Zoe talking about it at book club?"

Glenda bites her lip, thinking. "She didn't actually accuse you of writing the letter, did she?" Glenda asks.

"Not in so many words," Olivia admits. "But I could tell what she was thinking from the way she was looking at me." She looks at Glenda in misery. "I wish I could hide my feelings better, but you know what I'm like. She could tell I was upset, and why would I be, unless it was my son who broke into her house?" She props her elbows on the kitchen table and holds her head in her hands. She thinks about how it all started, just a few days ago, her and Paul grilling Raleigh about it in this very kitchen. "If I hadn't written those damn letters, she would never even have known he was there. Paul is going to be *furious* at me."

"It's not really your fault," Glenda says, trying to soothe her. "You didn't do anything wrong. Raleigh's the one who broke in. You acted out of a sense of decency. You were trying to do the right thing."

"And it blew up in my face," Olivia replies bitterly.

"Paul will understand."

"No, he won't. And Raleigh won't either."

"But you put those letters through the slots on Sunday night. You didn't see the lawyer till Monday. It's not as if you sent the letters *after* the lawyer said not to."

"No. But I knew Paul didn't like the idea. And I probably should have confessed to it right then, in the lawyer's office, but I didn't. At least this would all be out in the open, and I could go back to the lawyer and ask him what to do."

"You can still ask the lawyer what to do. But you'll have to come clean with Paul first. You'll have to tell him."

"I know," Olivia says miserably. "What a mess. And I'm so worried about Raleigh. Why did he do it? Why would he want to snoop around other people's houses?"

Glenda shakes her head helplessly. "I don't know."

"I suggested to Paul last night that maybe we should send Raleigh to a therapist. He told me I was overreacting, that it was just a phase. He's not in favor of it—in fact, he was quite adamant about it." It was the first real argument they'd had in years. The second one will be tonight, when she tells him about the letters.

"That's the worst thing about being a parent," Glenda says, "not knowing if you're doing the right thing, whether you should step in or step back. Our parents just ignored us. Maybe that was better."

"I know," Olivia sighs.

Glenda gives her an uneasy glance and then looks away. "I worry about Adam, all the time. Ever since he started drinking. It's not like Keith and I are problem drinkers."

"It's the kids he hangs out with," Olivia ventures.

"He didn't use to hang out with those kids. He used to be more sporty and academic. Now his grades are slipping and he's missing practice. And he's become so moody and insolent. Frankly, he's awful to be around."

Olivia can hear the strain in Glenda's voice. They all sound strained these days when they're talking about their kids. It didn't use to be this way. They used to sit around the wading pool, chatting and laughing, serene in the expectations that their kids would be bright and beautiful and untroubled. Parents always seem to have overly optimistic visions of their kids' talents and futures when they're toddlers, Olivia thinks—maybe that's how they manage to keep going.

Finally Glenda gets up to leave. "Not the way we thought it would be, is it?"

Glenda walks home thoughtfully. Everyone warns you that the teen years will be tough, but she wasn't expecting anything like what she's dealing with. She thinks about her own problems. Her son . . . What will become of him? She finds herself brushing away sudden tears. What will become of all of them?

She thinks back to the night before. A year ago, Adam would have been out at some kind of sports practice or game. She and Keith might have lingered over supper, had another glass of wine, and talked. That's something they don't do anymore. She doesn't buy wine very often at all anymore, because she doesn't want Adam to see them drinking. Is that why she stopped buying it, or was she afraid that Adam might sneak some of it himself? Probably both.

She and Keith don't talk much anymore. At home, things are strained. Oddly, she and Keith only seem like themselves when they're out of the house, with other people. She thinks back to the previous Friday night when she and Keith had gone to the Sharpes' for dinner. Maybe they'd overdone the drinking a bit themselves that night— letting themselves off the leash because Adam wasn't there to see them, and they'd only had to walk to the next street to get home.

Olivia and Paul had been in good spirits. They hadn't known then that their son was out breaking into houses. Olivia had made an excellent roast, and Glenda had drunk her wine and watched her still very handsome husband laughing with Paul, the two of them remembering some of the funny things that had happened over the years. It had been a great evening, like old times. If only they could turn back the clock.

FIFTEEN

Olivia waits until supper is cleaned up and Raleigh is in his room, plugged into his laptop with his headphones on, ostensibly doing homework. Paul is in the living room, glancing through the newspaper.

She stands quietly for a moment, watching him. She has to tell him.

She sits down near him on the sofa. Paul looks up from the paper. "We need to talk," Olivia says quietly.

Instantly a look of concern crosses his face. She doesn't usually start with this kind of opening. It sounds ominous. It *is* ominous.

"What's wrong?" he asks, also with a lowered voice.

"There's something I have to tell you, and you're not going to like it." Now he looks alarmed. He waits, his eyes focused on her, alert. She says, "I don't want Raleigh to hear this until we decide what we're going to tell him."

"For Christ's sake, Olivia, what is it? You're scaring me."

She takes a deep breath and says, "Last weekend, before we saw the lawyer, I wrote letters of apology to the people that live in the houses Raleigh broke into."

He looks back at her, incredulous. "But you didn't send them," he says emphatically.

She chews the inside of her cheek. "I did. I put identical anonymous letters through their mail slots."

He stares back at her with his mouth open, in obvious disbelief. Then he sputters, "What are you talking about?"

"I took Raleigh out in the car, when you were out golfing last Sunday, and made him show me the two houses he snuck into."

"And you didn't tell me?" he hisses at her, clearly furious.

"No."

"Why not?"

"Because I knew you wouldn't like it."

"Of course I don't like it!" His voice is rising. "I already told you that I thought an apology was a bad idea! And the lawyer agreed with me."

"I know. And I'm sorry. I did it before we saw the lawyer." She's beginning to cry. "I thought it wouldn't do any harm, and I thought some sort of apology should be made. There was nothing in the letter that would lead back to Raleigh."

He looks at her in cold fury. "I don't like that you went behind my back."

"I know," she says, almost as coldly. "And I'm sorry, but why should *you* get to make all the decisions? I don't like it when you tell me what I can and cannot do." She feels furious with him suddenly. Why *should* he get to decide everything? Even though, this time, he was absolutely right. She's still smarting because he overruled her the night before on the question of having Raleigh see a therapist. She takes a deep breath and exhales. "I made a mistake. You were right. I shouldn't have done it. I feel awful about going behind your back. And I felt terrible about not telling you. We've never kept secrets from each other before. We've always been honest with each other."

He turns away from her. "Let's just hope this doesn't jump up and bite us in the ass," he says. "How could you do this without talking to me? That's not like you."

Because you gave me no choice, Olivia wants to say, but she remains silent. A moment passes, but the tension between them doesn't dissipate.

"So why are you telling me this now?" Paul asks testily, turning back to her again.

"Because . . . there may be a problem."

"What problem?" His voice is tense.

Olivia steels herself to tell him the next bit. "A woman came here today. Her name is Carmine something. She lives next door to Zoe, from book club." Olivia pauses, but then forces herself to go on. "Raleigh broke into her house. She's been going around the neighborhood, telling people about the break-in, and showing them the letter."

"You didn't tell her the truth, did you?" Paul glowers at her.

"No, of course not!"

"Well, that's something," Paul snorts.

"But she may have guessed."

"How?"

"You know what I'm like!" Olivia exclaims. "I can't hide anything! I got really nervous. She asked me if I was okay. She could tell I was upset. Then she started asking if I had teenagers in the house. I'm worried that she may have figured it out."

There's a long, pained silence. Olivia can't even look at her husband. She stares miserably at the floor instead.

"Jesus," Paul mutters. "I can't believe this." After a moment, he asks, "What was she like?"

"What do you mean?"

"Is she the type to pursue this and press charges? Is she likely to come after him?"

"I—I don't know. Maybe. I mean, why was she going around knocking on doors in the first place?" Olivia hears a sound and looks up; Paul looks up, too. She sees Raleigh standing in the living room doorway, looking tense.

"Figured what out?" Raleigh asks. "What's going on?"

He looks anxiously at both of them. She glances at Paul. They have to tell him.

Raleigh asks, "Why are you crying, Mom? What's happened?"

Olivia looks at her husband, gauging the situation; he's already angry at her. They have no choice. She turns back to Raleigh. She hates the thought of Raleigh hearing about the letters, that he might be found out. He'll blame her. He won't take responsibility for his part in it, he'll just blame her for the letters. She pulls herself together. *This is what happens when you interfere*, she thinks bleakly.

Raleigh slouches into an armchair, facing them on the sofa, his expression alarmed. "Am I going to be arrested?"

"No," Olivia says.

"We hope not," Paul clarifies, and Olivia sees the quick flash of fear in Raleigh's eyes.

"I didn't take anything," Raleigh says quickly. "I'm never going to do it again. I *swear*."

"That's what we hoped," Paul says. "But your mother here, against my express wishes, slipped apology letters through the mail slots of the houses you broke into."

Raleigh turns to her in disbelief and obvious fear. "Why would you do that? The lawyer said—"

"I know what the lawyer said," Olivia breaks in. "I did it before we saw the lawyer. I thought *someone* should apologize to these people and let them know that their computers had been hacked. I still think it was the morally right thing to do." Her voice has become defensive. "And the letters were anonymous—there was nothing in them that could lead to you, Raleigh."

"Except that one of the people whose house you broke into came knocking on our front door today," Paul says. "And your mother got nervous and may have made the woman suspicious."

Raleigh looks like he's about to be sick.

"So it's not necessarily over yet," Paul says.

Olivia forces herself to say it. "The other house that Raleigh broke into was the Pierces'."

Paul looks back and forth between the two of them, his face showing disbelief. "And you're just telling me this now?"

"I didn't think it mattered," Olivia says lamely.

"You didn't think—Jesus Christ! The police have been all over that house!"

"I know," Olivia says.

"I don't suppose you wore gloves, Raleigh?" Paul says, turning to his son.

Raleigh shakes his head, looking frightened, and says, "I'm not a criminal."

"Oh, Christ," Paul says.

"The police don't have Raleigh's prints on file," Olivia says, her voice tense. "They can't connect Raleigh to the break-ins." *Surely they can't prove anything against Raleigh?*

"What if this woman goes to the police and accuses him?" Paul asks. "What if they take his prints? They'll know he was in both of those damn houses!"

Olivia sends a desperate, pleading look for forgiveness at her son, but he turns and flees upstairs, before he bursts into tears again.

Raleigh returns to his bedroom and slams the door behind him. He throws himself down on his bed and puts his headphones on and turns his music up loud. He wants to blot the scene downstairs from his mind, but he can't. He keeps thinking about it. How could his mother have been so stupid? He'd wanted to yell at her, but he didn't dare. And his dad—his dad is still furious at him, he can tell. And now his dad is furious at his mom, too.

Raleigh's angry at everyone, but he knows deep down that it's mostly his own fault.

He lies on his bed, heart pounding, wondering if he's going to be arrested. He will have to see that horrible lawyer again. He feels bad at how much money this might cost his parents. He will make it up to them. He'll be a better son. He'll start doing chores, work harder in school.

Raleigh is sick with fear. Every time someone knocks at the door, he's going to think it's the police, coming for him.

Becky rattles around in her empty house, which is far too big for just one person. It's Wednesday night. Her husband has been away on business all week, on the West Coast, although they have been in touch by phone. He'll be home tomorrow evening. She's proud of her husband, Larry, and grateful that he's been successful—she doesn't need to work—but sometimes it's lonely. With the long hours and travel, he missed so much of the kids growing up. She didn't really mind it when the kids were here, but since the twins went off to college, she's missed him. Working from home wasn't her first choice; she'd rather be out of the house. But she wanted to get back into bookkeeping, and the only work she could find was freelance. Now she's made such a mess of things that she wonders if she should just find a full-time job at a shop somewhere. Something that will get her out of the house. She needs to keep herself busy. Because she'd been thinking far too much about Robert Pierce, alone next door, and what they were like together.

She thinks uneasily about him now. He *did* suspect his wife was having an affair. It makes her uncomfortable, what he said to her, telling her what to do. He's lying, and he wants her to lie, too. He's clearly afraid of the police. She can understand that. He doesn't want her telling the detectives that he knew his wife was cheating. Well, she won't tell them. He doesn't have to worry about her.

Now she remembers something else—a night in the summer. It was before Becky slept with Robert the first time, but she was already hopelessly attracted to him, devoting far too much of her time to thinking about him.

Becky didn't mean to spy on them. But it was a hot night, and she had the upstairs windows open and she heard music coming from their backyard. Some slow jazz piece filtering across the sweet summer air, something romantic. She looked out a window, taking care not to be seen. Robert and Amanda were on the back lawn, wrapped in each other's arms. She felt an immediate stab of jealousy. Oh, to be young and in love again—dancing in the moonlight! Becky couldn't see their faces, but after watching them for a minute, she realized something was wrong. Something about the way they were holding each other. Amanda wasn't relaxing into her husband; she seemed to be moving stiffly as they danced, as if she were unwilling, almost as if she were being forced.

After a moment, Becky saw Amanda's shoulders convulsing. She was sobbing, her face buried in her husband's chest.

Now Becky wonders again about what she saw. She'd romanticized Robert, she knows that. What had been going on that night in the dark?

Robert couldn't have killed Amanda, Becky tells herself again, staring into the dark. Surely she would know if someone she'd had sex with was a killer? Surely she would be able to tell?

SIXTEEN

Carmine is lingering on her front walk on Thursday morning when she sees Zoe come out of the house and head for her car.

"Hey, Zoe!" she calls, and makes her way over to her next-door neighbor's driveway.

"Hi, Carmine," Zoe calls. "How are you?"

"Good." She reaches the driveway. "Have you heard anything more about that woman who was killed?"

Zoe shakes her head. "It's too awful. To have somebody murdered who lived so close." Her expression is solemn. She adds, "I'm sure the police will find out who did it." She pauses with her hand on the door of the car. "Any luck finding out who broke into your house?"

"I think so," Carmine says. "Do you know the Sharpes? On Sparrow? They have a teenage boy, right?"

"Yes, Raleigh." Zoe frowns and narrows her eyes, catching her meaning. "You can't think it's him."

"Why not?"

"Well, why would you? He's Olivia and Paul's boy. He would never do something like that. I know Olivia. She's in my book club."

Carmine remains quiet, watching Zoe.

"Why do you think it's him?" Zoe asks finally.

"I went by there yesterday afternoon," Carmine says. "The way she reacted, I'd swear she knew exactly what I was talking about. She looked very nervous, and guilty. I'd bet a hundred dollars she wrote that letter."

Zoe bristles. "I don't think so." She pauses. "We were talking about it at book club, and I didn't notice anything."

"Maybe you could talk to her?" Carmine suggests.

"What do you mean?"

"Find out if it was her son, and if she wrote the letter?" Carmine says.

"I'm not going to ask her that!"

"Okay," Carmine says, turning away.

"Wait!" Zoe calls. "What are you going to do?"

"I don't know yet," Carmine says and heads back inside.

Webb and Moen stand on Becky Harris's front step and ring the bell. They both feel that she is still holding something back, that she knows more than she's telling.

Her car is sitting in the driveway. The day is overcast and threatens rain. Webb rings the bell again, flashing an impatient look at Moen.

Finally the door opens. Becky looks like she hasn't slept much. Her hair is pulled back into a ponytail as if she didn't want to bother with it. She's wearing yoga pants and a shapeless sweater.

"What do you want?" she asks.

"May we come in?" Webb asks politely.

"What for?"

"We have a few more questions."

She sighs and opens the door reluctantly.

Webb wonders about her change of mood. The day before she had been weepy and terrified of exposure, but today she seems resigned. She's had a long, probably sleepless night to think about it. Perhaps she's realizing that it's inevitable that her indiscretions will come out. She leads them into the living room. She doesn't ask them to sit down or offer them anything; it's clear she doesn't want them here. He can't blame her. She's been sleeping with her neighbor, now the chief suspect in a murder investigation.

The two detectives sit down on the sofa; Becky finally slumps down in an armchair angled across from them.

"We appreciate that this isn't easy for you," Webb begins. Becky watches him uneasily, her eyes darting to Moen as if for support, and then back to him. "But we think there's more that you can tell us."

"I told you everything already," Becky says. "I don't know anything about Amanda's murder." She shifts restlessly in her chair. "I told you I don't think he did it. Someone else must have done it."

"It's just that we feel you're keeping something from us, Becky," Webb says. "There's something you're not telling us." She looks back at him with a stony, almost angry expression, but her hands are fidgeting in her lap. He notes that the skin around the cuticles is picked raw.

"I spoke to him yesterday afternoon, over the fence," she says finally. He waits patiently. She looks down at her lap. "He was outside, in the backyard. I saw him, and opened the back door. He called me over."

She seems to think for a moment, as if deciding what to say. Webb already doesn't trust the truth to come out of Becky's mouth, but some edited version of it.

"He asked me if I thought he'd killed Amanda. I told him of course not. He told me he didn't kill her, and I said I believed him. I told him that you knew about us. That I was worried about my fingerprints in his bedroom, and that my husband would find out—that it might ruin my marriage, destroy my family." Her eyes are starting to fill up. She puts her hands up to her face, covers her mouth. Webb finds himself staring at her ragged cuticles.

"Did he say anything else?" he prods, when she hasn't spoken for a while.

She shakes her head. "Not that I remember." She sniffles and then looks up at them. "My husband's coming home tonight. This is all going to come out, isn't it?"

Webb says, "The truth has a way of coming out."

She looks at him bitterly. "Then if it does, I hope all of it does. I hope you find the real killer and leave Robert alone. Because I don't think he did it." She pauses as if she's gathering herself. Something in her face has changed, as if she has come to some kind of decision. "There's something else I have to tell you."

Webb leans forward, elbows on knees, and looks at her intently. "What's that?"

"I know Amanda was seeing someone else."

"How do you know that?" Webb asks, feeling a prickle of excitement.

"I saw them together, and I knew. I didn't want to tell you, because I know him, and I know he couldn't have killed Amanda either. I knew you'd just go after him like you've gone after Robert, when she was probably murdered by some nutcase somewhere, not killed by her husband, or the man she was seeing, who may have been unfaithful, but wouldn't hurt a fly."

"Becky, who did you see Amanda with?"

She sighs heavily, regretfully. "It was Paul Sharpe. His wife, Olivia, is a friend of mine. They live down the street," she says miserably, "at Number Eighteen."

"Tell us what you saw, Becky," Detective Webb urges.

Becky is sick at what she's about to do, but feels she has no choice. Like the detective says, the truth will come out eventually. She's telling the truth now, no more, no less. "I saw Paul and Amanda together one night, a short time before Amanda disappeared. It was raining, and they were sitting in Amanda's car. It was about nine o'clock at night, and I was leaving the movie theater downtown. They were in a parking lot. There's a bar across from the parking lot. I wondered if they'd been in the bar together."

"And . . ."

She thinks back, trying to remember every detail. "They were in the front seat—she was in the driver's seat. There was a light in the parking lot shining on them so I could see them quite clearly. I was so shocked at seeing them together, I stopped in my tracks and stared for a minute, but they were so intent on one another that they didn't notice me."

"You're absolutely sure it was them?"

"I'm certain. Their faces were close together at first. I thought they might kiss. But then, after a minute, they seemed to be arguing."

"Go on."

"He was saying something to her, as if he were angry, and she laughed at him and pulled away and he grabbed her arm."

"So you think they were seeing each other?" Webb asks.

She nods. "That's what it looked like. They seemed . . . intimate. Why else would they be there together?" She looks down at her lap. "I felt awful for Olivia. She's a good friend of mine. Amanda always struck me as a flirt, but I never would have guessed that Paul would cheat on Olivia."

"Can you be more specific about the date?"

She closes her eyes for a moment, trying to remember. Finally she opens them and says, "It was a Wednesday—it must have been September twentieth." She watches Moen jot it down.

"Did you see them together any other time?"

She shakes her head. "No."

"Why didn't you tell us this earlier?" Detective Webb asks.

"I'm sorry," she says. "But I don't think Paul is capable of harming anybody. And Olivia's a friend. I hate to do this to her."

"Did you ever mention this to Robert Pierce?"

"No, absolutely not."

"You sure about that?" Webb presses.

"Yes, I'm sure."

"Do you happen to know where Paul Sharpe works?" Moen asks.

"Yes. Fanshaw Pharmaceuticals—the same company as my husband. On Water Street, downtown." She watches Moen write it down.

"Is there anything else you're holding back?" Webb asks; she hears the sarcasm in his voice.

She looks right at him and says, "No, that's it."

We need to talk to Paul Sharpe," Webb says to Moen, over the hood of the car. She nods. He looks at his watch. "Let's go."

The drive back to downtown Aylesford doesn't take long—a mere ten minutes. It's a small city, with newer buildings butting up against old in the downtown center. Fanshaw Pharmaceuticals is in a brick building, not far from the Aylesford Bridge.

Webb and Moen enter the building and are told that Paul Sharpe's office is on the fifth floor. There, they are greeted by a receptionist whose perfect eyebrows rise ever so slightly when they show their badges.

"We'd like to speak with Paul Sharpe," Webb says.

"I'll get him for you," she says.

Webb spends the time staring sightlessly at the expensively bland décor and thinking about Amanda Pierce. They don't wait long. A man in a navy suit enters the reception area. He's tall, well built, with very short salt-and-pepper hair, probably close to fifty. He's kept himself fit, and he walks toward them with the ease of someone who stays in shape. He casts his eyes over the two of them. He looks wary, Webb thinks. He opens his badge, introduces himself and Moen, and says, "Is there somewhere we can talk privately?"

"Sure, let me find a meeting room." Sharpe leans over the large reception desk and speaks to the receptionist.

"You can have conference room three, it's empty," she tells him in a discreet voice.

"Come with me," Sharpe says, and they follow him down a carpeted hallway to a glass-walled meeting room. They step inside. There's a long table and chairs, and windows that look onto the river and the bridge. The water is dark and choppy today. It has started to rain now, and it's coming down heavily. Sharpe closes the door behind them and turns to face them. "What can I do for you?" he asks, gesturing to them to take a seat.

Webb says, "We're investigating the murder of Amanda Pierce."

Sharpe nods, his face a careful blank. "Yes, I've heard about it, of course. She lived on our street, and worked here occasionally. It's a terrible thing." He shakes his head regretfully, frowning. "How can I help?"

"Did you know Amanda Pierce?"

He shakes his head again slowly. "No. I mean," he amends quickly, "she temped here sometimes, but it's a big company; she never worked for me directly. I knew her to see her, but I don't think I ever spoke to her."

"Is that right," Webb says, and waits. Sharpe flushes slightly, looks uncertain. Webb says, "Are you sure you never spoke to her?"

Sharpe looks down at the table, arranges his face as if he's concentrating, trying to remember something. Finally he says, "I think I did sort of meet her once, now that you mention it. Funny, I'd forgotten it." He looks up at them. "I was out for drinks one night after work, with some friends, and . . . I think she might have joined us for a drink, but I didn't speak to her. She wasn't sitting near me and it was loud, you know."

Webb nods. "When was this?"

Sharpe looks down and adopts his concentrating face again. Webb isn't buying it. But he waits to see what Sharpe comes up with.

"It wasn't that long before she disappeared. I can't remember when exactly."

"You can't narrow it down more than that? Even though she disappeared some time shortly afterward?"

The other man's eyes flash, a slight hint of temper. "I don't remember the date, it was unremarkable at the time. But it was shortly before I heard she disappeared."

"What bar was it?"

"Rogue's, on Mill Street. Sometimes we go there for drinks after work—not often."

"Who's we?" Webb asks.

"Well, it depends. It changes week to week. Just people from the office, whoever's up for it, you know."

"Can you remember who was there that night, when she joined you for a drink?"

Sharpe does the same thing again—looks down, furrows his brow for a moment. He's a poor actor, and a poor liar. "I'm sorry, I'm not exactly sure. But me, Holly Jacobs, Maneet Prashad, Brian Decarry, Larry Harris, Mike Reilly. That's the best I can do."

Moen is busily writing the names down.

"And why did she join you? Did she know someone?"

He shakes his head again. "You know, I'm not sure. Probably she was temping here that day and came along."

Webb nods. Then he leans in a little closer to Paul Sharpe and fixes him with his eyes. "You know, I'm having a hard time believing you."

"What?" He looks worried now. "Why?"

"Why?" Webb says. "Because we have a witness who saw you talking—intimately—with Amanda. Just the two of you, in the front seat of her car, downtown, at around nine o'clock at night. Not long before she disappeared. Wednesday, September twentieth, to be exact."

Sharpe's face drains of color. His facade has begun to crumble. He swallows. "It's not like that."

"Not like what?"

"I wasn't involved with Amanda, if that's what you're thinking." He exhales deeply, slumps a little in his chair. "I didn't want to say anything. Maybe I should have, but—" He runs his hand over his face, and suddenly the pretense seems to fall away. "Look, I didn't really know Amanda. I only spoke to her that one time, in her car. It was to warn her off. She was having an affair with someone here, someone I work with. I told her to stay away from him. I thought she was trouble. I didn't want to see his life fall apart. Maybe it wasn't my place. I wish now I hadn't done it. I should have minded my own business." He adds, "The night we had drinks at the bar—that was the night I spoke to Amanda, in her car. But I don't remember the date."

Webb sits back in his chair and considers the man in front of him. "So you weren't having an affair with Amanda yourself."

"God, no."

"Sharpe's name hadn't come up on her cell phone records.

"Do you have a burner phone?" Moen asks.

"No."

"Where were you the weekend starting Friday afternoon, September twenty-ninth, till the following Monday morning?" Webb asks.

Sharpe looks at him, appalled. "You can't honestly think I had anything to do with Amanda Pierce—with what happened to her," he says, his gray-blue eyes alarmed.

Webb says, "You were seen arguing with her shortly before she disappeared. We're just eliminating possibilities. If you can tell us where you were that weekend, we're good."

"Okay," Sharpe says, nodding. He appears to think. "The only thing that stands out is that on Sunday we had my wife's parents over for brunch. They stayed till midafternoon. I helped my wife prepare it and clean up afterward. Other than that, it was just a regular weekend at home, I think. We usually stay in on Friday and Saturday night. Watch something on Netflix. I imagine that's what we did."

"Okay," Webb says. "Tell us about this affair Amanda was having."

Sharpe sighs reluctantly, but begins to talk. "There was always talk about Amanda. She was a gorgeous woman. She could be a bit of a flirt. The gossip was that she cheated on her husband, that she sometimes got involved with men at work. That was the story, anyway—sex in the elevators, that sort of thing. A lot of it was probably bullshit, but she had a bit of a reputation. Ask around."

"We will," Webb assures him.

"When she disappeared, I thought she'd left her husband. There was no big hue and cry then, even though her husband apparently reported her missing. I thought maybe she'd run away with another guy." Sharpe hesitates and adds, "Like I said, there was a lot of talk about her. I didn't know if it was true or not—but then I saw it for myself." He pauses.

"So who is this person you work with who you thought was having an affair with her?" Webb asks.

Sharpe sighs heavily. "He wouldn't have hurt her, if that's what you're thinking."

"A name?"

Sharpe says it reluctantly. "Larry Harris. He lives next door to Amanda and Robert Pierce."

Webb shoots a glance at Moen, sees her eyes widen.

What interesting news, Webb thinks. It never ceases to amaze him what they dig up in the course of a criminal investigation—the secrets people keep. Or try to. "You'd better tell us exactly what you saw."

SEVENTEEN

Olivia comes to the door when Paul arrives home. He tosses his keys in the bowl on the side table in the hall and takes off his coat. It's slick with rain. Olivia is always affected by the weather, her mood attuned to its changes. Sunny days make her cheerful. Dark, damp, dreary days like this one always get her down.

Last night she and Paul had lain in bed not speaking for the better part of an hour, until Paul had finally started snoring. Olivia got up and went downstairs and paced the carpeted living room for hours, worrying about Raleigh—and about Carmine coming after him. She fretted about Paul's reluctance to send Raleigh to a therapist.

She thinks Paul is still angry at her. He said he'd forgiven her about the letters and that they needed to move on and deal with whatever happened, but it doesn't feel that way.

She notices now that Paul hasn't spoken to her. "That good, huh," she says lightly, but he barely looks at her.

"I'm going to change," he says, finally giving her an absent smile.

She sees that his trousers are drenched. "Do you want something to warm you up?"

"Scotch would be nice. I'm soaked."

She pours her husband a drink and checks on dinner. Paul comes back downstairs to the living room and picks up the newspaper. She brings him his scotch.

"Anything interesting happen today?" she asks.

"No," Paul says, not looking at her. "Nothing out of the ordinary." She hands him his drink and he takes a sip. After a moment he turns to her and asks, "Have you heard anything more from that woman?"

He means Carmine, she's sure.

"No," Olivia says. She adds fretfully, "I wish this would all just go away." But she doesn't believe that will happen. Instead, she feels as if Carmine is lying in wait for her.

Larry has only been home for an hour. His suitcase is still standing at the bottom of the stairs. Becky has made his favorite meal, lasagna and garlic bread. And pie. They're just finishing up the pie. They'd talked about Amanda's murder on the phone while he was away, and in more detail as they ate. It has clearly shocked him. She's told him nothing about her own involvement in the investigation. She knows she will have to explain, and she dreads it. But he just got home, and she's waiting for the right moment.

When the doorbell rings, she jumps up to answer the door. She sees the detectives dripping on her doorstep, and looks at them in disbelief. "He just got home," she says.

"I'm afraid this can't wait," Webb says. "May we come in?"

"We're eating dinner," she protests.

"Who is it?" Larry calls from the kitchen, and he appears behind her, wiping his mouth with a napkin. He comes up beside her. "Who's this?" he asks.

She knows there's nothing she can do. She says wearily, "They're the detectives I was telling you about. They're investigating Amanda's murder."

Her husband says, "Come in." Webb brushes past her, followed by Moen. "Can I take your coats?" Larry offers.

Becky watches her husband as he hangs up the detectives' wet coats. Her heart is pounding in her chest and her mouth feels dry. Larry will never forgive her.

Becky turns on a couple of lamps and they all sit down in the living room. The night outside is dark and the rain beats against the front window.

"I don't know how much your wife has told you—" Detective Webb begins, with a sidelong glance at Becky.

The bastard. "I haven't told him much of anything," Becky says. "I told you he just got home." Larry flashes her a nervous look. Suddenly she just wants to get it over with. She can't stand waiting for the ax to fall on her neck. "Larry, there's something I have to tell you," she says. She feels almost short of breath. "I would have told you anyway," she swallows, "I swear, I would have—"

"Told me what?" Larry says. He looks uneasy.

She blurts it out, looking down at the floor. "I slept with Robert Pierce. When you were away. They found out when they were investigating him about his wife." She finally brings her eyes up to look at her husband. He's sitting perfectly still, and has gone quite pale. "I'm sorry."

Larry looks completely shocked. Of course he's shocked. He would never expect this of her. She closes her eyes.

"How could you?" he says.

"I'm sorry," she repeats miserably, opening her eyes.

Larry looks pointedly at the two police detectives and says, "Maybe you'd better leave."

"I'm afraid we have some questions before we go," Webb says.

Becky turns bitter, resentful eyes on the detective and waits. She doesn't want to help them.

"We talked to Paul Sharpe," he says.

Becky remembers what she told these same detectives that morning. She thinks uneasily of Olivia.

"Paul?" Larry interjects in surprise.

It occurs to her suddenly that maybe Larry knew about Paul and Amanda. Becky says, "Paul was seeing Amanda."

"We don't know that," Webb says mildly.

She turns on him. "Did he deny it?"

"Yes, he did."

Becky snorts. She knows what she saw.

"He admitted speaking to her that night, in her car," the detective says. "But he said he was warning her off. He believed she was having an affair with a colleague at work, and he was telling her to back off." Webb is looking at her husband as he says this.

"A likely story," Becky says sarcastically, expecting her husband to back her up.

But Larry says nothing at all.

Webb continues. "In fact, he told us that he believed Amanda was having an affair with your husband—isn't that right, Larry?"

Becky looks at her husband, stunned.

Now Larry is shaking his head, slowly, back and forth, frowning. "No. I wasn't having an affair with her. I can't believe Paul told you that."

Becky's mind is spinning. They're all watching Larry.

"It's not true," Larry protests. "I wasn't sleeping with Amanda." He looks at the rest of them defiantly.

"Why would he tell us that if it wasn't true?" Webb asks.

Larry glances at them all nervously. "The fact is, Paul *thought* I was having an affair with Amanda. He spoke to me about it. I denied it, because it wasn't true. I thought he believed me. I can't believe he spoke to Amanda about it."

"Why would he think you were having an affair with Amanda? Even after you denied it?" Webb asks. "Any idea?"

Becky catches something sarcastic in the detective's tone.

"You have to understand what Amanda was like," Larry begins, sounding defensive. "She was very attractive. She sometimes worked at our office as a temp. She could be—inappropriate. She was in my office one day, and she was behaving improperly, and Paul saw it."

"You're going to have to spell it out for us, Mr. Harris," Webb says, and stares at Larry until he squirms.

Larry admits reluctantly, his face coloring with embarrassment, "She was performing oral sex."

"On you."

"Yes."

Becky stares at her husband, speechless.

"Paul saw it," Larry explains. "He drew the obvious—but entirely incorrect—conclusion. He confronted me and I told him I wasn't seeing her. He didn't believe me. I didn't think he'd go so far as to warn her off. I mean, that's just ridiculous. There was nothing going on—it was just that one time. That's just what she was like."

Becky wonders if her husband is telling the truth. She realizes that she has no idea. Suddenly she doesn't feel so contrite, so ashamed. Maybe her husband had his hand in the cookie jar, too. She watches the two detectives, trying to get a read on what they're thinking. She can't tell.

"Yes," Webb says, "Sharpe told us about that. In detail."

Becky watches her husband's face flush.

"That's all it was, I swear, that one incident. I wasn't *seeing* Amanda. I knew her from her temping at the office and they live next door, but we didn't have much to do with them. I think we had drinks with them once or twice." He adds, "I don't know what happened to her."

"Where were you the weekend that Amanda disappeared?" Webb asks.

"You can't be serious," Larry protests.

Webb just looks at him and waits.

Becky is staring in alarm at her husband. He glances at her. "I was away that weekend, and when I got back, I heard that she was gone and that her husband had reported her missing, but it was generally believed that she'd packed a bag and left him." He adds, "I was at a conference from Friday afternoon to Sunday afternoon." He looks up at them. "I wasn't even here."

"Where was the conference held?" Webb asks.

"At the Deerfields Resort."

"And where's that, exactly?"

"It's a couple of hours from here. In the Catskills."

"You don't say," Webb says.

EIGHTEEN

Olivia can tell that something is bothering her husband. He was restless the night before, tossing and turning through the night. When she asked him if something was wrong, he denied it. Perhaps he is simply worried, like she is, about Raleigh. Waiting for the cops to show up at their door.

She's upstairs in her office the next morning when the doorbell rings. She freezes. She's afraid that it's that woman, Carmine, back again. She hurries to the front window in the upstairs bedroom and looks out, but she can't see who is at the door. The doorbell rings again. She waits. The doorbell rings a third time. Whoever it is isn't going away.

Finally she steels her nerves and goes downstairs. She's determined to put a brave face on things and completely deny anything Carmine says. She's angry enough that she thinks she can do it.

She opens the door and is completely surprised to see her friend Becky standing on her doorstep. She'd last seen Becky at book club, on Monday night. Now it's Friday morning, and there's something about Becky's wary expression that puts Olivia on guard. And she looks like a mess. Her hair is neglected, and she's not wearing her usual lipstick.

"Becky," Olivia says. And then, "Is something wrong?"

Becky nods and says, "Can I come in?"

"Of course," Olivia says. "Come have coffee with me."

They make their way automatically to the kitchen. Olivia pours two cups of coffee from the carafe. "What is it? Something's obviously upset you."

Becky sits down at the kitchen table. "This is really awkward," she says.

Olivia sets the coffee mugs on the table and sits down. She wonders if Carmine has been talking to Becky. She steels herself again. "What is it?"

"It's about the investigation, about Amanda."

Olivia recalibrates. Not Raleigh, then. She feels a sense of relief, at least for herself, but she feels concerned for the woman sitting across from her. Why is Becky here?

"The police came back to talk to me yesterday," Becky says.

"Okay," Olivia says, taking a sip of coffee.

"Oh, God, I don't know how to tell you this."

"Just tell me, Becky." Olivia can feel her anxiety climbing.

Becky grips her coffee cup with both hands. She finally looks Olivia in the eye and says, "I saw Paul with Amanda, before she disappeared."

Olivia is stunned. Whatever she was expecting, it wasn't this. "What?"

"I saw Paul with Amanda in her car one night, shortly before she disappeared. They—it looked like they were fighting."

Olivia says, "Paul didn't know Amanda."

"I know what I saw," Becky says carefully.

"You must be mistaken," Olivia says coldly. He would have told her. Wouldn't he?

Becky says woodenly, "I'm not mistaken. Paul's admitted it. To the detectives."

Olivia feels her insides turn. She's suddenly light-headed. Paul has spoken to the detectives? "What do you mean?" she asks. "When did he talk to them?" She feels like she's standing on the edge of a cliff, and all Becky has to do is give her a gentle push.

Becky shifts uneasily in her chair. "Yesterday. They went to his office. They talked to him there."

"How do you know that? Why would they go see *him*?" She's trying to make sense of what Becky is saying.

"Because when they questioned me about Amanda I had to tell them that I'd seen Paul with Amanda in her car." She adds, "I didn't *want* to tell them."

"He never said anything to me about the detectives," Olivia whispers, in shock.

"I'm sorry," Becky says, and sits quietly, as if waiting for Olivia to put it together.

"You think Paul might have been seeing Amanda?" Olivia asks in disbelief, sitting perfectly still. "That's impossible." But she thinks of Paul, tossing and turning all last night. Apparently he'd spoken to the detectives earlier that day. What else has he kept from her? She can feel herself starting to tremble. A darkness passes before her eyes, like a shade, and she grips the edge of the table. Was Paul cheating on her? She's never suspected him of being unfaithful. Ever. But now another realization hits her: If Paul was having an affair with Amanda, he will be a suspect in her murder. She remembers him reading the article in the newspaper, his feigned lack of interest in the case. Her stomach churns.

Becky says, "He admitted to being in the car with her, but he denied having an affair with her."

Olivia stares at Becky. She has to know what the hell is going on. "How do you know? Why was he in the car with Amanda? I don't understand."

Becky says carefully, "He told the detectives that he thought she was having an affair with Larry, and he was telling her to stay away from him, but I'm sorry, that's just not true."

"*Your* Larry?"

Becky nods.

Olivia is astonished. "Why are you so sure Larry wasn't having an affair with her? And you're suggesting that Paul was?" Olivia protests.

Becky leans closer toward her over the kitchen table. "I don't *know* if Paul was having an affair with Amanda, but I saw them together, and I had to tell the detectives."

Olivia says, "Why would Paul say that about Larry, if it wasn't true?"

Becky sits back in her chair and folds her arms across her chest. "You remember what Amanda was like. Remember her at that party? Oozing sex appeal, basking in all the male attention. Apparently it was worse at the office. And Paul caught her behaving inappropriately with my husband once. But he says it meant nothing."

"Behaving inappropriately how, exactly?"

"I don't know the details," Becky says, averting her eyes.

"I *can't* believe that Paul was seeing Amanda," Olivia says.

"Well, I don't believe Larry was either." She reaches for her coffee cup. "Maybe it's all just a misunderstanding. Perhaps Paul misinterpreted the situation and overreacted."

"So—what, now the detectives are investigating Paul and Larry?" Olivia asks in disbelief. Becky nods uneasily. "And what do they think?"

"I don't know. They never say what they think. But they spoke to Paul yesterday, and came to our house last night after Larry got home, and accused Larry of having an affair with Amanda. He denied it." Becky turns her face away and looks bleak. "We had the most awful argument after."

Part of Olivia wants to comfort Becky, but another part of her hates Becky for bringing all this into her house and dumping it in her lap. She thinks about the argument she and Paul will have that evening. She doesn't believe that Paul was sleeping with Amanda. But he's obviously not telling her everything either. If he thought Larry was having an affair with Amanda, why didn't he tell her? Why didn't he tell her the police had come to his office yesterday?

"I thought you should know what was going on," Becky says, "in case Paul didn't tell you."

Olivia recoils, as if from a slap. Does Becky expect her to thank her?

Now Becky is staring down at the kitchen table. "There's something else. I probably shouldn't tell you this, but it's probably not going to stay secret for long. And I need to talk to somebody and I don't want you to think I've been lying to you."

Becky seems so distraught now, that Olivia feels a sudden twinge of sympathy for her. But what she feels most is a sense of foreboding. What more can there possibly be? "What?"

"It's about Robert Pierce."

Olivia sits back. She could tell, even at book club, that Becky had a bit of a thing for him. He's very attractive, and lives right next door to her. Larry is away a lot. Her children go to school out of town. "What about him?"

"I slept with him, when Larry was away," Becky confesses, looking up at her. "Twice."

Olivia just stares, shocked into silence.

"I must have been out of my mind," Becky admits. "But there was this chemistry between us. I don't know what came over me. I—I just couldn't resist him."

"My God, Becky. He probably killed his wife."

"He didn't. I'm sure he didn't."

"How can you be so sure?" Olivia says, aghast. "If people were aware of what Amanda was like—if *Paul* thought she was sleeping with Larry, even if it wasn't true—then her husband must have had some idea what she was like. He might have been jealous. Angry." She adds firmly, "He's probably the one who killed her."

Becky says, shaking her head, "I don't think he did it. I don't think he could kill her. I think it was someone else."

"Who, then?"

"I don't know. Some stranger—someone we don't know. Paul and Larry had nothing to do with it."

"Of course they didn't," Olivia says. "I still think it was her husband."

Robert Pierce looks coldly across the interview table at the two detectives who have become such a nuisance to him. When Detective Webb called him at home a short while ago, asking him if he'd be willing to come down to the station to answer a few more questions, he considered his position carefully before he answered. He suspected that if he refused, they would simply arrive at his door and place him under arrest. So here he is.

He knows they suspect him of murder, even if they won't say so. He must convince them otherwise.

"Am I under arrest?" he asks.

"No," Detective Webb says, "you know you're not."

"Then why does it feel that way?"

"You can leave at any time," Webb says.

Robert doesn't move.

Webb leans back in his chair and asks, "Did you know your wife was having an affair?"

Robert eyes him warily. "No. I told you that."

"Were you aware that your wife had a reputation for flirting, for—cheating?"

Robert feels his face darken but remains calm. "No, I certainly wasn't aware of it. But she was a very attractive, very confident woman. People will talk."

"Yes, they do talk." Detective Webb leans forward and says, "We spoke to a number of people who worked where Amanda was a temp. Some of the places she temped regularly. One of those was Fanshaw Pharmaceuticals."

"Yes, she liked working there."

"People there said she had a reputation," the detective says.

Robert stares back at him, refusing to rise to the bait.

"A reputation for having sex in elevators, for instance," Moen says.

He glares at her silently.

"In fact," Webb says, "we think we know who was having an affair with your wife."

Robert remains silent for a few seconds and then shrugs and says, "It's possible. I told you. I don't know what to think since I found out she lied to me about going away with Caroline. Maybe she *was* having an affair." He leans forward now himself. "But if she was, I didn't know about it."

"You absolutely sure about that?" Webb says.

"Yes. I trusted Amanda," Pierce says, leaning back again in his chair.

"And yet you cheated on her with your neighbor," Moen breaks in.

He fixes a hard look on her. He finds her annoying, picking away at him. "That was a moment of stupidity. Becky came on to *me*. I shouldn't have done it. Just because I did something wrong, it doesn't mean my wife did."

"Doesn't it?" Moen asks, arching an eyebrow.

He doesn't like her. He doesn't like either one of them. He considers getting up and leaving. He knows he's within his rights to do so—he's here voluntarily.

Moen continues to goad him. "You haven't asked who was having an affair with your wife."

"Maybe because I don't want to know," Robert says bluntly.

"Or maybe it's because you know already?" Webb suggests.

Robert gives the detective a hostile look. "Why would you say that?"

"We think she was sleeping with your neighbor, Larry Harris."

He is suddenly furious, but tries to tamp down his anger. "I didn't know."

"Sure, you didn't," Webb says pleasantly. "That's not why you slept with Becky Harris, is it, to get back at your wife's lover? You wouldn't do that, would you? Just like you wouldn't kill your wife."

NINETEEN

Glenda waits in the Bean for Olivia. She's late. Glenda glances at her watch again and wonders what's keeping her. It's not like Olivia to be late for anything.

Finally she arrives, flustered, and approaches. Glenda has deliberately chosen a table where they can't be overheard. Looks like maybe that's a good thing.

Olivia sits down. She's obviously upset. "What's wrong?" Glenda asks.

"You have to promise me you won't tell *anyone* what I'm about to tell you," Olivia says nervously. "Not even Keith."

Glenda sits up straighter. "Of course. I promise. I don't tell Keith a lot of stuff we talk about anyway. What is it?"

Olivia lowers her voice and says, "Becky Harris seems to think Paul might have been having an affair with Amanda."

Glenda feels a shock run along her spine. She stares at Olivia in dismay. "Why would she think that?"

As Olivia explains, Glenda tries to process everything she's hearing about Olivia's earlier conversation with Becky. But it's hard to square with the man she's known for years. "Paul wouldn't cheat on you," Glenda says. "I simply don't believe it."

"Me neither," Olivia says, her voice fraught with emotion. "But why isn't Paul telling me these things? Why didn't he tell me he spoke to Amanda? Why didn't he tell me he thought Larry was having an affair with her? Why didn't he tell me he was questioned by the police?"

Glenda hears the growing hysteria in Olivia's voice. "I don't know," she says uneasily.

"I thought we had a solid marriage. We're honest with each other. I can't believe he's been keeping these things from me."

"If Paul told the police he thought Larry was sleeping with Amanda, and he was warning her off, I believe him," Glenda says firmly. "I think it's much more likely that Larry was cheating on Becky than that Paul was cheating on you, don't you?"

Olivia nods; she seems relieved to hear someone else say it. "Actually, I probably shouldn't even tell you this, but . . ."

"What?"

"Becky confessed to me that she slept with Robert Pierce. Before Amanda disappeared."

Now Glenda is truly shocked; she certainly wasn't expecting this. Finally she says, "Well, well. There you go. There are obviously problems in *that* marriage." Then she leans anxiously over the table. "Listen, Olivia. You don't want the police to think Paul might have been seeing Amanda. Then he might be a suspect in her murder. You don't want that. You don't want them snooping into your life."

"It's too late," Olivia says miserably. "I think Paul is already a suspect. I think Becky already told them her suspicions about Paul and Amanda."

Glenda says quickly, "Well, you have to make sure that they drop that idea, fast. Tell them he was with you all weekend."

"He probably *was* with me all weekend!"

"So, that's okay then."

Olivia says, clearly tense, "I have to talk to him tonight when he gets home. I'll ask him why he didn't tell me about any of this. And I'll ask him straight out if he told the police the truth."

Glenda nods. "Let me know what he says." Now she notices Olivia looking at her more closely, as if noticing for the first time how tired she is. Glenda knows there are dark circles under her eyes—she'd studied herself in the mirror this morning.

"How are things with you?" Olivia asks.

"Not good," Glenda admits. "Adam seems to hate his father."

"Why?" Olivia asks.

"I don't know," Glenda says, looking away. "They clash constantly. I suppose it's normal for teenage boys to clash with their fathers. They have to separate themselves, stand on their own." She pauses. "Mind you, he doesn't seem to like me much better these days."

After they part, Glenda walks home, thinking more about what Olivia has told her. Surely Paul wouldn't cheat on Olivia. She's known them for sixteen years. But she's uneasy. She remembers what Amanda was like, the one time she ever really saw her, at the party last year.

It was a warm, sunny day in September. Amanda was wearing a short yellow sundress, showing off her sleek, tanned legs. Her toenails were perfectly painted and she was wearing high-heeled sandals. Glenda and Olivia had stopped wearing short sundresses a long time ago. Now they wore capri pants and flat sandals and talked about getting the veins in their legs fixed. But Amanda was young and beautiful and had never had children, so her legs were perfect, like the rest of her. Glenda remembers how she kept leaning forward, casually showing off a bit of perky breast and lacy bra every time she spoke to Keith, or Paul, or Larry, or any of the other men who had been there.

Had she paid particular attention to any of the men that day? She didn't think so. But they'd all made fools of themselves. Amanda had flirted with each of them, holding court like a Southern belle, while her own husband sat back and said little, drinking beer and watching her indulgently. Amanda would occasionally turn to her quiet, handsome husband and clasp his hand in hers, silently acknowledging that she belonged to him. At the time, Glenda thought he'd seemed proud of her. But now she wonders—is that how it was? Or was he annoyed with her, with the attention she was attracting, and the attention she was paying to everyone but him? Was he angry and jealous, and hiding it? Did he worry that she might be unfaithful?

Every marriage has its secrets. Glenda wonders what theirs were.

When Paul arrives home from work, Olivia is waiting for him. Raleigh's gone out for basketball practice. It will give them a chance to talk.

She hears him come in the front door and moves from the kitchen to the hall to confront him. She immediately notices how worn out he looks. In fact, he looks like hell. She doesn't have much sympathy. "We need to talk," she says. Her voice is tight.

"Can I take off my coat first?" he snaps. He reads her face and says, "Where's Raleigh?"

"Raleigh's at practice. He'll be home later." He walks past her and into the kitchen. She follows him and watches as he reaches into the cupboard for the bottle of scotch. Olivia says, unable to keep the anger out of her voice, "I know you've been talking to the police."

"So they came and talked to you, did they?" he says, with an edge to his voice. "Why am I not surprised?" He pours himself a drink and turns to look at her, leaning against the kitchen counter.

"No, they didn't come here. Becky told me."

"Ah, *Becky*," he says bitterly, and takes a deep gulp.

"What the hell is going on, Paul?" Olivia asks desperately.

"I'll tell you what's going on, if you're sure you want to know." He takes another sip of his drink. "Larry Harris had something going on with Amanda Pierce for ages. I finally confronted him about it but he denied it. So I told Amanda to back off. Then she disappeared. I didn't mention it to the police at the time, because I honestly didn't think it was relevant. And nobody asked. Everybody thought she'd just left her husband. But now . . . apparently Becky saw me talking to Amanda and stuck her nose in and told the police. So I had to tell them everything." He snorts. "I'll bet she's sorry she ever mentioned it." He lifts his head and looks tiredly at Olivia. "Now they're all over me. Asking me for an alibi." He lifts his glass high and tosses back the rest of his scotch.

"Asking *you* for an alibi," Olivia echoes.

"Oh, I imagine they're asking Larry, too," Paul says.

She has to ask. "Tell me the truth," Olivia says. She can feel her voice catching. "Were you having an affair with Amanda or not?"

He looks at her and something in his demeanor changes. The bristling anger falls away. "Hell no, Olivia. I wasn't sleeping with her, I swear. I've never cheated on you. I wouldn't. You know that."

"Then why didn't you tell me about this? Why all the secrets? You spoke to the police yesterday and you didn't even tell me!"

He hangs his head. "I'm sorry."

She waits.

He says, "I didn't tell you at the time about Larry, because I wanted to keep it just between him and me. I know you and Becky are friends. I didn't want to put you in that position, of knowing and wondering whether you should tell her. I thought if I told Amanda to back off, she'd stop carrying on with Larry. I didn't think their fling was important to her."

"How do you know she was seeing Larry?"

"I'd suspected it for weeks, but then I caught her giving him a blow job in his office."

Olivia is shocked. She wonders if Becky knows the details.

Paul continues. "I told the detectives everything. It wasn't so much that I was worried about Larry's marriage—it's not really my business. But I was worried that he was getting careless—and that somebody other than me would see them at the office and he'd lose his job. I didn't want that to happen."

Olivia can feel the tightness in her shoulders slowly starting to relax. "But why didn't you tell me yesterday, after you'd spoken to the police? Why did you keep that from me?"

He shakes his head. "I don't know. I just didn't know what to do. I should have told you. I'm telling you now." He sighs and adds uneasily, "They asked me if I had an alibi for the weekend Amanda went missing."

"What did you tell them?" Olivia asks.

"I told them the truth. That I was home all weekend. I told them that we probably stayed in and watched something on Netflix. That's what we usually do. When was the last time we went out on a Friday or Saturday night?"

She thinks back to that weekend. Then she says, "No, you went to your aunt's that Friday, remember?"

He freezes. "Shit. You're right. I forgot."

"You called me from the office and said you thought you'd better go see her."

"Yes," Paul says. "Fuck."

She remembers that evening. Paul had gone to his aunt's and she'd stayed home and watched a movie by herself. "You'd better tell them," Olivia says anxiously.

He nods. "I will. They're probably going to want to ask you, too."

"Ask me?"

"About where I was that weekend."

"Why does it matter where you were?" Olivia says, frustrated with the situation. "You weren't involved with Amanda. Larry was."

Paul snorts. "I don't think the police know who to believe." After a moment, he says, "Can we call it even?"

"What do you mean?"

"You know—you didn't tell me about those letters. . . ."

She'd forgotten all about the letters; they've been pushed from her mind by everything else that has been going on. She approaches him, puts her hands on his chest. "Yes." She can smell the scotch on his breath.

"When did you say Raleigh was getting home again?" he says, wrapping his arms around her and giving her a kiss.

"Not for a while yet," Olivia says. "Why don't you pour me a drink?" As he pours her one, Olivia says, "You don't think Larry could have had anything to do with—"

"No, of course not," Paul says.

TWENTY

Becky wanders restlessly around the house Friday evening, waiting for Larry to get home from work. The way they left things the night before, he won't be in a good mood when he gets home. He said he'd probably be late; he always has a lot to catch up on after a business trip.

Last night she slept in the guest room. She's not sure how the two of them are going to move forward. Maybe they won't. Maybe their marriage is over and all that remains is to find some way to tell the kids and figure out how to divide the spoils. In spite of her staunch denial to Olivia, she spends a lot of time wondering if Larry's insistence that nothing of consequence had happened between him and Amanda could possibly be true.

It's been a long day—a long week since they'd found Amanda Pierce's body—and Webb is feeling it. His eyes are burning and his limbs are tired. He's frustrated with the lack of progress on the case. But a picture has begun to emerge. They'd spoken to others at Fanshaw Pharmaceuticals, when they'd finished with Paul Sharpe, and had formed a clearer idea of who Amanda Pierce really was. Webb wondered how much of the talk about her was true. But Larry has admitted to the incident in his office. So some of it is true, at least.

Now, Moen is driving them back from the Deerfields Resort where Larry had attended a conference the weekend that Amanda was murdered. Webb stares out the window at the darkening scenery, reflecting on what they've learned.

Larry Harris was certainly at the conference from Friday night until Sunday afternoon. Lots of people on staff confirmed that. He checked in at 3:00 P.M. on Friday. But after that, there's a gap. The bar staff and waitstaff remember him, but none of them can remember with any certainty seeing him at the reception before 9:00 P.M. They agreed that he was one of the last to leave the event and make his way up to his room at the end of the night, at around 11:00. There had been no sit-down meal, where someone might have remembered him; just drinks and mingling in the ballroom. He could have arrived late to the reception, giving him several hours to meet—and perhaps kill—Amanda Pierce. Most damning of all, her car had been dumped in a lake not far from the resort.

The rest of the weekend seems accounted for. He was registered in various sessions and he was seen in those sessions throughout the weekend. But there is the tantalizing gap on Friday.

Webb points his finger. "Turn here."

Moen turns off the highway and goes down a gravel road. It's almost dark already. It's been a miserable, wet day, but it's warm and cozy in the car.

They're returning to the scene where Amanda's body was recovered. He's been timing it since they left the resort. Moen is driving a bit too fast for the gravel road. "Slow down. We can estimate for speed later," Webb tells Moen. She lets up on the gas.

The way is dark and winding. The car's headlights sweep around the bends in the road; trees rise on each side. Some of the trees are almost bare already; the weather has turned, and it seems much longer than a few days since they were out here, lifting the leaking car out of the cold lake.

"Are you sure you'll be able to recognize the spot in the dark?" Moen asks, driving more slowly now. "I'm not sure I could. I'm a city girl."

"I hope so," Webb says, looking intently at the dark landscape beyond the windshield. "We're getting close, I think. Slow down."

She slows the car around a curve and he says, "Here. I think this is it. Pull over."

He recognizes the curve in the road, the slope down to the beach, the edge of the lake. Moen pulls the car over and stops. She turns off the engine. Webb looks at his watch, glowing in the dark. "Twenty minutes."

Moen looks at him, nodding. "No time at all."

For a moment they sit in the dark, then they get out of the warm car into the chill of the night. Webb stands by the car door, getting his bearings, remembering the previous Monday morning when they'd made their gruesome discovery.

"Where's the murder weapon?" Webb asks. He walks down to the edge of the water and looks out over the lake. A sliver of moon emerges sharp and bright from behind dark clouds. He tries to imagine what went on here. Who put the windows down? Whoever it was wore gloves, because there were no prints on the window buttons, other than Amanda's. Who stuffed her body into the trunk and guided the car down the slope and into the water?

Webb thinks the killer is quite likely someone they have already met. He turns to Moen; her eyes are glinting in the dark. "Whoever killed her was probably counting on her car—and her body—never being found at all," Webb suggests. He looks out again across the dark lake. "Everyone thought she'd left her husband. And it's very hard to convict without a body." He glances again at Moen. "Somebody must be squirming. For somebody, this hasn't gone according to plan."

Becky hears the door downstairs open shortly after 9:00 P.M. She's upstairs in bed, and cocks her head, listening. She'd grown tired of waiting for Larry and had eaten and gone up with a book. Now she listens to him wandering around downstairs. After a few minutes, she puts the book aside, pulls on her robe, and leaves the bedroom.

She stops at the top of the stairs when she sees her husband standing at the bottom, looking up at her. Their eyes meet, but neither of them speaks for a moment.

Then she says, "Where have you been?" She doesn't think he's been at the office this late.

He doesn't answer her. Finally Larry says, "We need to talk."

She makes her way slowly down the stairs.

He says abruptly, "I need a drink." He slouches over to the bar cart in the living room and pours himself a stiff shot of bourbon.

"You might as well pour me one, too," Becky says.

She walks over to him and he hands her a glass. They each take a sip. All the things he might say are swirling around in her head.

She wonders how Larry must have felt when Amanda disappeared—and then when her body was discovered. Was he worried that the police would find out about him and Amanda? The way she'd worried that they would find out about her and Robert?

He gives her a conciliatory look. "I had nothing to do with what happened to Amanda. And you know it."

"Do I?" she says.

He stares at her, clearly shocked. "You can't honestly think—" He continues to stare at her, as if unable to find words.

"I don't know what to think," she says coldly. "And if *I* don't quite believe you, how do you think the police are going to see it?" As she stands there looking at him, this man she's been married to for twenty-three years, she allows herself for the first time to actually consider whether Larry might have killed Amanda Pierce. It gives her a chill.

"You can't be serious!" Then he laughs—a short, tight laugh. "Oh, I get it. You're already in divorce negotiations, is that it? You feel you have some leverage over me and you want to use it to your advantage."

She hadn't really thought of it that way, but now that he's mentioned it, she sees the possibilities. She doesn't really believe that he harmed Amanda, but it wouldn't hurt for him to think she does. She gave up her career. She spent her best years keeping house and raising children for this man, while he was out making a good living. She should get what's coming to her. She doesn't want to get shafted.

"You absolute bitch," he says.

She jumps a bit at his tone. It's so unlike him. Then she says, in a mild voice, "I'm not going to make things difficult for you, Larry, as long as you play fair with me."

"Is that so," he says. He comes closer and stares down at her; she can feel his breath in her face, smell the liquor. "I had *nothing* to do with Amanda's . . . disappearance."

It's like he can't say it. He can't say *death*. She stands her ground. "But were you seeing her?" Becky asks. "Tell me the truth. It wasn't just that one time in your office, was it?" She knows him. She knows he would want more. He can be greedy.

He slumps down onto the sofa and looks weary all of a sudden. His shoulders sag. "Yes," he admits. "We were seeing each other, for a few weeks. It started in July." He downs the rest of his drink in one long gulp.

She feels her entire body go cold. "Where?"

"We went to a hotel on the highway outside of Aylesford."

She stares at him in disbelief, swelling with incoherent rage. "You *idiot*," she whispers. "They'll find out."

"No, they won't," he says stubbornly, glancing up at her, and then shifting his eyes away again at the incredulous fury he sees there.

"Of course they will! They'll go around to all the hotels and motels with photos of the two of you and ask the staff!" *How can he think they won't find out?* She feels sick with fear now, and it makes her realize that she does care. People get arrested for things they didn't do all the time. She cares enough not to want to see her husband dragged through a murder investigation. She can't let that happen to her and the kids. She watched *The Staircase* on Netflix; she saw what that did to that family. It's not going to happen to hers. She thinks rapidly. "Maybe you should have told the police when they were here. It's going to be worse when they find out and you didn't tell them."

"I was afraid to tell them! I couldn't think. This has all been such a shock." He takes a deep breath. "Maybe they won't find out," he says. He looks up at her, infected by her alarm. "I had nothing to do with what happened to her. I didn't think our casual meetings meant anything. I thought she'd left him."

"It doesn't matter," Becky says, forcing herself to calm down. She can see that Larry is starting to go to pieces; she must remain calm. She has to think. "You couldn't have done it—you have a solid alibi." She sits down on the sofa beside him. "You were at that conference." She'd had a bad moment when the detectives were here, and she'd realized that the conference Larry had attended wasn't that far from where Amanda's body had been discovered. But he'd told the detectives that he'd been at the resort from Friday afternoon on, and it had reassured her. There would be people there who could confirm that, surely. But now she sees a terrible pallor come over him and feels the bottom drop out of her stomach. "What is it, Larry? What aren't you telling me?"

"I didn't kill her, I swear." But there's panic in his eyes.

She recoils a little. "Larry, you're scaring me."

"Her car was found near the resort," he says nervously.

How he avoids it, she thinks. Her car, not her body. Like he can't face it. She brushes the troubling thought aside. "But it doesn't matter," she insists. "Not if you were at the resort the whole time." But now it crosses her mind—what if he snuck out for an hour or two? What if he'd arranged to meet her? Would he have been able to kill her then? *Could he have?* She feels frightened at the realization that she doesn't know.

"But what if people don't remember seeing me?" he says, shifting his gaze around the room. He doesn't seem to want to look her in the eye.

"Larry, what are you saying?"

He finally looks at her in fear, imploringly, as if she can somehow help him. But she's afraid she can't help him.

"Larry," she says anxiously, "did you leave the resort?"

"No."

"So what's the problem?"

"I checked in on Friday and went up to my room. I didn't feel like seeing anybody. I—I'd had an argument with Amanda the day before—she said she didn't want to see me anymore—and I was upset, and exhausted. So I stayed in my room and did some work and then—I fell asleep. I didn't wake up till almost nine. I missed most of the opening reception."

She looks at him in disbelief and rage. Long seconds tick by, the room utterly still but for the pounding of her heart. Then she says, "Are you telling me the truth?"

"Yes, I swear."

"Even *I'm* having a hard time believing that," she says. She realizes he has no alibi at all. "Where did you have the argument with Amanda?" she asks, the gorge rising in her throat. "Did anyone see?"

"It was over the phone."

"What phone?"

He looks away furtively. "We used burner phones."

She can't believe it—her husband, *the father of her children*, with a burner phone. She asks furiously, "What happened to the phone?"

"I threw it from the bridge into the river."

"Which bridge? When? Fuck! They might have cameras, you know."

He looks up at her, ghastly pale now. "The Skyway. On Sunday, on my way home from the resort. She'd broken it off—I figured I didn't need the phone anymore."

"You stupid son of a bitch," she hisses, and walks away.

TWENTY-ONE

Robert Pierce sits alone in his darkened living room, sipping slowly from a glass of whiskey. He's thinking about Detective Webb—and his sidekick, Detective Moen—and what they might think. What they might have. They can't have anything on him. They're fishing.

They will certainly be looking at his next-door neighbor, Larry Harris, who was sleeping with Amanda. Robert doesn't understand what Amanda saw in him, but she'd always been attracted to older men. Oh, he knew. He's not stupid. He'd known about Larry for some time.

Then he got into Amanda's secret phone. It wasn't that hard—he just Googled *how to unlock Android lock screen without password*. And once he did, how enlightening it turned out to be. Her calls, her texts, those two secret numbers. He called one of them and a man answered. As soon as he heard the man's voice, he recognized it. Because after all, it was who he was expecting it to be. "Larry," Robert said.

"Who is this?" Larry asked, clearly startled.

"It's her husband, Robert."

Larry had hung up the phone in a hurry.

There wasn't any answer at the other number. It was this other number that concerned him more. The number that she sent those texts to, the ones sharing intimate, private details of their life together, the ones saying that her husband was a psychopath. Those texts enraged him. She must have been able to warn *him* that her husband had her phone.

And there were other things on that phone, too, that she hadn't sent to anyone, that made him angriest of all. And even afraid.

He thinks about Becky. By now she must know about Larry and Amanda, if those detectives are any good at all. He suspects that Becky's half in love with him. He hopes she keeps her mouth shut. It wouldn't do for the police to think he had a motive to kill his wife. If Larry Harris tells them about that phone call, Robert will simply deny it. There's no proof. No proof at all that Robert ever made that phone call.

No *proof* that Robert knew about her affair. Her *affairs*. As long as Amanda's burner phone is never found. It must never be found.

He thinks back to when they first moved here. That insufferable party that Amanda insisted on going to. Sitting there watching her, so lovely, so unwittingly cruel. He wonders now if she'd made her selections that day, which ones she was going to screw. They'd only been married a year. How little he knew her then, her proclivities—her childish, inexplicable need to seduce older men. And how little she knew him then—the dark, cold center of his soul. But they'd gotten to know each other better.

He knows that Becky and Larry are both home. There are lights on downstairs next door, even though it's very late. How he'd love to be a fly on *that* wall.

Raleigh waits until everyone in the house is asleep. He pulls on his jeans, a T-shirt, and his dark hoodie, and carefully opens his bedroom door. He knows his dad's a heavy sleeper; it's his mother he's worried about. But he stands still outside his bedroom in the hall and he can hear each of them snoring their separate, distinct snores. Relieved, he creeps down the stairs, careful not to make a sound.

He pulls on his sneakers in the kitchen. He doesn't turn on any lights. He's used to operating in the dark. Quietly, he slips out the kitchen door to the garage, where he keeps his bike. He puts on his helmet, flings his leg over the bike, and as soon as he leaves the garage, starts pedaling, fast, away from the house.

He knows it's bad, hacking into people's computers. He started hacking for the challenge. How can he explain that to someone who doesn't feel it? His parents wouldn't get it, but any fellow hacker would know exactly why he does it. It feels great—hacking into someone else's system makes him feel powerful, like he has control over something. He doesn't feel like he has much control over his own life. He promised his parents—and himself—that he would stop. And he will. The risks are too great. This is his last time. He wouldn't be doing it at all if he didn't know for sure that the owners were away. And this time, he's got a pair of latex gloves stuffed in his jeans pocket—he took them from the package his mom keeps in her cupboard of cleaning supplies. He's not going to take any stupid risks, and he's not going to leave any prints behind.

Raleigh studies the house. It's a dark night, and the moon is covered by cloud. The light is on at the front of the house, and there's a light on upstairs—probably on timers. He knows this because they have a cat. And the local pet sitter, who has a sign on her car, has been stopping by and going into this house for the last few days. Raleigh's seen her every morning on his way to school. How stupid can people be? Hiring a pet sitter with a sign on her friggin' car? It's like advertising that you're out of town, for fuck's sake.

He'd tried to talk himself out of it. But he just couldn't resist. He wants to break into a house where he doesn't have to worry about the owners coming home after a dinner out. He wants to relax and take his time—dig a little deeper, try a couple of different things before he retires.

Raleigh creeps around the back of the house. No one is watching. He studies the doors and windows carefully. No obvious sign of security. But the doors and windows are securely locked. He's been watching videos on YouTube, just in case. It's not as hard to break into a house as a typical homeowner might think. He reaches into his jeans pocket and pulls out his bank machine card. He slides it along the edge of the door where the lock is and starts to fiddle with the catch. The guys on YouTube do this in a couple of seconds, but it takes Raleigh almost a full minute before the catch gives way with a satisfying click. And just in time—he's sweating buckets, afraid someone might see him.

He slips inside the door and closes it quietly behind him, his heart thumping. He puts his card back into his pocket and takes out his phone. He turns the flashlight on. The door opens directly into the kitchen. He kicks something—a dish—and sends it clattering across the floor. Shit. He points the light down. There's kibble everywhere. He squats down, sweeps it into a pile, and picks it up with his gloved hands. Now there's a black-and-white cat brushing against his shins. He stops to pat it for a minute.

He doesn't waste time downstairs. The computers are almost always upstairs, in the bedrooms or the office.

The house is obviously occupied by a couple with a baby—there's a master bedroom, a baby's room, and an office at the back. He slips into the office at the end of the hall and sets about getting into the computer. With a USB boot stick and a few keystrokes he's created a backdoor and bypassed the passwords. After he has a quick look around, he's going to try something new—he's going to use this compromised computer to try to get into its owner's employer's network, if he's employed anywhere halfway interesting. Raleigh's feeling relaxed—the computer is at the back of the house, the blinds are drawn, nobody can see in—he can stay here all night if he wants to. He's engrossed in what he's doing when he hears a sound. Car doors slamming. He freezes. He hears voices outside. Fuck. They can't be home. Raleigh panics. He looks out the window. There's no way out there. No roof to climb out onto. He's not jumping out a second-story window.

While he dithers, the voices get louder. Now he hears a key in the front door. *Fuck. Fuck. Fuck.* He's up out of the chair now and standing frozen in fear near the top of the stairs. Can he get down the stairs and out the back door fast enough? But the front door is opening now, and a switch is flicked on, flooding the front hallway with light. He's so screwed. There's no way out.

He sees the cat enter the hall, brush against the leg of the hall table, and mew at her owners, but he can't see them.

"You take the baby up and put her down and I'll bring in the gear," he hears a man's voice say. They still have no idea that there's a stranger upstairs in their house.

Raleigh ducks back into the office at the end of the hall, barely daring to breathe. The computer is still on, but it faces away from the door and it's not making a sound. The room is dark. Maybe they won't notice. Maybe he can hide in here until they go to bed. He feels a bead of sweat trickle down his back. He hears a woman come heavily up the stairs, cooing to the baby. Raleigh wills it to start crying, but the baby stays quiet. The floorboards creak as the woman enters the baby's room in the middle of the hall. The husband is still outside with the car. Raleigh hears the trunk slam. Does he run for it now? Or wait? It's the longest couple of seconds of Raleigh's life.

He panics. He flees down the stairs as fast as he can, not even bothering to be quiet. He makes it to the bottom of the stairs before the man is at the front door. He hears the woman's startled cry behind him. He's halfway to the kitchen before the front door opens. He scrambles for the door in the kitchen, making his way in the dark, and kicks the cat dish again, sending it scattering. He hears the man behind him in the front hall—"What the fuck?" —and hears him abruptly drop whatever he's carrying and come after him. Raleigh doesn't look back.

He's out the door and running as fast as he can. He runs right across the backyard, hops the fence without even thinking about it, boosted on adrenaline. He doesn't stop until he's far away and his lungs are bursting.

He hides behind a bush in a park until his heart stops pounding and he gets his breath back. He still has to go back and retrieve his bike before he goes home—at least he'd had the sense not to leave it near the house. There's no way they won't call the police. They'll see that the computer is on, and see what he's done.

Carmine can't sleep. She's tried reading but nothing holds her interest. It's human company she wants. She misses her husband. He used to read in bed beside her; now he's gone.

She's downstairs in the kitchen making some hot chocolate when she hears something outside, in the street. Shouting. She freezes, listening. She hears banging, more shouting. She moves quickly to the front door but doesn't turn on the light. When she looks out, she sees a lean, dark figure, weaving on the sidewalk at the end of her driveway. He appears to be alone. He's got something in his hand, a stick of some kind. She creeps forward, and as she gets closer she sees that it's just a boy. A teenager, probably drunk, on a Friday night. He's standing still now, swaying, as if he can't remember what he was doing, and he's got what looks like a broken hockey stick in his hand. She thinks he's been smashing her recycling bin.

"Hey!" Carmine says, striding down the driveway toward him in her pink bathrobe. The boy looks back at her, as if dumbfounded at the sight of her. "What are you doing?" she says crossly. She's not afraid of him, he's just a boy. She's only a few feet away from him now and can see him clearly. She can also smell the booze on him. Something about him reminds her of her own son, Luke. He seems to be trying to focus, but his face is slack. He doesn't say anything, but he doesn't run either. Probably because if he tried to he'd fall flat on his face.

"You're not old enough to drink, are you," she says, the mother in her speaking.

He waves her away like he's swatting a fly and stumbles on down the street, dragging his broken hockey stick.

Concerned, she watches him stumble down the sidewalk, until he turns into a house farther down the street. She sees lights go on in the house. At least he made it home, she thinks. His own parents can deal with him.

The next morning, Saturday, Glenda calls Olivia and invites her to go for a walk. She wants to know what happened last night, when Olivia confronted Paul.

Glenda puts on a jacket and her walking shoes. It's a cold, crisp day, but at least the sun is shining again after yesterday's dreary rain. She closes the door behind her, and begins to walk toward Olivia's house. Her mind is full. If only she could solve everybody's problems. If only all this—*stress*—would go away.

Last night their son, Adam, had come home drunk, again. They'd given him a curfew, but he'd ignored it. They'd grounded him, and he'd snuck out of the house. Now, they don't know what to do.

"Maybe we just let him sow his wild oats," Keith had said this morning. "When he's tired of barfing in the morning, he'll straighten out."

She'd glared at him angrily, with her arms folded across her chest. *He* hadn't stayed awake all night keeping an eye on their son to make sure he didn't choke to death. Keith slept just fine. Nothing seems to bother him; it's like he's coated with Teflon.

Sometimes she wishes she could make her husband understand all the things she does, all the things she's done for their family. He doesn't appreciate her enough. He never will. He's oblivious.

And she'd had to clean up the mess in the bathroom.

"Make him do it," Keith had said unhelpfully, pouring himself a cup of coffee.

She'd glanced in at Adam moaning in bed, realized that wasn't going to happen, and did it herself. Now all she wants is to get out of the house, away from her husband and her son and the smell of barf and talk to someone reasonable. Someone who understands.

She sees Olivia approaching her on the sidewalk and waves. Soon they are face-to-face, and fall into step together. "Let's head for the park," Glenda suggests. On the way, she tells Olivia about the latest problem with Adam. As they walk together along the edge of the pond, Glenda says, "Sorry to vent. So, what happened last night? Did you talk to Paul?" She turns to look at Olivia and notices that she seems much less tense than she had the day before.

Olivia nods. "I did." She lets out a big exhale and stops, looking out over the water toward the trees beyond. "He wasn't seeing Amanda. He caught her giving Larry a blow job in the office and warned her off so that Larry wouldn't lose his job."

"Wow," Glenda says.

Olivia turns to her and laughs suddenly. "It's crazy, isn't it?"

Glenda shakes her head. "The things people do."

"I don't think Paul and I have anything to worry about. But Becky—I wouldn't want to be in her shoes." Olivia's expression sobers. "If anyone was having an affair with Amanda, it's most likely to be Larry, don't you think?"

Glenda feels herself relaxing. The walk outside, airing her own complaints, and hearing Olivia's news have all done Glenda good. She doesn't know what she'd do if she didn't have Olivia to talk to. Glenda says, "I don't imagine that marriage is going to last much longer." They stand side by side, watching the swans. Finally Glenda asks, her voice hesitant, "Do you think Larry could have killed Amanda?"

"No," Olivia says, shaking her head. "No way. Paul doesn't think so either. My money's on Robert Pierce."

TWENTY-TWO

Olivia leaves Glenda at the corner and heads back home, head lowered. Glenda seems very distressed lately. She's obviously worried sick about Adam. Olivia knows Keith isn't a very proactive parent, or even a particularly supportive one. He seems to be leaving all the parenting to Glenda, and it's a heavy weight to bear. Olivia is grateful that Paul isn't like that. They make decisions together and they usually see things the same way—except for sending Raleigh for therapy, of course. And the apology letters.

As she approaches her own house, she sees a sedan parked out in front. Her eyes go to her front door and she sees two people standing there, their backs to the street. Her heart begins to beat faster.

She hurries up the driveway as Paul opens the door. She sees the startled look on his face. Then his eyes meet hers, and it seems to ground him.

The man on the front step turns around and sees her. "Good morning," he says, as she approaches. He shows her his badge. "I'm

Detective Webb, this is Detective Moen. Sorry to bother you on Saturday, but may we come in? We won't be long."

Olivia nods. "I'm Olivia," she says.

"Come in," Paul says, and pulls the door open wide.

"I was just out for a walk," Olivia says, taking their coats. "Can I get you anything? Coffee?"

"No, thank you," Webb says, following her husband into the living room, Moen behind him.

Detective Moen smiles back at her. She has a kind face, Olivia thinks. She's more likable than her partner, who seems rather abrupt. Maybe that's why they work together, Olivia thinks. She and Paul sit side by side rather stiffly on the sofa.

Detective Webb turns to her. "As you probably know," he says, glancing at her husband, "we're investigating the murder of Amanda Pierce."

Olivia tells herself to relax. They have nothing to hide. It's good that the detectives are here—they can immediately clarify where Paul was on that Friday night.

"Yes, I know," Olivia says.

"We've already spoken to your husband and he's been very cooperative," the detective says.

Olivia nods. She still feels slightly nervous, but who wouldn't be nervous having police detectives in their living room?

"I understand that he was home with you the evening of Friday, September twenty-ninth?" Webb says.

Paul faces Detective Webb. "Actually, I was mistaken before. I completely forgot. I have an elderly aunt—my aunt Margaret, who lives alone and gets quite lonely. She calls me a lot, asking me to visit. She called me that day, particularly agitated, and asked me to come see her, and I did. I went right after work. I called Olivia first, to tell her." He glances at her.

Olivia nods. "That's right," she says.

Webb studies her for a moment and then turns back to Paul. "Where does your aunt live?" he asks.

Olivia sees Moen pull out her notebook, flip over a page.

"She's in Berwick."

"I see," Webb says.

Olivia feels uneasy. She knows what the cop is thinking. The small town where Paul's aunt lives is in the direction of Canning, out where Amanda's body was found. But Paul didn't have anything to do with Amanda. What he says is true—quite often Margaret calls and begs him to visit. It's a pain, really. Mostly he doesn't, but sometimes he'll make the trek out there. He's not especially close to her, but there's no other family to visit her and he feels guilty. She remembers that Friday. He told her that Margaret was being very demanding, that he hadn't been to see her in a long time, and that he felt he couldn't say no.

The detective says, "You say she lives alone?"

"That's right," Paul answers. "She's on a list for assisted living, but her name hasn't come up yet. So for now, she has people come in and help her."

"Was there anyone there with her when you visited her that Friday evening?" Webb asks. "Anyone who can vouch for you?"

"Well, no. It was evening. They'd gone home."

"But if we make a visit to your aunt, she'll confirm that you were there that night?"

Now Paul looks uncomfortable. He shifts a little in his chair. "Well, I don't know," he says. "You see, her memory is going. She's got quite bad dementia, too—so she's liable to get a bit mixed up. She won't remember a visit from three weeks ago."

"I see."

"What number did she call you at?" Detective Moen asks.

"She called my cell, while I was at work," Paul says. "She calls me quite a lot, actually. Pretty much every day."

"So if we were to check your cell phone records, it would show that she'd called you that day?" Moen asks.

Paul nods emphatically. "Yes, of course."

"And if we were to check your whereabouts by the location of your cell phone that night, it would show you were at your aunt's," Webb says.

Now Paul looks less sure of himself. He opens his mouth to speak but says nothing.

"Is there a problem?" Webb asks.

Olivia watches all this unfold in front of her, her heart picking up speed.

"I—I don't know," Paul says. "I had my cell phone with me, but it was very low on battery and I didn't have a charger with me, so I just turned it off."

"I see," Webb says.

Paul glances nervously at Olivia. It doesn't look like the detective believes him.

"What time did you get home, Mr. Sharpe?" Webb asks.

"I'm not sure," Paul says, looking at Olivia. "Around eleven?"

Olivia shrugs. "I honestly don't remember. I went to bed early—I was already asleep when you came in." She suddenly realizes that Paul won't actually be able to prove where he was that night. She studies the detectives, but she can't tell what they're thinking. She tells herself she has no reason to be worried. But she doesn't like the way they are looking at her husband. She feels a bit nauseated.

She wonders, sickeningly, if he's got anything to hide.

"And the rest of the weekend?" Webb asks, looking at Olivia.

"He was home, with me. Definitely."

"Could I have your aunt's address?" the detective asks Paul.

Robert Pierce is at home Saturday morning, enjoying a cup of coffee, when he hears his doorbell ring. He goes still. He decides not to answer it; maybe whoever it is will go away.

But the doorbell rings again, insistently. He thumps his coffee down, annoyed, and walks to the front door. He doesn't want to talk to anyone.

He opens the door and sees a pleasant-looking older woman smiling at him. "What do you want?" he says curtly.

"I'm sorry to bother you," the woman says. He looks back coldly at her—*does she honestly not know that his wife has been murdered?*—but she blithely carries on. "My name's Carmine. I'm a neighbor of yours. I live at Thirty-two Finch, one street over." She points over her shoulder.

He begins to close the door.

"I was broken into recently," she says hastily, "and I'm trying to find out if anyone else was as well."

He stops. He remembers the letter, the unexplained fingerprints in his house. He thinks about Amanda's phone, how he'd found it on top of the envelopes in his drawer when he was so sure he'd put it beneath them. He wants to hear what this woman has to say, but he doesn't want to let her know that he was broken into, too. He has already destroyed the letter. What if the police find out? What if they find out who it was, and ask him what he saw in Robert's house? He shakes his head, frowns. "No. Nobody broke in here," he lies.

"Well, that's good, I guess," she says. She sighs rather dramatically.

"Somebody broke into *my* house, and I'm going to find out who." She holds up a piece of paper. "I got this letter."

"May I?" he asks.

She hands it to him. He quickly realizes it's exactly the same as the letter he received. "When did you get this?" he asks.

"I found it last Monday morning. It was pushed in my door slot."

He looks up and hands it back to her. "How unusual," he says. He can't think of anything else to say.

She snorts. "You could say that. I don't know how unusual it is for kids to break into houses, but it's pretty unusual for the mom to write an anonymous apology letter." She adds, "I can't find anyone else who got the letter. But it clearly says there were others. And I bet this kid has broken into more homes than just the ones his mother knows about." She sighs again, heavily. "I suppose I should just let it go. Nothing was taken and the kid's parents have obviously dealt with it."

"Just some dumb teenager," Robert says, careful not to show how uneasy he feels.

She leans in conspiratorially and says, "Actually . . . I'm pretty sure I've figured out who it is. And from what I hear, he's got some pretty good tech skills."

"Really? Who?" Robert asks casually. But he's thinking, *What if the kid looked inside the phone?*

"If I find out for certain, I'll let you know. He snoops into my life, I'm going to snoop into his. And then I'm going to tell him what I think of him."

Robert nods. "Have you gone to the police?"

"No, not yet. I doubt they'd take it seriously."

"Probably not," Robert agrees.

"Well, keep your doors and windows locked," she says, turning away.

Robert closes the door and begins to pace the living room. Fuck. This fucking teenager. What if the kid looked in Amanda's phone, and saw what was on it? He writes down Carmine's name and address before he forgets them. And if he thinks he needs to do something about this kid, he will.

Raleigh looks on in surprise at the scene in front of him. He's never seen these two official-looking people sitting in his living room before. What are they doing here? Adrenaline shoots through his body. This must be about him—about last night.

"Raleigh!" his mom says, obviously startled. "What are you doing up?"

He'd gotten up early on purpose—it's not even noon—all part of trying to get back on her good side so he can get his phone back. But right now, she doesn't seem very happy about it.

"We're finished here anyway," the unfamiliar man says, flashing a dismissive glance at Raleigh.

Nothing to do with him, then. The relief almost makes Raleigh's knees buckle.

Raleigh realizes he's in his pajamas, and everybody else in the room is fully dressed. Well, he didn't know anybody was here. He slinks back into the kitchen, relieved and embarrassed, while his parents show the visitors to the door, somehow aware that he's stumbled into something that he's not really supposed to know about. He pours himself a bowl of cereal and waits.

He hears the front door close. His mom and dad don't come into the kitchen immediately. They're obviously discussing what to say to him. Finally they join him, and his mom busies herself tidying up.

There's an uncomfortable silence; nobody says anything for a minute and Raleigh wonders if they're just going to say nothing at all. Screw that. "What was that all about?" he asks.

His mom looks anxiously at him, and flashes a glance at his dad.

"It's complicated," his father says with a sigh, sitting down at the kitchen table.

Raleigh waits, his body tense. A wave of anxiety comes over him.

His dad says, "Those were the police detectives investigating the murder of Amanda Pierce, the woman down the street." He stops there, as if he doesn't know what on earth to say next.

Raleigh can feel his heart thumping. He looks at his father, then at his mother. She's silent, wary. He turns his attention back to his dad. He's never seen him at a loss for words before. "Why were they talking to you?" Raleigh asks. He's not stupid. He wants to know what's going on.

"It's just routine," his dad says. "They're talking to lots of people who knew Amanda Pierce."

"I thought you didn't know her," Raleigh says.

"I didn't, not really. She was a temp at the office sometimes, so I knew her, but not very well. She never worked in my department."

Raleigh looks at both of his parents; he senses there's more they're not telling him.

"Look, Raleigh, there's something you should know," his dad says carefully.

Suddenly he doesn't want to hear it. He wants to be a child again and run from the room with his hands over his ears and refuse to listen to what his dad has to say. But he can't. He's not a little kid anymore. His father gives him a man-to-man look across the kitchen table and says, "I saw Amanda carrying on with someone at the office.

It was improper. I warned both of them to stop it. Someone else saw me arguing with Amanda about it and put two and two together and got five. I've told the detectives the truth. I wasn't involved with her in any way. We weren't having a—relationship. I don't know who killed her. We can leave that up to the police to figure out. Okay?" He adds, "There's nothing to worry about."

Raleigh stares at his dad, disturbed by what he's just heard. He's pretty sure his dad's telling the truth. He can't think of a single time his dad has ever lied to him before. He sneaks a glance at his mom, but she's watching his father, and there's anxiety written all over her face. *She* doesn't look like she thinks there's nothing to worry about. He wonders if he can trust his dad.

Raleigh nods, frowns. "Okay."

His mom says, looking directly at him, "I don't think this is something anyone else needs to know."

Raleigh nods and says hotly, "I'm not going to say anything." Then he retreats back upstairs to his room.

After driving in silence for a while, Webb turns to Moen and says, "He turned his phone off."

Moen nods. "Right."

Webb says, "We'll get his phone records, but I bet we'll find a call from his aunt that day—if she calls him every day anyway. She lives out that way. She lives alone and has a bad memory, she's confused. What if he was relying on all of that, for his wife at least, and went out that night and met—and killed—Amanda? We can't trace where he was if his phone was turned off."

"It's possible," Moen agrees. "But we haven't actually established that he was seeing her."

"But it's possible. Becky Harris thought he was seeing her."

Moen nods and says, "His wife looked worried. What is she so worried about if he just went to visit his aunt?"

"We should get him down to the station," Webb says. "See if we can get anything else out of him."

TWENTY-THREE

When the detectives return to the station, there's news.

"We've got something," a young officer says, approaching them. He's one of the uniformed cops sent out to canvass the city and its surrounding area. "We found a hotel where one of the clerks recognized Amanda's picture. She came there occasionally with the same man. And then we looked at the security camera footage."

"And?" Webb asks, feeling an uptick of excitement.

"You have to see this," the officer says, and leads them to a computer.

They look down at the screen.

The quality is quite good. Webb sees Amanda first, flicking her hair over her shoulder. Then the man with her comes into the frame. He retrieves his credit card at the desk and then turns, his face caught squarely by the camera. Larry Harris.

"Well, well," Webb says. He glances at Moen. "See how they're coming along with the security cameras at the resort—we need to know if Larry Harris's car ever left."

———

Raleigh is no longer grounded. His mom couldn't stand him moping around the house without his phone and the internet to keep him busy, so at least he's allowed to leave the house again, not just for school and practice. He heads out on his bike, cycling around the neighborhood, trying to work off some of his stress. Without the internet, there's not much to do at home. And he had to escape the tension in the house. He cycles down the residential streets, past some of the houses he's snuck into.

He almost got caught last night. That's it—he has to stop. It isn't worth the risk anymore. Breaking and entering. Messing with people's computers. Even though he's not actually stealing anyone's account info, or distributing malware or porn or anything—he's not tampering—what he's doing is still a crime. The cops won't care that he's just doing this stuff for fun.

He rides slowly past the Pierce place, glancing at it as he goes by. He remembers being inside that house, how clean it was, how orderly. Maybe because there were obviously no kids living there. While he was on the computer, he'd glanced through the desk drawers and found a cell phone at the bottom of one of them. It looked like a cheap, pay-as-you-go phone. Maybe it was an old one, or a spare. He'd turned it on—it had a charge—but it didn't really interest him, so he turned if off again and tossed it back in the drawer and soon left.

Later, when he'd learned that the woman in that house had been murdered, it gave him a chill. The police must have found the phone when they searched the house. His one worry now is that his fingerprints are all over that phone, and in that house. He picks up speed, thinking uneasily about the woman, Carmine, and the letters.

Raleigh's starting to understand that everyone has secrets—he's seen what some people keep on their computers; nothing really surprises him anymore. Raleigh has secrets, and his parents obviously have theirs, too. Perhaps he should be snooping in his own house.

It's Saturday afternoon and the tension in the house is driving Olivia mad. Paul is upstairs in the office. Raleigh has gone off to his room. Olivia tries to talk herself out of going over to confront Becky. She's worried about what exactly Becky might have said to the detectives about Paul. Does she know more than she admitted to Olivia? Did she make things up to take the attention off her own husband? Has Becky been completely honest with her? In the end, she can't stop herself. She grabs a jacket and leaves the house without telling anyone where she's going.

On the walk over, she has a crisis of confidence and half hopes that Becky is not in. But Olivia keeps going, even though it makes her sick that she's left her own house and is going to see Becky to try to find out information about her own husband. She feels lately that everything she took for granted—her good son, her faithful husband—has to be reevaluated.

As she walks past the Pierce residence, she stares hard at the house. The blinds are all drawn, giving the house the look of a blank stare. She wonders if Robert Pierce is in there, behind the blinds. Suddenly she hates him, and Amanda, too, for coming into their quiet neighborhood and rocking it to the foundations. He probably killed his wife, she thinks bitterly, and they are all suffering for it.

As she walks up the driveway and to the front door of the Harris's place—a cute house with dormer windows—she has a bad moment when she realizes that Larry might be home. He won't be at the office on the weekend. She doesn't want to see him.

She rings the doorbell and waits nervously. Finally she hears footsteps and the door opens. It's Becky. She's obviously not expecting visitors; she's wearing yoga pants and a long T-shirt that looks like she might have slept in.

"Hey," Olivia says. Becky doesn't say anything. "Can I come in?"

Becky seems to be considering it, then pulls the door wide. Olivia enters the house, her nerves flaring. "Is Larry here?" she asks.

"Did you want to talk to him?" Becky asks in surprise.

"No," Olivia says. "I just want to know if we're alone."

"He's not here."

Olivia nods, sits down at the kitchen table. Becky doesn't offer to make coffee. She just stands there, her arms folded in front of her.

"We need to talk," Olivia begins. Becky just stares at her and waits. "I need to know if you've told me everything."

"What do you mean?"

"You implied Paul might be having an affair with Amanda. You saw him in her car."

Becky nods. "That's true, I swear."

"Is there anything else that you know, or saw, that you're not telling me? Is there anything else you told the police? I need to know," she says.

Becky takes a deep breath and exhales. "Olivia, we've been friends for a long time. I've always been honest with you. That's all I saw. Just that night, the two of them in the car, arguing. I assumed they were having an affair, because why else would they be there, at that time of night? And you know what a—a *siren* she was. Maybe I was wrong. That's all I know. And that's all I told the detectives."

Olivia exhales loudly, puts her hands over her eyes, feels herself tearing up. She nods.

"You want coffee?" Becky asks.

Olivia sniffs and looks up and nods again, suddenly unable to speak. She's so glad that they aren't going to be enemies. As Becky prepares the coffee, Olivia wipes her eyes with her hands and asks, "Have you heard anything more about the investigation? Do you know what's going on?" She doesn't want to ask directly about Larry. She waits to see if Becky will confide in her.

Becky finishes with the coffee machine and turns around and leans against the counter. She shakes her head. "No, I don't know anything. They're not saying much, are they? There's nothing in the news either."

"I hope they figure it out soon," Olivia says. "And that this will all be over."

Becky pours the coffee and carries the mugs to the kitchen table and sits down. "Olivia, I'm not trying to convince the detectives there was something going on between Paul and Amanda. I told them what I saw. It's up to the detectives to find out the truth. I'm not out to destroy your life to protect my own. I wouldn't do that."

Olivia looks at her gratefully.

"Why are you so worried about Paul?" Becky asks.

Olivia flushes slightly and says, "They were over at the house this morning, those two detectives."

"Really?"

Olivia nods. "They wanted to know if Paul had an alibi."

Becky stares back at her. "And does he?"

"No, not really," Olivia admits. "He was visiting his elderly aunt— and there's no way she'll remember it and be able to vouch for him." Olivia adds nervously, "She's got dementia." She doesn't mention that Paul's cell phone was turned off that Friday night.

"Looks like we're kind of in the same boat," Becky says. "Larry doesn't have much of an alibi either." Olivia looks at her, expecting more. "He was at a conference at the Deerfields Resort that weekend." She hesitates and then says, "You know where that is?" Olivia nods. "But that Friday he went up to his room and did some work and then fell asleep and missed most of the reception. So he doesn't have anyone to vouch for him either."

Robert Pierce paces restlessly around the house as evening closes in.

He thinks about Larry Harris, next door. Does he miss Amanda the way Robert does? He feels a cold, hard hatred for Larry Harris. He wonders how Larry felt when he found out that his wife had been sleeping with his next-door neighbor. Robert already knows how that feels. He wonders how Larry feels now, with the police snooping around, asking questions. Robert knows what that feels like, too.

Robert thinks, too, about the other man that Amanda was seeing. Have the police found out about him yet?

And he thinks about this kid who broke into his house. Worries about whether Carmine will, in fact, go to the police about it.

Next door, Becky has the local TV news on in the kitchen while she prepares supper. She hears the name Amanda Pierce and realizes that her shoulders are hunched up around her neck; she's holding her entire body so tightly that it aches. She takes a deep breath and consciously lowers her shoulders. This can't go on. She mutes the TV.

She has changed over the last few days. She thinks of herself a week ago, how silly she was—with her girlish fantasies about her next-door neighbor. She's not silly anymore. Amanda is dead, viciously murdered, and as far as she can see, the two most likely suspects are Robert Pierce and her own husband, Larry.

The infatuation she'd had for Robert Pierce has fallen away since he'd grown cold to her, and since she realized she might have been used—that Robert might only have slept with her to get back at Larry. Had he known? And if so, how? Had Amanda told him? Had she taunted him with it? Or had he followed her and seen her with Larry? Was Robert ever attracted to her at all?

Now when she thinks about Robert, she doesn't think of his sexy smile at her over the fence, or of how he was in bed with her. Instead, she remembers how he spoke to her that last time, over the fence— how smoothly he told her that he hadn't suspected Amanda was having an affair. But he was lying, and they both know it. He knew Amanda was having an affair. And she thinks the crafty bastard knew exactly whom she was having an affair with. He just wanted to be sure she wouldn't tell the police. Maybe she should.

She has too much to lose if her husband is hauled through the criminal justice system. She has her children to think of. She can't let this destroy them all.

Saturday night, the usual strife. Glenda rattles around the house, feeling like she's jumping out of her skin. She'd tried to get Adam to stay home, and not go out tonight. She's worried he'll drink too much again, do something impulsive, something they'll all regret.

She'd enlisted Keith's help, but he'd been just as ineffective as she was. Adam doesn't listen to either one of them anymore. Keith avoids her, and she wanders around the silent house, waiting anxiously for Adam to come home.

On Sunday morning, Webb and Moen are at the station when one of the officers approaches Webb and says, "Sir, there's a Becky Harris here to see you. She says it's important."

They escort Becky Harris into an interview room. Webb notes the change in her; the first time she came to the station she was nervous and tearful, afraid that her marital indiscretions would become known. Now she looks more composed, more wary. Like she has far more to lose. Or like she has something to bargain with.

"Can I get you anything?" Moen asks.

Becky shakes her head. "No, thank you."

"What brings you in?" Webb says, as they all sit down.

She looks briefly uncomfortable, but she meets his eyes and says, "There's something I didn't tell you, before."

"What's that?" he asks, remembering all the other things she didn't tell them, before. That she and Robert Pierce were lovers. That she'd seen Amanda arguing with Paul Sharpe. What will it be today?

"It's about Robert Pierce." She flicks her eyes nervously between him and Moen.

"Go on."

"That night we were together, on the Saturday the weekend that Amanda disappeared—he told me that he thought his wife was having an affair."

"Why should we believe you?" Webb asks. She's obviously startled by his tone. What had she been expecting, with her track record?

"Because I'm telling the truth!" she says.

"You said you were telling the truth before, too," Webb points out, "when you told us he never said anything to you about suspecting his wife. What's changed?" Perhaps, Webb thinks, her husband has confessed to the hotel visits with his lovely neighbor.

She gives him an annoyed look and takes a deep breath. "He told me not to tell you. He was rather intimidating about it."

"I see."

"He made me promise not to tell. It was—more like a threat." She leans forward. "So you see, he *did* think she was cheating. He had a motive."

"I thought you said he wouldn't be capable of killing his wife, that he wasn't the type?" Moen says.

"That was before he threatened me," Becky says, sitting back and glancing at Moen. "I saw another side of him. He was—different. He scared me."

"Anything else?" Webb says.

She looks back and forth between him and Moen and says, "Are you even interested in him as a suspect?"

"We're interested in lots of people," Webb says, "including your husband."

"That's ridiculous," Becky says, bristling.

"Not really," Webb says. "You see, we have security footage of your husband taking a room at a hotel with Amanda Pierce, on multiple occasions."

Becky stumbles out of the police station. For a minute, she can't remember where she parked her car. Finally, she finds it with the help of her keychain fob. She gets inside the car, out of the wind, and locks her door. She stares out the windshield, seeing nothing, breathing rapidly.

The police have video of her husband with Amanda Pierce at the hotel. She knew this would happen, as soon as he told her. The police aren't idiots. But that stupid bastard she married is.

She has to find out the truth. She has to *know*, one way or another, what happened to Amanda. And then she will figure out what to do.

She stifles a sob in the front seat of her car. How did she get here? She's just an average woman, married, with two almost-grown kids, living in the suburbs. It's unbelievable that she's caught up in this— *nightmare*. A woman she barely knew has been murdered by either her own husband or Becky's husband. If it was Robert, she no longer cares. No—she hopes he's caught and convicted, the bastard. If it was her husband, Larry—she can't even think about that right now.

TWENTY-FOUR

Early Sunday afternoon Carmine finds herself going for another walk around the neighborhood. She's spent the last week talking to everyone she can about the break-in. In the grocery store. At her yoga class. She's frustrated that nobody else admits to having been broken into. It bothers her that she appears to be the only one. Maybe it was a lie, that there were others. Maybe it was just her. Maybe she has been targeted, the object of some kind of prank. If so, it makes it more personal. Is it, she wonders, because she's new here? An outsider? She's more determined than ever to turn the tables on this teenage creep.

She's pretty sure that Olivia Sharpe is the woman who wrote the letter. But she's not going to approach her again—at least, not for now. She's going to talk to her son, Raleigh. She's been asking around about him. By all accounts, he's a nice kid. A whiz with computers. He even had a little business last summer offering to fix people's computers. She wonders if he did any snooping *then*.

She knocks on the door of 50 Finch and a sullen-looking teenage boy answers. She recognizes him immediately as the drunken boy at the end of her driveway the other night. She can tell by his wary expression that he recognizes her, too. But she's not going to mention it. He's got dark hair and eyes and he definitely reminds her of Luke at that age. She asks him if their house has been broken into recently, but he just looks at her as if she's grown two heads. So instead she asks him if he knows of any local boys around his age who might be good with computers; she's having problems with hers. Sure enough, he suggests Raleigh Sharpe.

At that moment a woman arrives at the door wiping her hands on a dish towel. She has short auburn hair and freckles and a pleasant expression. "Hello, can I help you?" she asks, as the boy slinks back inside.

"Hi, my name is Carmine." She holds her hand out. "I'm new to the neighborhood. I'm at Number Thirty-two."

The woman gives her a smile, shakes her hand and says, "I'm Glenda."

"My kids are all grown," Carmine says, trying to make conversation. "Nice-looking boy you have." She's not going to say where she's met her son before. "Do you have other kids?" she asks.

"No, just Adam," the woman says. She doesn't seem to want to talk. She probably wants to get back to her dishes.

"I was broken into recently and I've been going around talking to people, telling them to be on their guard. There was no one home here last time I knocked."

"Well, we haven't been broken into," the woman says rather abruptly, her pleasant expression disappearing.

Lucky you, Carmine thinks. "That's good," she says, hiding her disappointment. "Awful about that murder," Carmine says, thinking this will get the woman talking. She leans in conspiratorially.

"People seem to think that her husband did it." She adds, "Do you know him?"

"No, I don't."

"I actually knocked on his door, just to find out if he's been broken into. I didn't have the nerve to say anything about his wife. But he hasn't."

"Well, it's nice meeting you," the woman named Glenda says and shuts the door firmly.

The phone rings, shattering the quiet. Olivia jumps. She grabs the phone in the kitchen, hoping it's Glenda. "Hello," she says.

"Mrs. Sharpe?"

She recognizes the voice. It's Detective Webb. Her heart immediately starts to pound. "Yes?" she says.

"Is your husband there?"

Wordlessly, she hands the phone to Paul, who is standing in the kitchen watching her. He takes the phone from her.

"What? Now?" Paul says. Then, "Fine."

Olivia feels a sickening jolt of adrenaline.

Paul hangs up the phone and turns to her. "They want me to come down to the police station. To answer some more questions."

She tastes the acid in her throat. "Why?"

"They didn't say."

She watches him put on his jacket and leave the house. He doesn't ask her to come with him, and she doesn't suggest it.

Once he's gone, Olivia gives in to her anxiety, pacing restlessly around the house, unable to quiet her mind. Why do the police want to talk to Paul again?

"Mom, what's wrong?"

She turns and sees Raleigh watching her with concern. She imagines how wretched she must look, caught off-guard. She smiles at him. "It's nothing, honey," she lies. She makes a sudden decision. "I just have to go out for a bit."

"Where are you going?"

"I have to visit a friend who's going through a hard time."

"Oh," Raleigh says, as if not quite satisfied. He moves over to the refrigerator and opens the door. "Are you feeling okay?" he asks. "When will you be back?"

"I'm fine. I'm not sure exactly when I'll be back," Olivia says, "but definitely in time for supper."

Raleigh is up in his bedroom when the phone rings. He wonders who's calling. Both his parents are out. Maybe it's one of his friends, reduced to looking up the family's landline number because he still doesn't have his phone.

He makes it downstairs to the kitchen in time to snatch the phone off the hook. "Hello?" he says.

"Hi." It's a woman's voice. "May I speak to Raleigh Sharpe?"

"Speaking," he says, suspicious.

"I'm having some problems with my computer and a neighbor told me that you might be able to help. You fix computers, don't you?"

"Yeah, sure," Raleigh says, thinking fast. He didn't have many clients last summer, after he distributed his flyers; he certainly didn't expect anybody to call now. But he's happy to earn some spare cash and he's got time on his hands. "What's the problem?"

"Well, I don't know," she says. "Can you come have a look at it?"

"Sure. Now?"

"If you can, that would be great."

"What's your address?"

"It's a laptop. I thought we could meet in a coffee shop. Do you know the Bean?"

"Yeah, sure." He wouldn't normally be caught dead in there, but he can make an exception.

"See you there in fifteen minutes?"

"Okay," Raleigh says.

"I'll be wearing a red jacket and I'll have my laptop with me, obviously," she says.

Raleigh hadn't even thought to ask how he'd recognize her. But she'll be watching for him, and teenage boys don't really hang out in those kinds of coffee shops where his mom and her friends go.

Now that he's made the appointment, he's a little nervous. He's not really used to hiring out his services, but he's done a couple of small jobs before. He's never sure what to charge. But it should be easy enough. Sometimes all these housewives need to learn to do is turn the computer off, wait ten seconds, and turn it on again.

He grabs his jacket and heads for the coffee shop.

Webb regards Paul Sharpe, sitting across from him at the interview table. Sharpe is perfectly still. He doesn't pick up the water from the table; maybe he doesn't want them to see his hands shaking. "Thanks for coming in," Webb says. "You're here voluntarily, you can leave at any time."

"Sure."

Webb doesn't waste any time. He tilts his head at Sharpe doubtfully. "You know, I'm not buying it."

"Not buying what?" Sharpe says. He folds his arms across his chest defensively.

"That you were at your aunt's that Friday night."

"Well, that's where I was," Sharpe says stubbornly, "whether you believe it or not."

"We went to see your aunt," Webb says. He lets a moment go by. "She wasn't able to confirm that you were there that night."

"No surprise there. I told you she didn't have a clue," Sharpe says. "She has dementia."

"You say you got home quite late. Late enough that your wife was already asleep. Do you usually spend such a long time with your elderly aunt?"

"What is this? Am I a suspect?" Paul asks.

"We'd just like to clarify a few things." He rephrases the question. "How long do you usually spend with your aunt?"

Sharpe exhales. "It's a fairly long drive, and I don't go very often, so when I do I tend to stay a few hours. She's always asking me to do things for her, fix this and that. It usually takes awhile."

"It's just that—I'm afraid it puts you in the area where Amanda's car was found," Webb says, "at around the time she is believed to have been murdered. And because your cell phone was turned off, we don't know where you were."

"I told you why I turned it off. My battery was dead. I had nothing to do with Amanda Pierce."

"You were seen in her car, arguing with her, just days before she disappeared."

"You know why I was speaking to her," Sharpe says. "I told you the truth. I'm not the one who was having an affair with Amanda Pierce." He seems rattled.

"Do you know that area?" Webb asks. "Where her car was found?"

"I suppose so." He hesitates and then adds, "We have a cabin out there, on a small lake."

Webb raises his eyebrows. "You do?"

"Yes," Sharpe says.

"Where, exactly?"

"It's at Twelve Goucher Road, Springhill."

Moen writes it down.

"How long have you had this cabin?" Webb asks.

Sharpe shakes his head, as if to show him how ridiculous he thinks this line of questioning is. "We bought it when we were first married, about twenty years ago."

"Do you go out there much?" Webb asks conversationally.

"Yes, we go on the weekends, in good weather. It's not winterized."

"When was the last time you were out there?"

"My wife and I went out a couple of weekends ago, October seventh and eighth, to start closing it up."

"Do you mind if we have a look at it?"

Sharpe seems to freeze.

"Do you mind if we take a look?" Webb repeats. As the silence lengthens, he says, "We can always get a warrant."

Sharpe considers, looking back at him stonily. Finally he says, "Go ahead. I've got nothing to hide."

When Paul Sharpe has left, even unhappier than when he came in, Webb turns to Moen; she raises both eyebrows at him.

"Lots of people probably have cabins out that way," Moen says.

"I'm sure they do," Webb agrees, "but I want to get a look at this one."

Moen nods.

Webb says, "He has squat for an alibi. Maybe he'd arranged to meet her at his cabin. The family wasn't going up that weekend. He had the story for his wife—the aunt called him, begging for a visit. If it's true, why did he go this time? He usually didn't. Why did he turn off his phone?" He adds, "And that cabin isn't very far from where she was found. He knows the area. He would know where to dump the car."

"He would," Moen agrees.

Webb considers. "In the meantime, let's get Larry Harris in here and confront him with this surveillance footage."

TWENTY-FIVE

Olivia grips the steering wheel tightly as she drives over the bridge, out of the city. She's going to visit her husband's aunt Margaret. She knows where she lives. And she hasn't seen her in a long time.

Raleigh saunters up to the door of the Bean, trying to look like a techie on the way to see a client. But he feels like a teenager meeting somebody else's mother. He doesn't feel confident at all. He's only sixteen. He reminds himself that he can probably fix her computer and get out of there within fifteen minutes. Then he can tell his mom and she'll be happy that he did something useful and maybe he can broach the subject of getting his phone back.

He steps inside and immediately sees an older, blond woman in a red jacket waving at him. Ugh. Embarrassing. He quickly walks over and sits down across from her. He takes in the laptop—it's a Dell Inspiron, pretty basic.

"Hi, Raleigh," she says. "It's nice to meet you."

He nods awkwardly and says, "Hi."

"I'm Mrs. Torres," she says.

Looking at her more closely, he can see that she's older than his mom. "What's wrong with it?" he asks, gesturing at the laptop.

"I can't get it to connect to the internet anymore." She flicks her hand at the machine in frustration.

He pulls the laptop closer to him and looks at it. He quickly sees that it is in airplane mode. He hits the key with the little airplane on it. The internet connects to the wi-fi of the coffee shop automatically. "You had it on airplane mode," he says, stifling a smirk. *Jesus*, Raleigh thinks, *it's like taking candy from a baby.*

"Oh, my goodness, is that all it was?" the woman says.

"That's that, then," Raleigh says, feeling both relieved and disappointed there wasn't more wrong with the laptop. He can hardly expect to be paid for that.

"Hang on a minute, Raleigh," she says.

He notes a sudden change in her tone of voice and is momentarily confused. She's holding a twenty in her hand, but she's not offering it to him. Now she leans closer. Her smile is still there, but it's changed, it's not genuine. She lowers her voice and says, "You broke into my house."

Raleigh's face feels hot. His mouth has gone dry. It can't be the woman with the baby. This woman is too old. He doesn't know what to do. A long moment passes and then he realizes that he must deny it. "What?" His voice is a dry croak. He clears his throat. "No, I didn't. I don't know what you're talking about." But he knows he's not convincing. He looks guilty as hell. Because he is guilty as hell.

"Yes, you did. You snuck in and snooped around my house, and in my computer, and I don't like it."

"Why would I do that? Why do you think it was me? I never broke into your stupid house," he says, like a terrified child. He *is* a terrified child.

"I have no idea. You tell me. What were you looking for, exactly?"

He shakes his head. "It wasn't me. I don't do that kind of stuff."

"You can deny it all you want, but I'm onto you, Raleigh."

He has to know how big a problem he's got here. "Maybe somebody broke into your house, lady. But what makes you think it was me?" Raleigh sputters, trying to keep his voice low.

"Because I know your mother wrote those letters."

"What letters?" He's thinking fast.

"The letters of apology your mom wrote about you breaking into our houses. I got one of them. So I know it was you."

Raleigh feels a growing terror. She must be the one who spoke to his mom. His fingerprints are all over her house. And he's just handled her laptop. *Fuck.* With a sudden, desperate bravado, he leans over the table toward her and speaks very clearly. "I was never in your house. Ever. You can't prove it. So back off and stay out of my way." He can't believe he just spoke that way to an adult. He stands up. "I'm going."

She calls out after him, "This isn't over!"

He can feel other people's startled eyes on him as he strides out of the coffee shop, his face burning.

It's about an hour's drive to Aunt Margaret's place, worse in traffic. But it's Sunday afternoon, and the traffic is light. As she drives, Olivia thinks about how pointless this trip probably is. Margaret won't remember if Paul visited her that night. She almost turns around and goes back home.

But something keeps her driving forward along the highway and into the Catskills, and soon she arrives in Berwick. Margaret's house is a small bungalow, not as tidy as it used to be, but Margaret can't do much anymore. Olivia parks in the empty driveway—Margaret had given up her car a couple of years earlier—notices the fading paint, and knocks firmly on the front door. She wonders if anyone else will be there.

For a long time, nothing happens. She rings the doorbell and knocks again. She has a terrible vision of Margaret perhaps lying on the floor with a broken hip, unable to get to the door. She feels a sudden shame that she's taken so little interest in Paul's aunt's well-being, so busy with her own life. How often do people come to help her? Does she even have an alarm to use if she falls down?

Finally the door opens, and Margaret stands there blinking at her in the sunlight. "Olivia," she says, in a weak, wavering voice. Her face breaks into a slow, surprised smile. "I . . . wasn't . . . expecting . . . you . . ." she says, out of breath after the effort of getting to the door.

It must be a good day, Olivia thinks. She knows the dementia comes and goes, that some days her head is clearer than others. "I thought you might like a nice visit," Olivia says, entering the house. "Paul wanted to come, but he couldn't today," she says.

The old woman totters into the living room and sinks slowly into her rocking chair. She has the TV on low, with captions running along beneath. She reaches laboriously for the remote and turns it off. Now that she's here, Olivia is engulfed with sadness. That life comes down to this. This loneliness, this waiting—for suppertime, for a visitor, for death. Olivia sits down on the sofa, turned toward Margaret. The air is stuffy and she longs to open the windows, but thinks Margaret probably wouldn't like the draft. "Can I make you some tea?" she asks.

"That would . . . be . . . lovely . . ." the old woman answers.

Olivia makes her way into the kitchen and fumbles around looking for the tea things. It doesn't take long. The kettle is on the stove, the tea bags are on the counter, and she finds the mugs in the first cupboard she opens. There's a carton of milk in the refrigerator. She sniffs it, and it seems okay. In fact, the fridge seems relatively well stocked.

When it's ready, she takes the tea out to the front room. "Tell me who you have coming in to help you," Olivia says. She listens patiently while Margaret tells her about her arrangements, and how she hopes she gets into assisted living soon.

"I imagine you like to have visitors," Olivia says.

"I have a few," Margaret says. She names some friends who come regularly, if they can.

"And Paul comes to see you, sometimes," Olivia says, feeling a twinge of guilt about what she's doing.

"Not very often," Margaret says darkly, the first hint of her petulant side. "I call him but he never comes."

"I'm sure he comes as often as he can," Olivia soothes.

"The police came."

"Did they?" Olivia asks, alert. "What did they want?"

"I don't remember." She slurps her tea. "You should come more," Margaret says. "You're good company."

"You probably don't remember the last time Paul was here," Olivia says.

"No," she says. "My memory isn't very good, you know."

Olivia's heart sinks.

Margaret says slowly, "That's why I keep a diary. I write in it a little every day, to keep my mind sharp. The doctor said it would be good for me." She points at a leather journal, peeking out from underneath the newspaper on the coffee table. "I write in it a little bit every day, the weather, who came to visit."

Olivia feels her heart begin to beat painfully. "What a good idea. When did you start to do that?"

"A while ago."

"Can I have a look?" Olivia asks. She must see what she wrote for September 29. Margaret nods, and Olivia leafs through the pages, hoping to find the relevant date. But the diary is a mess. It's mostly blank, words scrawled in a shaky hand in the middle of the page, some random dates, but nothing makes any sense. Barely a coherent sentence anywhere.

"Could you get us some more tea, Ruby, dear?" the old woman asks.

TWENTY-SIX

Webb decides that Larry Harris doesn't look as confident in casual clothes. When Webb saw him last, he was still in a suit, his jacket off, his tie loosened—an executive back from a business trip. Today he's wearing jeans and an old sweater, and he doesn't seem to have the same presence or authority. Or maybe it's that he's just not comfortable being brought in for questioning to the police station. That usually flusters people. Especially if they have something to hide.

Larry is staring at the table in the interview room. He has been read his rights. For now he has declined to exercise his right to an attorney.

"Larry, we know you were seeing Amanda Pierce."

He closes his eyes.

"Did your wife tell you? What we have?"

He nods. Webb waits for him to open his eyes. Finally he does. He looks at Webb and says, "I saw her for a few weeks. We met sometimes at that hotel. I don't know what she told her husband." He flushes. "It was wrong, I know. I shouldn't have done it. I'm not proud of it."

"We have the dates on the surveillance video," Webb says. "You saw her at the Paradise Hotel starting in July. You were with her there on the Tuesday before she disappeared, September twenty-sixth. No one saw her after the following Friday. So . . . what happened in that hotel room that night, Larry? Did she tell you it was over?"

He shakes his head firmly. "No, it was the same as usual. We were getting along fine." He sits back in his chair, seems to deliberately assume a more open position. "Look, it's not like we were in love. I wasn't planning on leaving my wife for her or anything. She wasn't putting pressure on me. It was just—physical. For both of us."

"But now she's dead," Webb says.

"I didn't have anything to do with that," Larry says sharply. "Just because I slept with her doesn't mean I killed her."

"When was the last time you saw Amanda?" Webb asks.

"That night, at the hotel. She wasn't temping at our offices that week. She was at some accounting firm, she told me."

"When was the last time you spoke to her?" Webb asks. Larry hesitates briefly, as if considering a lie. "That was the last time I spoke to her," he says.

Webb doesn't believe him. He decides to let it go, for now. "How did you communicate with Amanda? Did you call her at home?" Webb asks. He knows he's needling him.

"No, of course not," Larry says, shifting uneasily in the hard chair.

"So how did you communicate?"

"Phone," Larry answers sullenly.

"What phone would that be?" Webb asks.

"I had a separate phone, for her."

"I see," says Webb. "This would be an unregistered, pay-as-you-go, burner phone?" Larry nods reluctantly. "And did Amanda have a second, unregistered phone as well?"

He nods again. "Yes."

Webb glances quickly at Moen. They haven't found her burner phone. They found her regular cell phone in her purse, in the car. But no burner phone has turned up. They need to find that phone. He focuses in on Larry again. "Do you have any idea where it might be?"

"No."

"And where is your burner phone now?"

"I don't have it anymore."

"Why not?"

"After Amanda . . . disappeared, I didn't need it anymore. And I didn't want my wife to find it."

"How did you get rid of it?" Larry takes so long to answer, that Webb repeats the question. "How did you get rid of it?"

"I didn't kill her," Larry insists suddenly.

"What did you do with the burner phone?"

"I threw it into the Hudson," he says nervously. "I went for a walk along the river one night and tossed it in."

"And when was that?"

"It was about a week after she'd left. I mean—everybody thought she'd taken off on her husband."

Webb stifles his frustration. He'll never find that phone, or Amanda's phone either. His bet is that she had it with her when she was murdered, and her killer got rid of it. Same as the murder weapon. He shifts gears. "Why can't we find anybody who saw you at the resort on Friday afternoon? After you checked in, nobody saw you until around nine o'clock."

Larry exhales heavily, looks from Webb to Moen and back again.

"I worked in my room all afternoon, and then fell asleep. I missed most of the reception."

"And we're supposed to believe that?" Webb asks.

"It's true!" Larry says, almost violently. "Why don't you check with the resort? I never left my room, I swear. They must have cameras on the parking lot. They can tell you that my car never left."

"Where did you park your car?" Webb already knows Larry didn't park in the indoor parking lot at the resort; he's had people watch all the tapes.

"In the outdoor lot, to the right of the hotel."

"Right. We've checked, and there are no cameras there, apparently. Only in the indoor parking area." He adds, "As I'm sure you know."

Larry looks frightened now. "I didn't," he protests. "How would I know that?"

Webb says quickly, "Did you know that Amanda was pregnant?"

He shakes his head, frowning, off balance. "No, I didn't know, honest. I always used a condom. She insisted on it. She didn't want to get pregnant." He says angrily, "Why don't you arrest her husband? If anyone killed her, it was him. She told me once that if he ever found out that she was cheating on him, he would kill her." He adds, regretfully, "I didn't believe her at the time. I should have."

Webb looks carefully at Larry and tries to tell if he's lying. Webb thinks Robert Pierce is capable of murder, but he wonders if Larry is making this up.

"Robert Pierce is a cold son of a bitch," Larry says. "Amanda told me about him, how he treated her. She told me that she would leave him someday, so when she disappeared, I thought that's what she'd done. If anyone killed her, it was her husband."

Webb stares him down. "There's something else," Larry says

finally. "Robert Pierce—he knew about me and Amanda. And he knew she had a burner phone."

"How do you know that?" Webb asks, alert.

"Because I got a call from her burner phone, and it was Robert on the other end. He said, 'Hi, Larry, it's her husband, Robert.' I hung up."

"When was that?" Webb asks.

"It was the day she disappeared. Friday, September twenty-ninth. Around ten in the morning."

Webb meets Moen's eyes.

TWENTY-SEVEN

B ecky Harris stares out the glass doors to the backyard. She'd wanted to accompany Larry to the police station when the detectives came to bring him in for questioning, but he insisted that she stay here. She could tell he was worried.

They're both plenty worried.

When she'd returned from the police station and told Larry about the video surveillance of him at the Paradise Hotel, he'd looked so panicked that she didn't even bother to say, *What did I tell you, you idiot?* Instead she said, "They're going to bring you in for questioning." She'd had to steel herself to stop her body trembling. "Larry," she said, "tell me the truth. Did you kill her?"

He looked back at her, an expression of shock on his exhausted face. "How can you even think—"

"How can I think it?" she stormed at him. "The evidence, Larry! It's piling up against you. You were having an affair with her—it's on tape. You were in the area near the lake where her body was found and can't account for your whereabouts. God help you if they find out you argued with her the day before she went missing. And then you go and throw your phone off the Skyway early Sunday evening on the way back from the resort, *before anyone even knew she was missing.* I don't know, Larry, but you *look* guilty as hell!"

"I didn't know she was dead when I tossed the phone," he protested. He grabbed her arms and said, "Becky, I had nothing to do with this. You have to believe me. I know how bad it looks. But I didn't hurt her. It must have been Robert. He knew she was cheating on him. He found her burner phone. He called me from it, and I answered. He already knew about me and Amanda. He said 'Hi, Larry' before I even opened my mouth. *He* must have killed her."

So Robert did know. She nodded slowly. "He must have," she agreed. She forced herself to take deep breaths. When she looked at her husband, she couldn't believe, even in the face of all the circumstantial evidence, that he could actually have killed someone. That he could have beaten a woman to death.

"When you talk to the police, you have to tell them all that," she said at last. "But tell them you threw the phone into the river someplace from the shore, in case there are cameras on the bridge. They could check them and see when you did it. Tell them it was a few days after she disappeared, not the same weekend."

He nodded back at her, obviously terrified, relying on her now to help him. She was thinking more clearly than he was.

"And whatever you do, don't tell them you had an argument with Amanda the day before she went missing," she said, "and that she'd broken it off with you."

Then the detectives had come to take him down to the station for questioning and she'd worked herself into this frenzy of doubt and fear.

She doesn't think Larry is capable of planning a cold-blooded murder. If he was, he wouldn't be in this mess. But a moment of uncontrolled anger? Could he have struck Amanda in a rage, not meaning to kill her?

She's afraid that might be exactly what happened and that Larry is lying to her still and frightened for his life.

Her mind strays uneasily to an incident that happened a couple of years ago. Their daughter Kristie was being harassed by a teenage boy whom she refused to date. He kept bothering her at school, and then he made the mistake of coming around the house, calling her names. Larry had charged out of the house and rammed the boy up against the wall so fast it had made Becky's head spin. She still remembers the fear and shock on the boy's face. And how Larry looked, his left hand grasping the boy's shirt by the collar, his right hand drawn back as if he were about to punch the kid hard in the face. Kristie was crying behind her inside the house. But something stopped him. He shoved the boy down the driveway and told him to leave his daughter alone. Becky had worried that the kid might press charges, but they never heard from him again. Now, she forces herself to thrust the incident from her mind, returning to the present.

Robert *is* the cold-blooded type. She thinks now that he might be quite capable—smart enough, calculating enough—to plan a murder and carry it out. And if he did, she's pretty sure he would know how to do it so that he never got caught.

She has to know who killed Amanda—was it Robert or her husband?

Impulsively, she leaves her own house, crosses the lawn, and knocks on Robert's front door. As she waits, she looks nervously over her shoulder, wondering if any of the neighbors are watching her. She knows he's home. She'd seen him passing in front of the windows earlier, and his car is in the driveway.

She's about to turn away, defeated, but then the door opens. He stands there looking at her. His mouth doesn't quirk up in that charming smile of his. They're done with all that.

"Can I come in?" she asks.

"What for?"

"I need to talk to you."

He seems to consider it for a moment—*what's in it for him?*—but she sees curiosity get the better of him. He steps back and pulls the door open. It's only when he closes it behind her that she realizes that maybe she's been stupid. She's a little afraid of him. She doesn't really think he's going to harm her—he wouldn't dare, under the circumstances. But what does she expect to learn? It's not like he's going to tell her the truth. All at once she's tongue-tied; she doesn't know how to start.

"What did you want to talk about?" he says, folding his arms across his chest, looking down at her. He's much taller than she is. They're still standing in the front hall.

"Larry's at the police station," she says. "They seem to think that he might have killed Amanda." She's tried to say it bluntly, but her voice has a quiver in it.

"Because he was having an affair with her," Robert says matter-of-factly.

She stares back at him, nods slowly. "That's why you slept with me, isn't it? You knew Larry was sleeping with Amanda all along, so you slept with me."

"Yes," he says. He smiles.

He seems to be enjoying himself. How could she have been so seduced by him? There's no sign of that warmth and boyishness that charmed her anymore. But it doesn't matter. She's over that now.

He doesn't seem to care that she knows. If he killed his wife, he must be very sure now of not getting caught. "Larry's going to tell the police," she says, "that you knew about them. He told me about the burner phone, that you called him on it."

"I'm not worried," Robert says. "He has no proof. It's his word—and yours—against mine."

She looks up at him; he seems to tower over her now. She feels small; he could snap her neck with his hands if he wanted to. "Larry didn't kill her," she says.

"You can't possibly know that," he says. "In fact, I think you're worried that he *did* kill her."

"I think it was *you*," she whispers, goaded into saying it.

"You can think what you like," Robert says, "and tell the police whatever you want, but they know you'd say anything to protect your husband."

"Do you have an alibi?" she asks desperately.

"Not really," he admits.

"*You* killed her," Becky says wildly, as if repeating it will make it true.

Robert leans in close to her, so his face is just inches from hers. "Well, it was probably *one* of us," he says icily, "and you don't know which one. I guess you have a problem, don't you?"

Becky stares back at him for a moment in horror and then sweeps past him, yanks open the door, and flees back to her own house.

TWENTY-EIGHT

When Olivia returns home from her drive to Margaret's, she's exhausted. The house is quiet.

"Where have you been?" Paul asks. He's sitting in the living room, a drink in his hand.

She looks back at him warily, ignoring his question. "Where's Raleigh?"

"He's in his room."

"What did the police want, Paul?" Olivia asks nervously.

She sits down beside him while he tells her what happened at the police station.

"Why do they want to see the cabin?" she asks in disbelief.

"I don't know."

"Well, they must have said something, given some reason." She feels her anxiety skyrocket.

When he answers, he sounds irritated. "Like I said, they asked me if I was familiar with the area where her body was found, and I had to tell them about our cabin. How would it look if I didn't, and they found out afterward?" He looks at her steadily. "I have nothing to hide, Olivia." He certainly doesn't sound paranoid. He sounds like he thinks this is an inconvenience, an intrusion, nothing more.

"No, of course not," she says.

"They said if I didn't give consent, they would get a warrant." Paul crosses his arms in front of him as he tells her, "It was like a threat. I should have said no, on principle. Let them get their fucking warrant."

"We have nothing to hide, Paul," Olivia says uneasily. "We should just let them go ahead. They won't find anything, and then they'll leave us alone."

He glares at her. "You know how I feel about this sort of thing. It's an outrage, it really is."

She slumps tiredly. She has no energy left. She doesn't want him to be difficult about this. "But you told them yes, didn't you?" she asks. If he makes a fuss about this, she might really have cause for alarm— she might think he's actually hiding something. And they'll get the warrant anyway.

"Yes," Paul says at last. "There's nothing to find. It's not like we're hiding anything. But it's ridiculous, and a waste of resources. It's not a good thing that police can ask to search your home, knowing that they'll just get a warrant anyway; it's intimidation. It's an erosion of privacy."

"I know how you like your privacy," Olivia says, a hint of acid in her voice.

He turns on her. "What's that supposed to mean?"

"It just means I don't see why you have to be difficult about this! I want this to end, Paul."

"I'm not being difficult," Paul says tersely. "They're meeting me out there tomorrow morning. I'm taking the day off work."

She feels her body sag. She just wants to be done with this. And she's not going to tell Paul about her visit to his aunt Margaret.

Raleigh can hear raised voices on the floor below; it sounds like his parents are arguing, but the voices quickly recede. He couldn't make out what they were saying. It's not like his parents to argue, but lately, the house has been tense. He blames some of it on himself. He knows his parents are fighting partly because of what he's done. He doesn't dare tell them about what happened this afternoon at the coffee shop—how that horrible woman tracked him down, tricked him, and accused him. It took him ages to stop shaking afterward.

If he told his parents, his mother would probably have a breakdown. But what if that woman shows up at the house and confronts his mother again, and tells her about the meeting in the coffee shop? What if she decides to go to the police? He feels trapped, and he doesn't know what to do. The only people he would feel comfortable going to for help or advice for anything are his parents, and he can't go to them with this. Not now. Not with everything else they're dealing with.

And they all continue to pretend that everything is just fine.

Becky bolts inside her house and locks the door behind her. Now that she's away from him, she begins to shake. Only a psychopath would toy with her the way Robert just did. *It was probably one of us and you don't know which one. I guess you have a problem, don't you?* What kind of person would say something like that? When it's his own wife who's dead? He's sick.

She realizes, with a hideous feeling, that Robert *wants* Larry to be charged with the murder of his wife. After all, Larry was the one sleeping with her. Perhaps he's set the whole thing up somehow. He doesn't miss Amanda at all. He put on a good show of grief in the beginning, but he's not bothering to pretend for her anymore. He's let her see who he really is. He's dropped the mask. She paces the living room anxiously, picking relentlessly at her cuticles.

She hears a key in the lock. Larry comes in and looks at her.

"Why do you have the door locked?" he asks, his face gray.

He looks shattered. She doesn't answer. Instead, she says, "Well?" She doesn't even wait for him to take his jacket off.

"I told them what you said."

"Did they believe you?"

"I think so."

"You *think* so?" She can't keep the edge of hysteria out of her voice.

"Christ, I don't know!" he almost shouts back at her. "I don't know what they think!" He lowers his voice again. "But Becky, there's another problem."

"What problem?" *How much worse can it get?*

He tells her, haltingly. "At the resort, I parked in the outdoor parking lot, not the indoor lot. Apparently there's no camera on the outdoor parking lot—so I can't prove I never left."

She stares at him for a long moment.

"But they can't prove I did either," he says.

"Maybe it's time we got you a lawyer," she says dully.

"What does that mean?" he says. "Don't you believe me?"

"Yes," she says automatically, even though she doesn't know if she believes him or not.

He strides into the living room to the bar cart. "I need a drink."

"I went over to see Robert Pierce while you were out," Becky says, her voice a hoarse whisper, as she watches him pour himself a stiff whiskey.

He whirls around to look at her, the bottle in his hand. "What? What the hell did you do that for? He probably murdered his wife!"

She's staring into space. Now that it's over, she can hardly believe she did it. She must have been out of her mind. "I told him that the police think you might have killed Amanda."

"Jesus, Becky! That's insane! What did you tell him that for?"

She focuses on him now; he seems to have gone a shade paler. "I wanted to see what he'd say."

"And?"

"He said it was probably either you or him who killed her."

Larry looks horrified. "Becky—he's dangerous. Promise me you won't go near him anymore. *Promise.*"

She nods. She doesn't want to go near Robert Pierce ever again.

Detective Webb drives across the Aylesford Bridge spanning the Hudson, and turns north on the highway, Moen beside him in the passenger seat. It's early Monday morning, exactly a week since they found Amanda Pierce's abandoned car, her violently beaten body shoved into the trunk.

It's a cold, crisp day, but the sun is out, and it's a pleasant drive. At first the river is on their right. Soon they turn west, deeper into the Catskills, in the direction of the small town of Springhill. The wilderness stretches out all around them as the road curves and winds through the mountains. Eventually they turn off the highway and take a series of smaller, winding roads. The drive to the Sharpes' cabin takes them right past the spot where Amanda's body was found. Paul Sharpe must know this stretch of road well.

At last they turn down a gravel road and finally stop at a classic wood cabin that looks weathered, nestled in among the trees.

Webb sees a car parked in front. Paul Sharpe is here ahead of them. No surprise there.

They climb out of the car. The air is fresher here, and smells of earth, wet leaves, and pine needles. Breezes rustle through the remaining leaves on the trees overhead. They can see a small lake farther down, a dock jutting out into the water.

The door to the cabin opens and Paul Sharpe steps out, looking wary. His wife, Olivia, is right behind him.

Olivia decided to come along because she couldn't stand the thought of staying home and worrying about what was going on out here.

Olivia had tossed in bed the night before, unable to sleep, thinking about the cabin. It wasn't the same, now that Raleigh was sixteen. He still enjoyed the cabin, loved the lake, but he didn't look forward to it with gleeful excitement the way he had when he was little. By Sunday afternoon he was usually missing his friends and his wi-fi, so they tended to go back earlier than when he was a little boy, when she and Paul practically had to drag him into the car to go home.

She hadn't noticed anything different about the cabin two weekends ago when they'd come up to start closing it up for the winter. It had been Columbus Day weekend, the weekend after Amanda had disappeared, the weekend before they'd had the Newells over for dinner and Olivia had found out that Raleigh was breaking into houses. Everything had been just as it was the last time they were at the cabin. She doesn't understand what the hell the detectives want.

She's always loved their little cabin in the woods. It's not fancy— just one large room that's part kitchen, part living room, with a view down to the lake along the back, and two bedrooms and a small bathroom on the other side of the living area. The floor is linoleum, the walls are wood paneled, the furniture is mismatched but comfortable, and the appliances are outdated, but that's all part of its charm. She

SHARI LAPENA

hopes that this doesn't spoil it for them. They didn't tell Raleigh what was happening today. He'd gone to school early for basketball practice, leaving before they did. It will be over soon enough, and he will never have to know that the police were even here.

She steps out of the cabin behind her husband and is surprised to see that it's just Webb and Moen. She was expecting an entire team. It makes her relax a little bit. "Good morning," she says. She knows that Paul will be brusque with them; that's the way he is. She must try to smooth things over. "Can I offer you some coffee?"

"That would be great, thank you," Webb says, smiling his quick smile.

"Yes, that would be lovely," Moen says, warmly. "Beautiful spot you've got here."

They all go inside and Olivia turns away and busies herself with the old, serviceable coffee maker. She takes down four blue enamel cups. These old, chipped cups comfort her, remind her of relaxed, happier times. Morning coffee on the deck, with the mist rising off the water; hot cocoa for Raleigh when he was little, wrapped in a red-and-black plaid blanket against the chill. She glances over her shoulder and sees the detectives each pulling on blue latex gloves, and just like that, all her happy feelings abruptly disappear.

TWENTY-NINE

S he brings the coffee over to the detectives; they accept it gratefully. Olivia finds the sight of those latex gloves holding her cups
unsettling. The detectives begin to go about their work. Olivia and
Paul sit silently at the kitchen table, trying to pretend that they don't
mind, that they're not watching the two cops' every move.

When the detectives leave the main room of the cabin and go into
the bedrooms, Paul gets up and follows, taking his coffee with him.
Olivia gets up, too. The detectives open drawers, look under mattresses.
They put everything back the way they found it. She has no idea what
they expect to find. They return to the kitchen and go through it
methodically, silently. The longer it goes on, the more anxious Olivia
becomes. She watches as Webb studies the navy curtains carefully. Silently, he waves Moen over. Together they look at the curtains, both
sides, with the aid of a flashlight. Webb's face seems to turn grim.

Finally, Webb turns to Olivia's husband and says, "Do you have
any tools?"

"Tools?" Paul repeats.

Olivia wonders if they want to take something apart. She's not going to allow that, and she's sure Paul won't either. If they want to start tearing up the floorboards they will have to get a damn warrant.

Paul must be thinking along the same lines she is, because he says, "What for?"

"Where do you keep them?" Webb asks, avoiding the question.

Without answering, Paul leads them outside to a small shed, not far from the cabin. It's full of firewood, plastic lawn chairs, a lawn mower, and other accumulated junk. Olivia peers around Paul as he opens the door to the shed, and points. Webb pulls out his flashlight and flicks it on, playing the light over the interior of the shed. There's a hatchet leaning up against the wall. The light lands on a battered red metal toolbox. The detective steps inside and squats down and opens it. He uses an index finger to search inside the toolbox, his blue gloves stark and clean against the dusty interior. Olivia wonders what the hell he's looking for. She can see the tension in Paul's shoulders.

"Do you have a hammer?" Webb asks.

"Yes," Paul says, "it should be there." He bends down to look inside the toolbox.

"It doesn't appear to be here now," Webb says, and turns his attention to Paul. "When was the last time you saw it?"

"I have no idea," Paul says. "I don't remember." The two men stare at each other for a long moment.

Olivia feels her stomach drop. She's been telling herself that the detectives are on a fool's errand, that they won't find anything, and then they'll leave them alone. But there it is again, the doubt niggling at the back of her mind—*Do the detectives know something that she doesn't?*

Webb looks up at Moen and says, "I think we need to get the crime team out here."

"You're going to need a warrant for that," Paul says angrily.

Olivia stares at her husband, her heart pounding.

"I can do that," Webb says, "with a phone call. And I can have a forensic unit out here within a couple of hours."

Webb watches Paul Sharpe, standing by the shed in the sunlight filtering through the trees, his hands down by his sides.

"What's going on?" his wife blurts out suddenly, her face ashen. "Paul had nothing to do with Amanda Pierce! Why aren't you after *her* husband—he's probably the one who killed her!"

"Olivia, you're not helping," Sharpe says. "They've obviously made up their minds. Let them search. There's nothing to find."

While they wait for the crime scene team to arrive, Webb and Moen explore the area outside the cabin, while the Sharpes stand by mutely and watch. Finally they all turn as a couple of police cars and a white crime scene van pull up to the cabin.

Webb knows that if this cabin is a crime scene, it has already been compromised. But they must search it regardless. Webb points out the suspicious stains on the kitchen curtains—the stains that look like blood—to the technicians. If it is blood, they will be able to get DNA from the stains. Webb and Moen watch silently while the technicians close all the blinds and curtains to darken the room. A tech begins to spray luminol in the kitchen. The kitchen floor lights up near the back windows and shows a path from there to the sink on the opposite side of the room.

The tech gives the detectives a meaningful glance.

"What's that?" Paul asks.

"The lit-up areas show the presence of blood," Webb says, "even when it has been cleaned up and is invisible to the eye." He looks at the couple standing at the edge of the kitchen. Webb doesn't know who looks worse. Olivia Sharpe looks like she's about to faint. Paul Sharpe is standing completely still, staring at the floor, his face slack with incomprehension and shock.

The tech then sprays the area around the sink and it lights up, too. But as they proceed, the biggest area where blood has been scrubbed clean—at least to the human eye—is at the back of the kitchen on the floor in front of the windows that face the lake. There is evidence of wiped-up blood spatter on the walls and even the ceiling as well. The luminescence fades after a few moments, but they have all seen it.

With the help of the chemical, it has become obvious that Amanda Pierce—or somebody—was attacked in the kitchen near the back windows, and that something—probably a weapon—was carried from where the attack occurred to the kitchen sink. The evidence of blood spatter arcing on the nearby walls and ceiling indicates that she was struck violently and repeatedly with something hard. The missing hammer.

Webb steps forward and says to Paul Sharpe, "You are under arrest for the murder of Amanda Pierce. You have the right to remain silent. Anything you say can and will be used against you in a court of law. You have the right to speak to an attorney, and to have an attorney present during any questioning. If you cannot afford a lawyer, one will be provided for you at government expense. Do you understand these rights?"

Olivia Sharpe slides to the floor before anyone can catch her.

THIRTY

Olivia is so disoriented that she can barely function. She hardly remembers the drive back to the city. Her husband went in the police car—handcuffed—on his way to the police station. She followed in the back of the detectives' car, her mind numb, Webb driving, while Moen drove the Sharpes' car back to the station and the forensic team was left behind to finish processing the scene.

Now she's sitting at the station, waiting for someone to come out and tell her what's happening, and what will happen next. She couldn't bring herself to meet Paul's eyes when he was arrested. She keeps seeing the lit-up areas where the blood had been in their cabin. She has to fight down the bile that's rising in her throat. That stain had been there, but invisible, since Amanda was murdered. Olivia had stood on it a couple of weekends ago, the last time they were at the cabin, looking out at the water in the morning, holding her coffee, thinking that everything was right with the world. The last normal weekend. The weekend before she found out Raleigh had been breaking into places.

The weekend before Amanda's body had been found. But nothing had been right at all. These things had already happened, and she had simply been unaware of them. It seems like a lifetime ago. She's appalled at her own monumental ignorance. She'd had no idea that a murder had taken place where she stood. She can't get it out of her mind, can't stop seeing it, the lit-up pattern on the floor, the evidence of blood spatter on the wall and all the way up to the ceiling. She thinks about their missing hammer—heavy and familiar, its old wooden handle with layers of white paint on it. Did Amanda know she was going to die? She must have screamed. Out there, no one would have heard her. Olivia imagines the hammer coming down on the woman whose face she knows only casually, and from that one photograph they keep showing online. When Olivia closes her eyes, she sees the trail leading from where she was murdered to the kitchen sink. Her sink, where she washed the dishes two weekends ago, while Paul stood beside her and dried, making idle chatter, knowing all the while what had happened there the week before, what he'd done. Thinking he'd cleaned it all up.

She remembers Paul's face, pale as chalk, as they took him away, and he said to her, "I didn't do this, Olivia! You must believe me!"

She wants to. But how can she believe him?

What will she tell Raleigh?

Suddenly she needs a toilet, but there's no time—she throws up all over her own lap, the chair, the floor.

Detective Webb pauses outside the door of the interview room. Moen is already in there, with Paul Sharpe. Webb is tired, and takes a moment to prepare himself mentally. Then he opens the door.

Sharpe is slumped in the chair, his cuffed hands on the table in front of him. He looks terrible. His eyes are watery, as if he's trying not to cry.

What had he expected? Webb thinks. Why do they always think they can get away with it? He remembers what Sharpe was like at the beginning. He denied knowing Amanda Pierce. Then he admitted to being in the car with her, but only after they told him that he'd been seen. The story about Larry Harris—it had had the ring of truth because it was true; they'd subsequently confirmed that Larry *had* been seeing Amanda. But why had he been "warning her off" Larry, as he claimed? Maybe it wasn't because he was trying to protect a friend; maybe he was jealous. Maybe he was involved with Amanda himself. He'd argued with her that night, a little more than a week before she went missing. What happened that Friday night? They couldn't confirm he'd been at his aunt's. He could have been at the cabin. He could have met Amanda there, killed her with the missing hammer, thrown the murder weapon in the lake. He could have driven her car to that spot at the neighboring lake and sunk it and walked back to his own car at the cabin. The walk would have taken a little over an hour. He could have done it. They don't know what time he got home that night.

Webb sits down across from Sharpe and looks at him for a moment. "You're in a lot of trouble," he says. Sharpe raises his eyes to him and gives him a look of pure fear.

"I want a lawyer," Sharpe says. "I'm not talking to you without a lawyer present."

"Fine," Webb says, standing up again. He hadn't expected anything else.

Glenda hears the ping, glances down, and sees the text on her cell phone. *I'm at the police station. Please come.* It's from Olivia.

What is Olivia doing at the police station? Glenda doesn't tell Adam, just home from school, where she's going, just that she's going to see Olivia.

She parks the car and rushes up the steps into the police station. She asks for Olivia, and is directed to a small waiting area. The smell of vomit assails her and she sees immediately that Olivia has been sick, but someone has tried to clean her up.

"Olivia, Christ, what's the matter? What's happened?"

Olivia starts to tell her, crying, and Glenda gets the gist of it, feels her body growing colder and colder as she pieces things together from Olivia's sobbing account. The worst possible news. She's stunned. Paul, arrested for the murder of Amanda Pierce. Evidence of blood found in the cabin. Olivia has her face buried in Glenda's shoulder; Glenda is grateful that for the moment, at least, Olivia can't see her horrified expression. Glenda must pull herself together; Olivia needs her.

Finally, she pushes Olivia away gently, so that she can look at her. "Olivia," she says. "I'm going to help you get through this." Olivia looks back at her as if she is the only thing keeping her together. "Okay?"

Olivia nods dumbly.

"You need to get Paul a lawyer. The best one we can find."

Olivia nods again, almost distractedly, and whispers, "What am I going to tell Raleigh?"

I don't know, Glenda thinks. They can't hide it from him. She says, "We'll figure it out. We'll tell him together. Come on, let's get you home."

"Wait," Olivia says.

"What?"

Olivia looks at her desperately and lowers her voice to a whisper. "Do I tell Raleigh that he didn't do it?"

Glenda doesn't know how to answer. Finally she says, "What did Paul say?"

Olivia averts her eyes. "He said he didn't do it."

"Then that's what you tell Raleigh," Glenda says.

She bundles Olivia into her car and drives her home. Paul's car can stay there overnight—she'll come back for it in the morning. The sight of the familiar house as they pull up makes Glenda's heart sink. She's dreading what's to come. But she will stick by Olivia, no matter what. No matter how ugly it gets. That's what friends are for.

Raleigh must wonder where she's been all day, Olivia thinks dully. She'd texted him somehow from the station, saying she'd be home soon. Olivia doesn't know where to find the courage to tell him. How do you tell your son that his father has been arrested for murder?

She wants to believe it's all a terrible mistake. The police make mistakes all the time. But then she remembers the bloodstains. She can't forget them.

When she opens the door, she hears Raleigh's steps hurrying down the stairs to greet her. His face falls when he sees her and Glenda; he can tell something's wrong.

"Mom, where have you been?" he asks.

Olivia wants to protect him. But she can't protect him from this. Everyone will know. She can't keep it from him. Her son's life is going to be ripped apart in the next few minutes. You try so hard to do everything right, but then—

Suddenly she is so tired that she can hardly stand.

"Let's sit down," Glenda says, and leads Olivia into her own living room, guiding her by the elbow until she slumps down on the sofa.

"What's wrong?" Raleigh demands, in a hollow voice. "Where's Dad?"

"Your father is at the police station," Olivia says finally, trying to keep her face from crumbling.

He looks back at her with blank incomprehension. But then he seems to get it; she can see it in his face, the dawning dread.

"He's been arrested," she says.

"What?" Raleigh asks. "For what?"

"For the murder of Amanda Pierce," Olivia says, her voice breaking.

There's a stunned silence.

"That's crazy!" Raleigh protests after a moment. "Why? Why did they arrest him?"

This is so hard. She has to tell him. "They searched our cabin today. And they found—evidence."

"What evidence?" Raleigh demands, his face contorted with emotion. "Dad didn't kill her! He didn't really know her, right? He just saw something, he was covering for somebody, that's all. That's what he said."

It hurts her to look at her son, struggling with this. It feels so brutal, what she must tell him now. "They found some bloodstains in the cabin. They're going to do some tests and see if it's Amanda Pierce's blood." Her voice is a rough whisper.

"How can they arrest him if they don't even know it was her blood?" Raleigh says desperately. "They must have something else."

"Our hammer is missing." There's another long silence. Finally Olivia says, "Your father has told them he didn't do it."

"Of course he didn't do it!" There are tears in Raleigh's eyes.

She says, her body limp, "The police want all of us—Keith and Adam, too—to give our fingerprints tomorrow, because we've all been at the cabin. They want to see if there are any other prints there that they can't account for."

Olivia lies in bed, rigid, eyes wide open and staring sightlessly at the ceiling, thinking of her husband in a cell. Glenda is in the next room, staying over for support. She'd made Olivia have a bath, thrown her soiled and smelly clothes in the washing machine, and made everyone soup and toast that mostly went uneaten.

Olivia glances at the digital clock on her bedside table. It's 3:31 A.M. Her mind has been going around in circles, an endless loop of horror and disbelief. Paul calling from work that day, saying he was going to see his aunt. Had he been lying? Her thinking nothing of it, watching a movie on her own that night—choosing something she knew he wasn't interested in seeing. Him creeping in late, after she was already asleep—she has no idea what time he came home. This is what trust does. You don't notice these things, you don't question them, because you think you have no reason to. Now she wishes she'd been less trusting; she wishes she'd paid attention.

What was he wearing when he came home? She has no idea, because she was asleep. Was he still in his office clothes? She certainly didn't notice anything like bloodstains on his clothes the next day— she would have noticed that, and remembered, no matter how trusting she'd been. If he killed Amanda, he must have gotten rid of his clothes somehow.

She gets up, turns on the bedside table lamp, and starts searching through his closet, clawing through his chest of drawers. All his suits seem to be accounted for. But Paul has a lot of clothes, especially old jeans and T-shirts. She can't think of anything that isn't there. He keeps clothes at the cabin, too. Something might be missing, and she wouldn't necessarily know.

He must have been seeing Amanda. She remembers watching all the men fawning over her at the party in the park. Some of the neighbors had got a permit to barbecue. They'd all chipped in twenty bucks per family for hot dogs and hamburgers and soda and beer, and most of them had brought a salad or some kind of dish. There was a bouncy castle for the younger kids and some balloons, but most of the teenagers didn't bother showing up. Olivia was tidying up the ketchup and mustard dispensers, occasionally throwing a glance at the semicircle of people talking and laughing in the white plastic chairs that had been rounded up for the occasion. She watched the new woman, Amanda something, who had recently moved in on their street. She was absolutely gorgeous and completely aware of it. Why was she bothering to flirt with their much older husbands? She had a hot-looking husband sitting right beside her.

None of the women liked her.

Glenda had come up and stood beside Olivia, following her gaze, watching in apparent disbelief as Amanda let her hand—with her long, red nails—rest on Keith's forearm. "Who the hell does she think she is?" Glenda said.

Then Becky came up on the other side of Olivia, and the three of them stood watching their husbands, clearly in thrall to this new woman.

They should all have been more on their guard, Olivia thinks, coming back to the present. Perhaps Becky's instincts were right after all, and Paul and Amanda had become lovers. Did they meet at the cabin that night? Did Paul beat her to death with their hammer? And then stuff her body in her trunk and sink her car? And then scrub everything clean and come home and behave as if nothing had happened? What other explanation can there be?

Olivia gets out of bed and pads down the hall quietly, past the spare room, careful not to wake Glenda, who she can hear snoring lightly through the partly open door. She reaches her son's room and quietly pushes his door ajar. She watches him sleep, completely unaware of her. For the moment at least, he's peaceful.

She moves closer and looks down at him. His young face is angular, and constantly changing these days. He's growing some whiskers. It's a face she adores. She would do anything to protect him. She wants to sit down on his bed beside him and stroke his hair, the way she used to when he was little. But Raleigh doesn't want his mother stroking his hair anymore, not like when he was very young. He doesn't want her hugs and kisses anymore; he's almost grown up. And he keeps things from her—he never did that when he was little. He told her everything. But now he has secrets. Raleigh is keeping things from her. Like his father. They both have secrets.

She's the only one in the house who has nothing to hide.

THIRTY-ONE

Becky Harris stands staring down at the morning newspaper in her hands. The headline screams in large print ARREST IN AMANDA PIERCE MURDER. Her first thought is, *They've arrested Robert.* She feels an intense relief. And then, as she reads, *Oh no.*

She can't believe it. She thinks of Olivia. She can imagine what she's going through because Becky's been imagining herself going through the very same thing.

She takes the paper through to the kitchen. She's alone in the house; Larry has already gone to work.

The evidence—as much as the article reveals—sounds damning. Blood found in the Sharpes' cabin, now thought to be the scene of the murder. A missing hammer, the possible murder weapon, yet to be recovered. And the car with her body in it found not far from there, on a route familiar to Paul Sharpe. Stunned and incredulous, Becky thinks back to that time she saw Paul with Amanda in her car. Was she right? Were they lovers after all? Was he jealous of the affair she was having with Larry? Maybe that's why he told her to break it off with Larry, rather than any altruistic concern about Larry getting into trouble at work.

She hadn't thought Paul was capable of hurting anyone. But she hadn't thought Larry was either. She imagines how it must have been. They argued at his cabin and he struck her. Maybe the hammer was lying close by, and he acted impulsively. He was probably horrified at what he'd done, probably regretted it immediately. But then—he covered it up. He put her body in the trunk and sank it. What must life have been like for him since it happened? Especially since the body was found. It must have been a living hell.

There will be a trial. Larry will have to testify about his affair with Amanda—his sordid meetings with her in that awful hotel. The thought of all of this out in the open sickens her. How horrible it will be for her and the kids.

But it will be far worse for Olivia and Raleigh.

She rereads the newspaper article. Things look very bad for Paul. But at least she knows now that her own husband, despite all his failings, didn't kill Amanda Pierce. She really hadn't been sure.

Carmine Torres is shocked by what she reads in the newspaper Tuesday morning. They've arrested Paul Sharpe for the murder of Amanda Pierce.

She thinks of the poor woman she spoke to at the door—Paul Sharpe's wife—and how ill she looked that day. Maybe she knew. Maybe it wasn't only her son she'd been worried about.

Paul Sharpe has lawyered up, but Webb still hopes to get somewhere with him when they question him this morning, with his lawyer by his side. His lawyer hadn't been available the night before, but now that Paul Sharpe has had a night in a cell to think about his situation, maybe he will be more cooperative.

As he enters the room, he sees Sharpe sitting, no longer cuffed, beside his attorney. He looks as if he hasn't slept at all. He has to be scared shitless. Good. Maybe he's ready to talk.

Sitting next to Sharpe is Emilio Gallo, a well-known criminal lawyer from a respected firm. Webb has dealt with him before. He's good. Expensive. Gallo will stop at nothing to help a client, as long as it's legal. His dark, nicely tailored suit, pressed shirt, and smart silk tie contrast starkly with the rumpled jeans and wrinkled shirt of his client. Sharpe is tired and scruffy and Webb can smell the sweat and fear coming off him. Gallo is well rested and well groomed, smelling faintly of expensive aftershave.

Webb and Moen sit down. The tape is turned on. "Please state your name for the tape," Webb directs.

"Paul Sharpe," he says, his voice shaky.

"Also present are Emilio Gallo, attorney for Paul Sharpe, Detective Webb, and Detective Moen of Aylesford Police," Webb begins. He doesn't mince words. "Your client is going to be facing a murder charge," he says, looking directly at Gallo.

"Good luck with that," Gallo says mildly. "My client didn't do it."

Webb turns his gaze on Paul Sharpe. He waits until Sharpe finally looks up at him. "I want to hear it from him."

Sharpe says, "I didn't do it."

"The evidence against you is pretty compelling," Webb says.

"It's all circumstantial," the attorney counters. "A missing hammer? Blood on the floor? You haven't even confirmed that it's the dead woman's blood."

"When we do, perhaps you'll see things differently," Webb says.

"I don't think so," Gallo replies. "Anyone could have been in that cabin, anyone could have found the hammer in the shed and used it. You have nothing against my client except that he wasn't home that night. And he has a perfectly reasonable explanation for where he was."

"That he can't prove," Webb says. "He was seen arguing with the victim before she disappeared."

"And he has a perfectly good explanation for that, too," the attorney says smoothly.

"Maybe we don't believe him."

"It doesn't matter what you believe," Gallo says. "What matters is what will hold up in court." Now the attorney leans a little closer and says, "I think we both know you'll have a tough time getting a conviction. There are other rather obvious suspects in this case—the husband, who may have known about his wife's infidelity, and her lover. I understand there was a lover? My client denies having any kind of relationship with the victim. Lots of reasonable doubt, if you ask me. You'll never get this to stick."

Webb sits back in his chair, lifts his chin at Paul Sharpe, and says, "She was murdered in *his* cabin."

"And anyone could have killed her there." The attorney stands up, indicating that the interview is over. "You either have to charge my client or let him go." Webb turns the tape off.

"We can hold him a bit longer," Webb says.

After Sharpe has been taken back to his cell and his attorney has left, Moen says to Webb, "With Gallo representing him, he's never going to break down and confess."

"So we have to build a case," Webb says. "We have work to do."

Olivia looks back at her husband. He's sitting across from her in a small room at the police station. There is a guard nearby. She stares at him in his messy, slept-in clothes. He is barely recognizable as her husband. Is he, or is he someone else altogether? She doesn't trust her own judgment, her own senses anymore.

"Gallo thinks he might be able to get me out of here," Paul says.

She can't speak.

"Olivia—say something," Paul demands. He is distraught. His eyes are bloodshot, and he already smells—of the cells, of fear, and desperation. She can't stop staring at him. He looks so different. He already looks more like a prisoner than he looks like her husband of a week ago, going off to work in an ironed shirt, a good suit. The world has gone all tilted, and she can't find her balance.

"What did he say?" she asks finally.

"He said that they'll have trouble getting a conviction."

He looks both desperate and hopeful at the same time. A drowning man reaching for a life raft. *Does she extend her arm and help him, or does she push him away?* "Why did he say that?" she asks. She feels and sounds like an automaton. Surely he's wrong, she's thinking. Why would he tell his client such an obvious lie? Somewhere in the back of her mind she's also thinking that this is going to cost them a fortune. Probably everything they have. If he did it, maybe it would be better for everyone if he just admitted it and pleaded guilty, she thinks.

"We know *I* didn't kill her," Paul says. "Which means somebody else must have."

She looks at him, wanting to believe him. She would rather he be wrongly accused, to *know* in her heart that he is innocent, and stand by him and fight tooth and nail to get this sorted out. But she's not sure. She needs convincing. She *wants* to be convinced. She wants to believe him.

"What did Gallo say, exactly?" she asks, daring to hope he has some good news.

"He said there are other, better suspects—her husband. Larry, who probably *was* having an affair with her. They need to prove it beyond a reasonable doubt, and there's plenty of room for reasonable doubt."

She was hoping for something more conclusive. Something that would exonerate her husband, clear him once and for all. She doesn't want him to simply *get away with it*. If he did it—if he was sleeping with this woman, and killed her in a rage, and covered it up—she wants him to go to prison for the rest of his life. She will never forgive him. If he did it, she doesn't ever want to see him again.

"Gallo said anybody could have used our cabin," Paul says. "Taken our hammer, and killed her and cleaned it all up, and we would never even know."

"But the cabin was locked," she says.

"Someone could have broken in. Or found the hidden key." He lowers his voice now to a whisper and another look comes over his face, a pleading look. "We could say we'd had break-ins before, but since nothing was ever taken we didn't bother to report it."

She whispers back, "That would be a lie."

"Just a small one," he says very quietly. "I didn't *do* it, Olivia. And my life is on the line."

She looks back at him, her dread growing, and starts shaking her head. "No, we can't do that. Raleigh would know it was a lie."

He slumps in his chair and looks down at the table, suddenly defeated. "Yeah, you're right. Forget it." Finally he looks up, completely exhausted, and says bleakly, "How is Raleigh doing?"

"Not good. Not good at all."

He hasn't asked about her.

Robert Pierce is biding his time in his kitchen. When he picked his newspaper up off his front step that morning, there was already a crowd of reporters on the street in front of his house. They saw him and started to surge toward him, but he quickly stepped inside the house and slammed the door. He looked down at the front page of the *Aylesford Record*.

As he read, a slow smile came over his face. They'd made an arrest. And it wasn't him.

The news has put him in a very good mood. Maybe he will be able to relax now. Maybe he will be able to return to work. It's been wearing, the police always at his door, always looking at him as if it's just a matter of time until he screws up. But now they have arrested Paul Sharpe. All attention will be on him. Robert can start living his life again, put all this behind him.

He looks out the window and sees that the reporters are still out there. He knows they will wait all day until they get a statement from him. He's something of a celebrity. He goes up to his bedroom and dresses carefully. A nice pair of pants and a dress shirt. He combs his hair, admires himself in the mirror. And then he goes downstairs and opens the front door and steps out.

The cameras flash repeatedly; he keeps his expression suitably serious. A bereaved husband, grateful at last that his wife's killer has been arrested.

THIRTY-TWO

An officer sticks his head in Webb's office door and says, "The Sharpes and the Newells were all fingerprinted this morning, sir. And something very interesting has turned up."

Webb looks down at the report. *What the hell was Paul Sharpe's son doing in Amanda Pierce's house?*

Olivia sits on her bed and looks at herself in the dresser mirror. She's ashen. The detectives have called and want to see her again. They have asked her to bring Raleigh, too.

Raleigh is in his room, having stayed home from school. Glenda is sticking by Olivia and Raleigh—showing people that she supports them. Olivia feels better having Glenda here. She remembers how people had stood and watched outside of Robert Pierce's house, not that long ago, thinking that Robert Pierce had murdered his wife. And now there are people outside of her house, thinking that Paul is a killer.

When she and Raleigh arrive back at the station, she is directed into an interview room, while Raleigh is asked to wait outside. Webb and Moen are there waiting for her. She's caught them in the middle of a conversation, which they abruptly break off.

"Mrs. Sharpe," Webb says. "Thank you for coming in. Just so you know, this interview is purely voluntary; you are free to leave at any time."

Detective Moen brings her water and looks at her as if in sympathy. *Men can be such shits.*

Olivia's mouth is dry. She swallows. There's absolutely nothing she can tell them, one way or the other. She doesn't know anything. Nothing that happens in this interview will change anything. She must just get through it.

Webb says, "Lab results confirm that the blood found in your cabin is Amanda Pierce's."

Her head swims at the news, but she already expected it. Who else's blood could it be? He waits for her to say something.

"I don't know anything about it."

"You must have given it some thought," Webb chides her.

"I think someone else must have killed her in our cabin."

"Who do you think that might be?"

"I don't know." She pauses and says, "Her husband, possibly."

"What would her husband be doing in your cabin?"

"I don't know." Olivia wants to cry, but refuses to. She can't explain it. She can't explain any of it. Why won't they just leave her alone? They know they've got him. Why torture her like this? She can't help them. Can't they see that she's suffering enough?

"Is there anyone we don't know about who may have had access to the cabin?" Webb asks.

"No."

"Did the Harrises ever visit?"

"No, never."

"Did you ever tell them where it was, exactly?"

"No."

"Anyone else?"

"No."

"Okay, thank you. That's it for now. We'd like to speak to your son. You can stay if you like."

They bring Raleigh in. He looks anxious and very young. He sits down beside her and she tries to give him a reassuring look. She wants to put her arm around his shoulders and give him a squeeze, but she suspects he wouldn't like it.

"Raleigh, I'm Detective Webb, and this is Detective Moen. We'd like to ask you some questions, if that's all right."

Raleigh looks at him uncomfortably. "Okay."

"You see, Raleigh, we found your fingerprints in the Pierce house. Can you explain that?"

Olivia freezes at this second blow. Her son shoots her a look of alarm. No one says anything for a long moment.

Finally, Raleigh asks, "Do I need a lawyer?"

"I don't know, do you?" Webb says.

"I want a lawyer," Raleigh says, his voice breaking.

"We'll get you one," Webb says, rising out of his chair. "Stay put."

Raleigh has conferred privately with his lawyer—a young man named Dale Abbot—and his mother, and they have decided on a course of action. Raleigh is petrified. The interview resumes, Webb and Moen on one side of the table, Raleigh, his attorney, and his mother on the other side.

"So, Raleigh," Webb says, "are you going to tell us what your fingerprints are doing in the Pierce house?"

Raleigh glances at his lawyer, who nods at him, and says, "I snuck into their house."

"When was that?"

"It would have been early October. I don't know exactly."

"Before Amanda Pierce's body was discovered?"

"Yes."

"How did you get in?"

"Through a basement window. It wasn't locked."

"And why did you do that?"

"Just—for fun." Raleigh's going to try not to admit to the hacking. It's all about damage control now.

"I see." Webb sits back in his chair, glances at the attorney. "That's breaking and entering, Raleigh."

He nods.

"Did you take anything?"

Raleigh shakes his head. "No."

"What were you doing there?"

"Just—snooping."

Webb nods thoughtfully. "Snooping. Did you see anything interesting?"

Raleigh glances at him. "Not really."

"Did you see a cell phone anywhere?" Webb asks.

Raleigh nods. "Yeah. In a bottom drawer of the desk. One of those pay-as-you-go kind. You must have found it when you searched the house."

"No, we didn't."

"I didn't take it, I swear!"

"Did you look inside the phone, Raleigh?"

"No, I wasn't that interested."

"It's okay if you looked inside the phone, Raleigh."

"I didn't."

"Okay." Webb sits back again, as if disappointed. Then he says, "Did you kill Amanda Pierce?"

Raleigh recoils in shock. "No! I just went in their house, looked around, and left."

Webb stares back at him. Finally he says, "I'm afraid we'll have to charge you with breaking and entering."

Raleigh sits back in his chair. It's a relief, really. He can't believe how much of a relief it is. It feels so good that he suddenly blurts out, "I broke into another house, too. Thirty-two Finch Street." He doesn't want to have to worry about Carmine anymore. He'll admit to those two. They can't prove he was in the last house he hit—the police must know about that one already, but he was wearing gloves. He's not going to admit to any more than he has to.

Glenda makes something comforting for supper. Mac and cheese. But the three of them simply pick at their food. Glenda watches Olivia and Raleigh with concern. She has no appetite either. They're both sitting quietly at their places, faces drawn, each lost in their own private hell. Neither of them has said anything about what happened down at the police station, and although Glenda's dying to know, she doesn't want to ask.

Raleigh says, "Mom, maybe you should go lie down."

"Good idea," Glenda agrees. Olivia looks like she's about to collapse. "Why don't you go lie down in the living room? I'll clean up."

She tucks a blanket around Olivia on the sofa and glances out the window to the street. Everyone has gone away. She imagines they will be back tomorrow. Murder is always big news.

Why did Robert and Amanda Pierce ever have to move here? she thinks bitterly.

Olivia falls asleep on the sofa. Finally, around nine o'clock, Glenda decides to go. She can't stay at the Sharpes' forever; Adam needs her at home. She leaves a note that she'll be back in the morning, and walks home in the dark, her footsteps echoing hollowly on the pavement.

When she arrives at home, Adam tells her that they're out of milk and bread. "Fine," she says, not even taking off her coat. "Why don't you come with me to the store then?"

He puts on his jacket and heads out with her.

"How are they doing?" Adam asks, obviously worried.

"They're going to be okay. Everything's going to be all right," Glenda says. She doesn't know what else to say. They walk the rest of the way in silence.

The bell on the door chimes as they enter the convenience store. Glenda is completely drained and just wants to pick up her things and go home. As she turns away from the refrigerator with her milk, Adam trailing behind her, she spots Carmine in the aisle in front of her. *Shit.* She definitely doesn't want to talk to her. She's a busybody, and Glenda is in no mood for it. She resents the way she's been sticking her nose in everywhere about the break-ins, hounding Olivia. She wishes she'd leave Raleigh alone. And she certainly doesn't want to talk about Paul being arrested—Carmine will be all over that. Glenda considers putting the milk down quietly on the floor and making a quick exit. Too late—at that moment, Carmine turns her head and sees them. A smile of recognition lights her face. *Shit.*

"Glenda, isn't it?" Carmine asks, approaching her.

"Yes," Glenda says, making her way briskly to the front of the store where the bread is, avoiding her eye. But Carmine follows her. She's really not great at reading social cues, Glenda thinks.

"Hi, Adam," Carmine adds.

Glenda notices that her son is trying to avoid Carmine, too.

"You know, you remind me of my own son a bit," Carmine says to Adam. "Same dark hair and eyes."

Adam looks as if he wishes he could disappear, and Glenda wants to tell Carmine to get lost.

"My Luke was a bit of a handful. He used to get up to all kinds of trouble. Drinking, taking my car without permission."

Glenda stares at her.

But Carmine focuses her eyes on Adam and says, "Did you tell your mom that I saw you the other night?"

Glenda says, "What are you talking about?"

"Oh, nothing. Never mind," Carmine says, as if finally getting the hint. "Have a good night." And she wanders off to another aisle.

Glenda makes her purchases, eager to get away from Carmine.

Late at night, Olivia pads down the carpeted hall to look in on Raleigh. She silently pushes open the door. She stands there for a moment in the dark, studying the bed. Then, alarmed, she flicks the light switch on. Her son isn't there.

Her heart speeds up and she turns away from his bedroom and creeps downstairs. The kitchen, living room, and den are dark. He's not there either, sitting alone, brooding in the dark—she turns on the lights to be sure. She returns to the kitchen and opens the door to the adjoining garage. Raleigh's bike is where it should be, his helmet hanging from the handlebar.

She returns upstairs and quietly makes her way to the only room she hasn't checked—the office at the end of the hall. The room is completely dark, except for the slight glow coming from the computer. It's her husband's computer, and Raleigh is engrossed in its contents.

"Raleigh, what are you doing?" she says.

THIRTY-THREE

Webb arrives very early at the station the next morning, after a poor night's sleep. He grabs a coffee and heads to his office, then he sits back in his chair, gazing at the wall opposite, his mind busy.

They can't hold Paul Sharpe in custody much longer before the prosecutor has to charge him or let him go. It's Amanda Pierce's blood in his cabin. His hammer is missing. Sharpe was seen arguing with the victim shortly before she disappeared, but his story that he was warning her away from Larry Harris has a certain plausibility—they know Larry was seeing her.

Olivia Sharpe said that Larry Harris had never been to the cabin. Is it possible she was wrong? Could Harris have arranged to meet Amanda at the Sharpes' cabin that weekend, while he was at the conference? Maybe he killed her. He parked in the outside lot at the resort and had his story ready that he was working and fell asleep. No one seemed to care that he missed most of the reception—until he became involved in a murder investigation. The only thing that went wrong is that they found Amanda's car with her body in the trunk. She'd made that convenient fib to her husband, so it would look like Amanda had arranged her own disappearance. Paul Sharpe was the only one who knew about the affair, and he wouldn't say anything, especially if he hadn't known they'd been at his cabin.

Possibly. But Paul Sharpe might have said something. When she disappeared, staff at the hotel might have come forward about seeing them together, and then Harris would have been under a microscope. But still, with no hard evidence—and especially no body—it would look as if an unhappy, unfaithful wife had run from her life.

Or maybe Robert Pierce is the killer. Pierce has been lying to them. According to Harris, Pierce had access to Amanda's burner phone and knew about their affair. And Raleigh Sharpe saw the burner phone in Pierce's desk *after* Amanda had disappeared. But it wasn't there when they searched the house. Pierce must have gotten rid of it. Maybe he'd been watching her. He seemed the type. Maybe he knew where she was going that night, drove up to the cabin, saw her with her lover—Larry Harris? Paul Sharpe?—waited for her to be alone, and bashed her head in. Pierce doesn't have an alibi either.

He'll talk to the prosecutor. They'll let Paul Sharpe go for now, and see how everybody reacts. Webb has time. Time to get under everybody's skin. There's no statute of limitations on murder.

Olivia is startled by the kitchen phone ringing early Wednesday morning. It's Detective Webb, telling her that they are releasing her husband without charge. She hangs up and stands perfectly still. Her drive to the police station passes in a blur. She feels numb.

Olivia sits in the waiting area at the station, watching for Paul to appear. Torn between relief and dread, she wants to put the moment off. But it's come; she hears footsteps and stands up. Then she sees Paul. She walks up and hugs him, like she's done a thousand times before, but this time is different. She's not sure about him. She can feel both their hearts beating. After a moment, she pulls away.

He looks at her warily.

"Let's get you home," she says, and turns away so he can't see the doubt in her eyes.

She's already texted Glenda with the news, telling her not to come by.

Raleigh waits anxiously for his mom to return home with his dad. She'd told him she was going to pick him up. Raleigh's not going to school again today.

His father is innocent, he tells himself. They're letting him go. But Raleigh's relief is tinged with uneasiness. He can tell that his mother has her doubts. Raleigh has doubts, too. He's not sure of anything anymore. He hadn't found anything illuminating on his dad's computer. But Raleigh also knows something that they don't. And he's going to have to tell them.

When his parents arrive home, it's awkward. His mom smiles at him as if everything is fine, but he can tell from her drawn face that things are far from fine. His father looks awful and smells like he could use a shower. Raleigh can feel the tension emanating from both of his parents.

They all end up in the kitchen and his mom says, "I've told your father that you're being charged."

"It'll be okay, son," his dad says, pulling him into a hug.

Raleigh nods, swallows. But it's not himself that he's worried about right now, it's his dad. Raleigh has to confess to his parents, and he's dreading it. Raleigh must tell them the truth.

Beginning is difficult. "There's something I have to tell you," Raleigh says. He can see at once from the closed look that comes over his mother's troubled face that she doesn't want to hear it. She's got enough to deal with. He hates to hurt her more than he already has. But he must say this. He can't seem to get the words out.

"What is it, Raleigh?" his father says tiredly. He's been humbled, obviously, by his own recent history. He's not on his high horse now, Raleigh thinks.

"I lied to you," he says. "I lied to both of you. About the break-ins."

His mother looks more anxious than ever; his father looks deeply weary.

"I told you—and the lawyer—that I only broke into two houses, but it was more." He watches his dad's brow darken. "It was more like nine or ten," he confesses.

His dad looks at him sharply; his mother looks horrified.

"There's something else I need to tell you," Raleigh says uncomfortably. "I didn't want you to know, but—I broke into the Newells'."

"What? When?" his father asks.

Raleigh swallows. "It was the night they were over here having dinner—I knew that Adam would be out that night, too."

His mom gasps. "You broke into our dearest friends' house while they were over here having dinner with us?" She looks utterly betrayed. "How *could* you? Why?"

Raleigh feels himself coloring. He gives a helpless shrug. "I was hacking. I was serious about it. . . . It's a skill, and it takes practice. So I snuck into people's houses when they weren't home and hacked into their computers." He risks another glance at his parents. They're staring at him in disbelief. "I was getting really good," he says, "but I'm not doing it anymore." They're still staring at him, appalled. There's a pregnant silence. "I knew you wouldn't approve. But I never did any harm. It's not like I ever stole any data, or shared it, or put anything on anyone's computers, or told anybody what I found," Raleigh protests. "I never tried to blackmail anybody or anything," he offers in his own defense.

"Blackmail!" his mother repeats, her hand at her throat.

"Mom, relax, I never did anything like that! It was more just—getting experience."

"Experience—is that what you call it," his dad says.

Raleigh doesn't like his tone. It's the old dad tone, and it pisses him off.

"Yeah, well, maybe you should listen to me for a change," Raleigh says sharply.

"What are you talking about?" his mom asks.

"I know things, about your dearest friends," Raleigh says.

Olivia feels her heart freeze. She stares at her son, not so sure she wants to hear what he has to say. She feels dizzy, shocked. What secrets could Glenda and Keith have? She glances at her husband, but he's watching Raleigh intently, as if he's struck a nerve.

"What are you getting at, Raleigh?" Paul says.

"I saw things, on their computer," Raleigh says.

"We gathered that," Paul says in a tight voice. "What did you see?"

"Keith is a prick," Raleigh says with energy.

"Don't talk that way," Olivia says sharply.

"Why not? It's true! You should see what was on his computer! I saw his emails—he's been cheating on Glenda, seeing someone else behind her back. I couldn't tell you because they're your friends."

Olivia feels sickened; she can't speak.

"When was this?" Paul asks.

"I told you—it was that night they were here for dinner, the night before mom saw the texts on my phone and found out what I was doing," Raleigh says miserably.

Olivia tries to focus. Keith is cheating on Glenda, and Glenda has no idea. Olivia is certain that Glenda doesn't know. Now what does she do? Does she tell her? Or leave her in ignorance? Olivia glances at her husband and remembers when Becky came over to tell her her suspicions about Paul. She realizes, her heart sinking, that she's going to have to tell Glenda.

"Are you sure about this?" Paul asks.

"Of course I'm sure. I saw it with my own eyes. There was no way to misinterpret what he wrote. I even sent some emails back to his girlfriend from his account, and they weren't very nice."

Olivia watches her son, feels her jaw drop open.

Raleigh says, "So at least now he probably knows that somebody was in his computer and knows what he's doing." He snorts. "I hope he's been losing sleep over it. Maybe he thinks it was Adam. Why do you think Adam drinks so much? He drinks to forget that his dad is such an asshole."

"Raleigh," Paul begins, looking unnerved. "You can't just mess with people's lives like that."

"He's an asshole. Serves him right."

Olivia wonders if Glenda ever told Keith that Raleigh was breaking into houses, even though she promised she wouldn't. Olivia sometimes lets things slip to Paul that she said she wouldn't share.

"The emails were hidden," Raleigh continues. "You wouldn't know they were there unless you were looking, like I was."

"How did you find them?" Paul asks.

"It's easy if you know what you're doing. I can get into a powered-off computer in about three minutes—I just use a USB flash drive to boot up the computer—most computers allow you to boot from a live USB and that way you can get around the internal security. Then with a few commands, I can create a backdoor and I'm in. Once I was in Keith's computer, I could tell he was trying to hide something because he was deleting his browser history. But he didn't delete the cookies, so I was able to get the username and password for his hidden email account. And then I could get into his account and see his emails and pretend to be him and send whatever I wanted."

Olivia doesn't know whether to be horrified or impressed. "Do you know who the woman was?" she asks.

"No. It was some silly name on the email account. Something made up."

"Jesus, Raleigh. You shouldn't have done that," Paul says.

Raleigh looks at his father as if challenging him somehow and says, "Do you think he could have been seeing the woman who was murdered?"

Olivia watches the two of them, stunned into speechlessness.

"No, of course not!" Paul says. "That's . . . ridiculous."

"He knows our cabin," Raleigh says.

"Are you suggesting that *Keith* murdered her?" Paul says, clearly horrified at the idea. "Keith can't possibly be involved with this. He can't be a murderer. He's my best friend."

THIRTY-FOUR

Becky jumps when the door opens and her husband walks in. He'd been too upset to go into the office this morning, and then the detectives had called him to come down to answer more questions. She can see that he is shaken. But he's home from the police station. He hasn't been arrested.

"What happened?" she asks.

"They asked me if I'd ever been to the Sharpes' cabin." Larry sinks, clearly exhausted, onto the sofa in the living room. "They're still acting like they think I killed her. Why do they think that, Becky? I had an affair with her, but I swear I didn't kill her." He looks up at her, worried.

She sits down beside him. Then, "It's just us now, Larry. You've never been to that cabin, have you?"

"No! Absolutely not. I swear, I don't know where it is."

But he's lied to her before. He could have known about the Sharpes' cabin somehow.

It's been on the news this morning, online, that Paul Sharpe has been released without charge. She can't be the only one who finds that odd. But they obviously don't think he did it. They must think some-one else killed her in his cabin. And they must think it was either Robert Pierce or her husband, Larry.

Back to square one. Which of them did it? She doesn't know.

Robert Pierce can't believe it. Yesterday he was in the clear—gave a press conference and celebrated alone with a few beers; today he learns that Paul Sharpe has been released without charge. He reads about it in the news, and then those damn detectives show up on his doorstep around lunchtime.

"Mr. Pierce," Webb said. "We'd like to have another little chat with you."

"About what?" Robert said suspiciously.

"About your wife."

"I thought you caught the guy," Robert said. "Quick work, by the way. What do you want with me?"

"Well, you see, we had to release him. Not enough evidence."

"You're kidding, right?" Robert said, his heart pounding harder. "My wife's blood on the floor of his cabin isn't enough for you?"

"Oddly enough, no," Webb replied. "We'd like you to come down to the station."

"Now?"

"Yes."

And so here he is, back in this claustrophobic room, but this time he has been read his rights, and the interview is being taped. The detectives have let Sharpe go. They will be after him now, the hus-band. They always think it's the husband.

"We think you knew your wife was seeing someone else," Webb begins.

Robert says nothing.

"We know she had a burner phone. We haven't been able to find it, but we know she had one."

Robert remains warily silent.

"Do you know where it is?" Webb presses.

Still, he says nothing.

"We know she had one," Webb continues, "because Larry Harris told us."

Robert isn't going to rise to the bait.

Webb gets right in his face and says, "We know you had her burner phone, because Harris told us that you called him from it. On the morning of Friday, September twenty-ninth, the day your wife disappeared."

Robert shrugs. "That's not true. You've only got his word for it. He was screwing her—he'd say anything."

"We don't just have his word for it. We have a witness."

"What are you talking about?"

"A local boy broke into your house and found the burner phone in your desk drawer after Amanda went missing. But it wasn't there when we searched the house a few days later. What did you do with the phone, Robert?"

He doesn't answer. His heart is racing. Instead he says, "What boy?"

But the detective ignores his question. "We know you lied to us. We know you knew she was seeing Larry. Was she seeing Paul Sharpe, too? Did you know about that? How many numbers were in that phone? Was she sleeping with both of them? That must have been hard to take. We know you had the phone, so you must have known she was planning to meet someone that weekend at that cabin. Which one was it? And you went there, and saw them together, and once she was alone, you bashed her head in."

Robert says nothing, but his heart is pounding.

"Maybe the burner phone is at the bottom of a lake somewhere, like the hammer," Webb says.

"I want to call my attorney," Robert says.

Olivia," Paul says to her, in a troubled voice, when they're going to bed that night, "what if Keith *was* seeing Amanda?"

She'd been thinking the same thing herself, all day, and all evening. Part of her dismissed the idea as improbable. Surely Keith didn't really know her. He'd met her at the neighborhood party, like everyone else, but he didn't work in the same company as Paul and Larry, where she was a regular temp. The chance he was seeing Amanda seems like a stretch. Glenda had never given any hint that she suspected Keith might be having an affair. On the other hand . . . She answers him quietly, "Do you think it's possible?"

"I don't know. I don't think they ever met, other than the party a year ago. He certainly never mentioned her to me. I never thought he was the type to have an affair."

"They could have met online," Olivia says. "They could have met anywhere."

Paul looks back at her, radiating tension. "Olivia, Amanda Pierce was killed in our cabin. I didn't kill her. But who do we *know* has been to our cabin?"

And that's why she's unsure. Glenda and Keith come to their cabin every summer, for at least a weekend or two. They know the cabin very well. Their fingerprints are everywhere, and perfectly explainable. Keith could have met Amanda there that weekend, and nobody would have known. Because Keith probably would have known that they wouldn't be using the cabin that weekend.

"But how would he get in?" Olivia asks.

"Keith knows where we hide the spare key," Paul says.

"He does?"

Paul nods, biting his lip. "I told him once how we drove all the way to the cabin that time and forgot the key, and how after that we hid a spare in the shed under the oilcan."

They look at each other, an uneasy dread spreading across their faces. Could it have been Keith, Olivia considers, and not Amanda's husband, or Larry, *or Paul*, at all?

"What should we do?" Olivia asks.

"We have to tell the police," Paul says. "Let them look into it. They can seize his computer."

Can she do that to Glenda? Keith probably wasn't even seeing Amanda. But he was seeing someone. Olivia looks at her own husband, who must surely still be a suspect, and knows that they must.

"If you go to the police," she says, "you'll have to tell them how you know. You'll have to tell them that Raleigh broke into their house, too—and looked in his computer."

"I won't. I won't tell them how I know."

"That's so naive, Paul. If they seize Keith's computer and find he was seeing Amanda, Keith will be a suspect in a murder investigation. *Everything* will come out."

"We'll just have to cross that bridge when we come to it," Paul says bluntly.

As she settles under the covers and tries to sleep, she can't stop thinking that if Keith did kill Amanda, then he was willing to let his best friend take the fall, and say nothing at all. She feels a deep chill, and she doesn't know if that chill will ever go away. She pulls the covers more tightly around her and lies in the dark, eyes wide open.

It's late. Carmine is reading in bed when she hears the knock at the door. How odd. She hears it again. There's definitely someone there. She gets up and slips on her terry robe, wrapping the tie around her waist as she descends the stairs. When she gets to the bottom, she flicks on the light switch. She peers out the window and then hesitantly opens the door a crack.

"Hi," she says, smiling uncertainly.

"Sorry to bother you so late, but your lights were still on."

"No problem. What can I do for you?"

"Can we talk?"

"Okay," she says. She steps back and opens the door wide. Then she turns her back to her guest, closing the door. Everything changes in a fraction of a second. There's a sudden movement behind her and then she feels something around her neck pulling tightly. It happens too fast for her to scream. She can't breathe and the pain in her throat is excruciating. She can feel her eyes bulging, her vision blurring as she tries desperately to grab at the cord around her neck. But her knees are buckling and now she's being pushed forward, her own weight working against her as she leans into the cord around her neck. She realizes with surprise that she's dying. No one thinks this is how they're going to die. And then everything goes black.

THIRTY-FIVE

Glenda is surprised to find Olivia on her doorstep the next morning.

"What is it?" Glenda asks quickly. "What's happened?" Olivia always calls first, she doesn't just show up unannounced like this. She'd texted her yesterday when Paul was released and told her not to come over. Her husband has been released without charge—why does she seem so distraught?

"Are you alone?" Olivia asks nervously.

"Yes, they've gone already. Come in," Glenda says.

"There's something I have to talk to you about," Olivia says, not meeting her eye.

Glenda starts to feel apprehensive. "Okay."

They sit down in the kitchen. "Do you want coffee?" Glenda asks.

"No."

"Olivia, what is it? You're freaking me out."

"The detectives matched Raleigh's fingerprints to some found in the Pierces' house," Olivia says. "He's been charged with breaking and entering."

"Oh, no," Glenda says.

"But that's not why I'm here," Olivia says. "Raleigh told us some things yesterday." She hesitates and then comes out with it. "He told us that he broke into your house. The night you and Keith were over for dinner."

Glenda is shocked. Her mood changes abruptly. "Why would he do that?" she asks.

"I'm so, so sorry, Glenda."

Everything about Olivia is begging for forgiveness. She looks abject. But Glenda feels betrayed, violated. She had no idea that Raleigh might have broken into *their* house. That's different. All the smooth, glib assurances fall away. Now what she's thinking is, *How dare he?* She doesn't say, *Oh, that's okay, Olivia. I know how upsetting this must be for you. Please don't worry about it.* She doesn't try to make it better. She doesn't say anything. She folds her arms in front of her chest, not even aware of how defensive she looks.

"I don't know why he did it," Olivia says. "Just teenage stupidity, I guess—you said it yourself. Teenagers do stupid things."

They're sitting at the kitchen table, across from one another. It feels awkward, although they've sat here together a hundred times. "Okay, thanks for telling me," Glenda says finally. "I guess there's no real harm done, is there?" She says it rather grudgingly, and she's pretty sure Olivia knows how she really feels.

But there's something in Olivia's face, and Glenda knows that there's more coming. What is Olivia afraid to tell her? Because she looks frightened to death. "There's something else, isn't there?" Glenda says.

Olivia nods. Her face is pale, her lips are quivering, and she looks so sorry that Glenda almost forgives her in advance. Whatever it is, it can't be that bad, Glenda thinks.

"You know Raleigh was snooping around on people's computers," Olivia begins.

Glenda's sure there's nothing on their computers they need to worry about. She and Keith share the same home computer. What is Olivia getting at?

"He found some emails on your computer. . . ."

"What emails?" Glenda asks sharply.

"Emails that show that Keith's been having an affair."

Glenda feels like she's been kicked in the stomach. For a moment she can hardly breathe. "No," she says. "Raleigh's lying. There are no such emails. Why would he say such a thing?"

"I don't think he's lying," Olivia says carefully.

"You *know* he's a liar," Glenda snaps back. "He told you he was at the movies when he was out breaking into houses. Why do you even believe him?"

"Why would he lie about it?" Olivia says. "He's not saying it to get himself out of trouble. Why would he make it up?"

"I don't know," Glenda says, at a loss. "But I use that computer all the time. And I even admit—I do look through Keith's emails some-times. And it's all work stuff. There's nothing there to any other woman. If there were, I'd know."

Olivia looks even more uncomfortable and says, "Raleigh says they were hidden. You have to know what to look for. And Raleigh knows."

Suddenly Glenda knows it must be true. Hidden files. How could she have been so stupid, so blind? She shakes her head, she can't even speak. She wants to kill him.

"I'm so sorry, Glenda. But I thought you should know."

Finally Glenda finds her voice. "Who is it? Is it anyone we know?"

Now Olivia shakes her head. "I don't know. Raleigh says it was a made-up name."

"That son of a bitch," Glenda says.

"Do you think," Olivia says, venturing cautiously, as if over thin ice, "that he might have been seeing Amanda?"

Glenda turns cold eyes on Olivia. "Amanda. Why would you ask that?"

"I don't know," Olivia says quickly. "He probably barely knew her."

"Then why mention her?"

Olivia shakes her head, backtracking. "I'm sorry, I shouldn't have."

"Maybe you should leave, Olivia," Glenda says.

"Don't hate me, Glenda, please," Olivia begs. "I didn't want to tell you, but I thought if it was me, I'd want to know."

Glenda replies acidly, "Or maybe you thought you could shift the attention away from Paul, is that it? One more possible suspect. Are you going to tell the police about this?" She looks at Olivia's face. "My God, you *are* going to tell the police!"

Olivia sits in front of her, biting her lips.

"Get out," Glenda says.

Olivia scrambles to her feet.

Glenda doesn't even get out of her chair as Olivia turns to leave. Glenda hears the front door close, and then the house is silent. She feels terribly alone.

For a long time she doesn't move. Then she springs from her chair and climbs the stairs to the spare bedroom they use as an office. She sits down at the desk and turns on the computer. She tries everything she can think of, which isn't much. She can't find the hidden emails. But she believes that they're there. And though she wishes she didn't, she believes Raleigh is telling the truth.

Finally, fighting back tears of frustration, she gives up and collapses onto the spare bed against the wall. And then she reaches for her phone to call her husband.

Webb hears someone tapping at his office door. An officer pops his head in. "Paul Sharpe here to see you, sir."

Surprised, Webb says, "Show him into an interview room. I'll be right in." He sees Moen on the way; she's coming toward him down the hall. "Paul Sharpe just came in. Let's go." She changes direction and falls in beside him. As they enter the interview room, Webb hopes this might be a breakthrough in the case. He can sense the same anticipation in Moen.

"Mr. Sharpe," he says, having reminded him of his rights and turned on the tape, "is there something new you want to tell us?"

"Yes."

Webb looks at him inquiringly and waits. He doesn't look like a man about to confess to murder. And he hasn't brought his lawyer with him.

"I might be completely wrong about this," Sharpe begins, "but I thought I should let you know. I've learned that a friend of mine was cheating on his wife. And I think he may have been seeing Amanda Pierce."

"And why are you just telling us this now?"

"I just found out."

"How did you find out?"

Sharpe looks uncomfortable. "I'd rather not say."

Webb looks back at him, mildly annoyed, and exhales heavily. "Why are you wasting my valuable time, Mr. Sharpe?" He doesn't answer, merely looks stubborn. "What makes you think this man was seeing Amanda Pierce?"

Sharpe says nervously, "He knows our cabin. He's been there."

"Who?"

"Keith Newell."

The name is familiar. "Right, his fingerprints were in your cabin; we eliminated him."

Sharpe nods. "He and his wife visit us there every year."

"And you now think he was seeing Amanda, but won't tell us why you think so?"

"I don't *know* that he was seeing Amanda, but he *was* seeing someone. He was having an affair. I don't know who with. And he knows where we keep the hidden key. I told him, when he was out at the cabin last summer."

Webb chews the inside of his cheek. "I see."

"Look on his home computer," Sharpe says. "Look for the emails to his girlfriend. Maybe you can figure out if it was her."

"And how do you know about these emails? Did he tell you about them?"

"No." Paul Sharpe looks away. "But I know they're there."

Keith," Glenda says tersely into the phone. "I think you'd better come home."

"What? Why? I'm just heading into a meeting."

"Olivia was here this morning. She says Raleigh broke into our house. He got into our computer."

"What? What the hell are you talking about? Why would Raleigh do that?"

She hears the fear in his usually calm voice. She ignores his question. "What are you hiding on our computer? Emails to another woman? To Amanda *Pierce*?" Her voice climbs.

The stunned silence on the other end of the line tells her everything she needs to know. She could kill him.

"I'll be right home," Keith says, sounding panicky.

THIRTY-SIX

Detective Webb knocks on the door firmly. He's obtained a warrant to search Keith Newell's computer. The two men with him and Moen are tech experts; they'll get his computer and other electronics.

A woman answers the door. "Mrs. Newell?" Webb asks, holding up his badge. He notes the woman's pallor; she's clearly been crying.

"Yes," she says.

"Is your husband at home?" They'd already called his office, expecting to find him there—wanting to question him—but were told he'd been called home suddenly. Webb notes her reluctance to answer.

Finally she says, "Yes, he is."

"We'd like to talk to him," Webb tells her.

She seems to know what this is about. She opens the door without saying anything further.

Webb steps into a front hallway, and she leads them into the living room. "I'll get him," she says.

Webb wonders if Keith Newell is at the computer, hurriedly deleting files. It doesn't matter. They can recover just about anything.

A few moments later, Keith Newell comes down the stairs looking nervous.

Webb says, "I'm Detective Webb and this is Detective Moen. We'd like you to come down to the police station to answer a few questions."

"About what? Who are they?" Keith says, indicating the two silent techs.

"They're the technicians who are here to get your computers, laptops, tablets, smartphones, and so on."

"You can't do that."

"Actually, I can. I have a warrant." Webb holds it up, sees the fear in the man's eyes.

Keith Newell looks from him to his wife, obviously feeling cornered.

They leave the techs behind in the house with Newell's wife, and drive him to the police station. There they lead him into an interview room and advise him of his rights. He says he doesn't need a lawyer. He says he's done nothing wrong. "So," Webb begins. "Did you know Amanda Pierce?"

Newell looks warily at them. "Yes, I knew her."

"Were you having an affair with her?"

Newell looks as if he's poised on the edge of a precipice. The panic in his face tells Webb the truth, no matter what he might say next. But Newell says, "Yes, I was having an affair with her. But I didn't kill her."

"Tell us about it."

"We didn't want anyone to know. Her husband was very jealous. He made her life miserable at times. She wanted to leave him."

"Did you ever see her at the Sharpes' cabin?"

He nods. Exhales deeply. "Just once. The weekend that she disappeared." He stops as if he can't go on. His hands are shaking.

"What happened, Mr. Newell?" Moen asks quietly.

"I knew the cabin would be empty that weekend—I knew the family wouldn't be going up. I knew where they kept the spare key. Amanda and I wanted to see each other and I didn't want to go anywhere we might be recognized. Then I thought of the cabin." He clears his throat, takes a sip of water, his hand trembling badly.

"She told me that she could go away for the weekend, that she would tell her husband that she was going away with her friend Caroline, shopping. So she packed an overnight bag and I gave her directions to the cabin. She knew I couldn't stay all weekend. I told her that. I told her I could come out late Friday afternoon for a while but that I'd have to go home, and that I'd come back for most of the day on Saturday, but I couldn't just leave my family for an entire weekend—it would look too suspicious. She was fine with that. She was happy to spend time with me, but she also liked her alone time. She liked to have time to be away from her husband.

"So I went up there on Friday afternoon, around five. She arrived about a half hour later. I stayed for a while, but I couldn't stay too late. I left around eight. Everything was fine when I left her. I went home. The next day, I told my wife I was going golfing, and I went back to the cabin. The first thing I noticed was that Amanda's car wasn't there. I thought that was odd, because I'd brought up everything we'd need. I thought maybe she'd just gone for a drive. I was a bit annoyed because it's a long drive up there and back and I couldn't stay late. The door to the cabin wasn't locked. I went inside and everything was all tidy. None of her things were there. She'd gone. I found the key on the counter. You couldn't tell she'd ever been there.

"There was no note or anything. I checked my phone—there was no message, no text—but she'd already warned me that her husband had found her burner phone. I wondered if she'd changed her mind about the weekend, or maybe about me. Or maybe something had come up at home. Anyway, I waited around for a long time, until it was time to go—hoping she'd come back, I guess. But she didn't. And then I locked up the cabin and put the key back under the oilcan and just went home. I didn't know what else to do. I couldn't tell anyone.

"On the way home, I drove past her house to see if her car was there, but it wasn't. The next day I drove by her place again and her car still wasn't there, but the garage door was closed and I thought it might be inside.

"I had no way to reach her. My texts and emails would go to her burner phone, but her husband had it. I didn't know what to do. I was a mess, but I had to pretend that everything was fine. Then I heard a couple of days later that she'd been reported missing by her husband."

He looks up at Webb, his face haggard. "He's the one who killed her, I'm sure of it. Back then, the rumor going around was that she'd left him, because she'd told her husband she was going away with a friend and he found out it wasn't true. But I know she lied to him to be with me. I think now that he knew, and he killed her. But at the time, I thought—I hoped—that she really had just left him. After she was found—" He hides his head in his hands.

"After she was found, you didn't come forward with any of this," Webb says, not bothering to hide his contempt.

Newell shakes his head, looking remorseful. "I know. I'm not proud of it." He takes a shuddering breath. "Her husband must have killed her. She told me sometimes that she thought he was a psychopath. He wasn't the man she thought she'd married. He was manipulative, he played games. She wanted to leave him." He runs a hand through his hair nervously. "She'd send me texts, telling me what their marriage was like. It was—abnormal."

"What are we going to find on your computer?" Webb asks after a bit.

"Emails to Amanda."

"You hid them."

"Of course I did. I used a burner phone mostly for Amanda, but sometimes I sent emails to her burner from my laptop. I didn't want my wife to see them. If it weren't for Raleigh, nobody ever would have known any of this."

"Raleigh Sharpe?" Webb asks.

Keith snorts. "He broke into our house and found those emails and told his parents, who obviously told you. The little shit."

"I see," Webb says. "And what happened to your burner phone?"

"I smashed it to pieces and threw them in a passing garbage truck."

After a moment's pause, Webb asks, "Did you know about the other men she was seeing?"

"Amanda? She wasn't seeing any other men. Just me."

Webb can't believe the man's gullibility, or perhaps it's his ego. "Seriously? You didn't know? She was meeting someone else at the Paradise Hotel, quite regularly. We have video evidence of it."

Newell's face drops and he looks away. "No." He asks, "Who?"

"Larry Harris." Webb feels a certain satisfaction at the look on Newell's face. "How do we know that *you* weren't the jealous one?" Webb asks. "You were at the cabin with her that Friday. You went back again on Saturday. She hasn't been seen since that Friday. As far as we know, you were the last one to see her alive. You knew she'd told her husband she was with Caroline, that it would look like she'd simply left. Did you know she was pregnant? Did that not fit with your plans? Did you argue about it?"

Newell looks back at him in growing fear. "No. I mean, yes, I knew she was pregnant. But we didn't argue about it. She was going to terminate it."

"I'm not sure I believe you," Webb says.

"I want a lawyer," Newell says, his voice frightened.

Webb gets up to leave the interview room and signals to Moen to join him. He sends an officer in to facilitate Keith Newell's call to his lawyer. They'll let him sweat and shake while he waits for his lawyer to arrive.

Glenda paces restlessly around her house. The two techs left long ago, taking all of their computers and electronics with them. She's terrified. Keith told her he'd deleted the emails, but she's afraid that isn't good enough; she's pretty sure that the police know how to recover deleted files. That's what they do.

Keith has been gone for hours. She doesn't know what's happening and it's driving her mad. They obviously suspect him of murdering Amanda. He was seeing her; he admitted it to her and will probably admit it to them. They'll find the emails. They'll charge him and try him for murder. What will she tell their son?

She thinks regretfully of Olivia. She has never needed a friend more than she does at this moment, but Olivia's the last person she wants to talk to right now.

When Adam gets home from school, Glenda is waiting for him. He drops his heavy backpack to the floor just inside the front door with a familiar thud, and sweeps past her on his way directly to the kitchen for something to eat. He doesn't even seem to register that she's standing there.

"Adam," she says. She follows him into the kitchen. "We need to talk." He opens the fridge door and then looks over his shoulder at her warily. She swallows. "Your father is down at the police station." He goes still as a stone. "He's being questioned about Amanda Pierce."

A look of dread comes over her son's face. There's a drawn-out silence. "They're questioning everybody, though, right?" Adam says.

"Yes."

"They'll let him go," Adam says. "Like Raleigh's dad. They let him go."

"I don't know," she says, her voice tight. "I don't know what's going on at the station. But the police took your father's computer away."

Adam stands completely still for a moment longer, his face pale. Then he turns away from her abruptly and leaves to go upstairs. "Wait, Adam, I need to talk to you."

But he's taking the stairs two at a time.

Raleigh is a wreck. He's the one who saw Keith Newell's emails. Because of him, his dad went to the police. Because of him, Keith Newell is sitting in the police station, probably suspected of murder. Raleigh just got a frantic text from Adam.

Raleigh finally got his cell phone back from his parents after he told them the truth about the break-ins and swore he was done with hacking. But now he almost wishes they hadn't given it back to him. He stares at the text again. Well, what did he expect? He knew that as soon as he told the truth about Adam's dad, his parents might go to the police. He didn't feel like he had a choice, with his own dad still under suspicion of murder. Raleigh knows that Keith Newell is an asshole, but could he actually be a murderer? It's less outrageous than the possibility of his own father being a murderer.

He looks again at Adam's text, then tosses the phone aside.

He won't be able to contain it. It will all come out now, that he broke into the Newells' house and their computer, too. If Adam's dad goes on trial, Raleigh will have to testify about those emails. Everyone will know. Raleigh could be in big trouble. But if Keith Newell killed Amanda Pierce, at least his own father will be free.

Webb enters the interview room again, late that afternoon, Moen behind him. Keith Newell now has his lawyer beside him.

They resume the interview. Newell stubbornly shakes his head back and forth. "I didn't kill her. When I left her there Friday evening she was fine. When I came back on Saturday, at around ten thirty in the morning, she was already gone. Everything was cleaned up. I thought she'd changed her mind. I had no idea what had happened to her." He stifles a sob, the exhaustion and the strain getting to him. "I knew something was wrong as soon as I saw her car was gone. I tried to open the door but it was locked. I got the—" He stops suddenly.

Webb feels Moen snapping to attention beside him. "It was locked," Webb repeats into the silence.

"No," Newell says quickly, shaking his head. "I'm sorry, I'm tired. It wasn't locked. I walked right in and saw that the place was empty."

"You said it was locked. *I got the*—you were going to say you got the key, is that right?" Webb says.

"It was definitely not locked," Newell repeats. "I went right in and the key was on the counter." He looks at his lawyer, seems to signal something to him with his eyes.

"No more questions," the lawyer says. "My client is tired. That's it for now." The lawyer stands up. "Are you going to detain him?"

"Yes," Webb says. "We certainly are."

Olivia arrives at Glenda's door. It's late, after ten o'clock. The street is dark, and it's cold out. She pulls her coat closer. She's tried calling, but Glenda isn't picking up the phone. Olivia knows she's home; Raleigh told her that Adam has been texting him because he's worried about his mom, and asking him to send his mother over to help. So she's not exactly imposing; she's been invited over. But she's nervous because she's pretty sure Glenda won't want to see her.

Glenda doesn't answer the door. Olivia rings the bell again. Finally she hears the sound of footsteps. The door opens, but it's not Glenda there, it's Adam. He looks distraught. And maybe not completely sober. She can smell liquor on his sixteen-year-old breath. It makes her heart sink. She steps inside, into darkness. "Where's your mother?"

He nods with his head toward the living room. She steps farther into the house, not stopping to take off her jacket. She sees Glenda sitting in the darkened living room. Olivia automatically reaches for the light switch. The light floods the room and Glenda blinks, as if she's become unused to light. She might have been sitting here for hours.

"Glenda, are you all right?" Olivia asks anxiously. She's never seen Glenda look like this. Her face is haggard. Usually she's pretty resilient, even in times of crisis; she's the one who holds the family together. Olivia glances at Adam, who is staring at his mother. He seems to be swaying slightly on his feet. Olivia feels the weight of it all pressing on her chest. How has everything come to this? She steps forward until she's closer. "Glenda," she says. "I'm here." Her voice breaks. Glenda is her closest friend. How can this be happening to her, to her family? To all of them? "I'm so sorry."

Glenda finally looks up at her and says, "It's not your fault."

Adam stands watching, swaying. "Why don't you go back upstairs, Adam," his mother says. Adam flees, obviously relieved.

"It's going to be okay," Olivia says, and sits down on the sofa next to her. She doesn't believe it, but she doesn't know what else to say. She remembers Glenda sitting beside her in the police station that day, when their positions were reversed. She wants to comfort her. "They've been questioning everybody, you know that. They'll talk to Keith and then they'll let him go, just like Larry, like Paul. He didn't kill Amanda. You know that." But she's thinking, *It's someone we know.* And truthfully, she thinks it might be Keith.

For a moment Glenda doesn't answer. Then she says, "He's been there a long time."

"They kept Paul for a long time, and then they let him go."

Glenda whispers, "I'm so worried about Adam."

Olivia nods. She's almost afraid to ask, but she must. She must know. "Did you find out who Keith was seeing?"

"That's it, isn't it?" Glenda says. "We all want to know if Keith was seeing *her.*"

Olivia waits for the answer. When Glenda falls silent, Olivia says, her voice a whisper, "Was he?"

Glenda lowers her voice to a whisper, too. "Keith told me, before the police came. He admitted he was seeing her. He said he deleted everything from the computer, but they'll be able to recover it, won't they? And then the police will know. They must know already; he must have admitted it. It's been hours."

Olivia feels the blood pounding in her ears, terrified of what she might hear next.

Glenda leans toward Olivia and says, "Keith says he didn't kill her. But I don't know if I believe him."

Olivia looks back at her, remembering her own doubts about her own husband, her heart breaking for Glenda.

THIRTY-SEVEN

Webb paces his office while Moen sits tiredly in the chair opposite his desk and watches him. It's late. But they've got two people being held in the cells—Robert Pierce, who's been detained since the day before and who must soon be charged or released, and Keith Newell. "Newell slipped up when he said the door to the cabin was locked," Webb says. "Before, he said the door was unlocked and the key was left on the counter." Webb stops pacing and looks at Moen. "That's what he wants us to believe. Why would he lie about that?"

"Maybe he *was* just confused, like he says," Moen says.

But Webb knows they both believe that Keith Newell slipped up—it was obvious. Why else the backpedaling, and the sudden, silent plea to his lawyer to stop the proceedings? "You don't believe that either," Webb says with a snort.

"No, I don't," Moen admits. "I think he made a mistake in there a little while ago, and he knows it."

"He says he arrived before she did on that Friday," Webb says. "So he probably retrieved the key from under the oilcan in the shed before she got there. She probably didn't know about the hiding place. He never said she did."

Moen is nodding. "And he left the key with her, because she was staying, and then he came back, and if it was locked—"

"And he had to get the key—he would get it from the usual hiding place." Webb looks down at his notes. "He said, *I tried to open the door but it was locked. I got the*—and then he stopped." Webb continues. "If the key was hidden somewhere else, he wouldn't have known where to find it."

"He's protecting someone," Moen says.

"Whoever killed Amanda Pierce must have known that the spare key was kept under the can in the shed, and put it back there. Keith came back the next day, found the door locked, and automatically went to the shed for the key. But afterward he must have realized that the only other people who knew about that hiding place were the Sharpes. Robert Pierce didn't know about the hiding place."

"Unless Pierce saw Newell pick up the key."

Webb considers. "If Pierce was there, hiding, watching, he might have seen him go into the shed, but he certainly wouldn't have been able to see him get the key from under the oilcan. It's way inside the shed, against the wall. He might figure out the key was kept in the shed, but not where."

"Newell is trying to protect Paul Sharpe."

Webb nods. "What if Sharpe somehow knew that they would be using the cabin that weekend? What if he came up to the cabin after Newell left, knowing that Amanda would be there? He kills her, cleans everything up, dumps her body and car in the lake—and gets home in the middle of the night." Webb exhales loudly. "Newell goes up the next day, finds the place deserted and locked, the key under the can."

Moen says, "Sharpe must have been rattled, not thinking clearly.

He forgets Newell will come back the next day and find the key in the usual hiding place—a dead giveaway that he'd been there."

Webb nods again. "Then Newell would be rattled himself. He wouldn't have known what happened, but he must have realized that Sharpe had at least been there. When we questioned him, he knew that if he said the door was unlocked and the key was left on the counter, it meant anybody might have killed her—from her husband to a complete stranger."

"Right."

"Pierce wouldn't have known where to put the key," Webb says. "We're going to have to release him."

"I wonder how long Keith Newell has known," Moen muses, "that his best friend is a murderer?"

Friday morning they head in to interview Keith Newell again. "I want one more shot at him, then we'll talk to Paul Sharpe again," Webb tells Moen.

Keith Newell has spent the night in a cell, and looks it.

"Let's get started," Webb says, flashing a glance at Newell's attorney. Then he looks at Newell. "I'm inclined to believe you," he says. The other man looks at him mistrustfully. "I don't think you killed Amanda Pierce, after all." Newell glances at his lawyer. "But I think you're covering up for the person who did."

"What? No. I'm not covering up for anybody. I don't know who killed her." He's agitated, but trying not to show it.

"I think you do."

Newell shakes his head vigorously, looks at his lawyer for support, and then turns back to Webb. "I don't know anything about it. I told you. I never thought any harm had come to her until you found her."

"And what did you think then, Newell?" Webb leans in close and fixes him with his eyes.

"I—I don't know."

"You must have had an uncomfortable time since her body was found. You knew *someone* had killed her—who did you think it was?" Newell doesn't respond, but his eyes look haunted. "When you got to the cabin that Saturday, the door was locked."

"No, it wasn't. It was unlocked, and the key was on the kitchen counter," Newell says stubbornly. But he won't look at him; he's staring at the table.

"Do you have a point to make?" the attorney asks. "Because we've been over this, and he's told you quite clearly that the door was unlocked."

Webb gives the attorney a hard look. "He also slipped up and told us that it was locked and that he had to get the key. And we think he got the key from the usual hiding place. Amanda Pierce was brutally murdered in that cabin. And whoever *cleaned up* put the key back in the usual hiding place. Who else knew about that hiding place, Newell?" He sees that the man's face has gone ashen.

"I—I don't know."

"You don't know. Well, let's see. Paul Sharpe is the one who told you about it, so he certainly knew, didn't he?"

Keith Newell looks at his lawyer, and turns back to Webb.

"Who else?" Webb demands.

Olivia recoils when she goes to answer the door and finds Detectives Webb and Moen standing on her doorstep looking grim. What can they want now? When is this going to end? Do they want them to help put the final nail in Keith Newell's coffin? She wants to be done with this; she wants it all to be over.

"Good morning," Webb says, all business. "Is your husband at home?"

"Yes," she says, automatically opening the door. She turns her head when she hears Paul coming up behind her.

"What do you want?" Paul says guardedly.

"We have a few more questions," Webb says.

"I've already answered all your questions," Paul protests. But he looks worried, Olivia can tell. He doesn't want to talk to them about Keith either.

"We'd like you to come down to the station," Webb says.

"What for? Can't you ask me here?"

"No. We want to interview you again on tape."

"What if I refuse?"

"Then I'm afraid we'd have to arrest you," Webb says, without batting an eye.

Olivia is suddenly frightened. Why are they back for her husband? What has changed?

Raleigh appears on the stairs. "What's going on?"

Olivia looks at her son in dismay, unable to find the words to tell him.

"We'd like you to come, too, Mrs. Sharpe," Webb says. "We have some questions for you as well."

They've left Paul Sharpe in an interview room, waiting for his attorney. In the meantime, Webb has also asked Glenda Newell to come in for an interview. They will talk to the two wives while they're waiting for Paul Sharpe's attorney. They start with Mrs. Sharpe.

She sits nervously in the interview room. Webb gets directly to the point. "Mrs. Sharpe, this won't take long," he says. "I understand you kept a spare key for your cabin hidden in the shed underneath an oilcan."

"Yes," she says.

"Who knew about the hidden key?"

She clears her throat. "Well, we did, of course. My husband and I."

"Anybody else?"

"My son knew." He waits. She says quietly, "And Keith Newell knew about it. My husband told him last summer that we started putting it there after we drove all the way to the cabin once and forgot the key."

"Anyone else?"

She shakes her head miserably. "No. I don't think so."

"You see, here's the problem," Webb says. He waits until she's looking in his eyes. "We don't think Keith Newell killed her. But whoever did, cleaned up the scene and then returned the key to that hiding place."

She stares at him in horror as the penny drops.

THIRTY-EIGHT

G lenda watches the detectives, unsure of how to behave, what to
do. The interview room is bare except for a table and chairs. It's
intimidating. This is where her husband has been spending so much
time. All those hours when she couldn't imagine what was happening
at the station—she's beginning to be able to imagine it now. He's still
here, somewhere, in a different interview room, probably just like this
one. What has he told the detectives? What do they think? Are they
going to tell her? Or are they just going to ask endless questions and
try to get her to implicate him?

"Mrs. Newell," Webb begins.

She looks back at him with dislike. She's angry at him; she's angry
and afraid. She will ask for a lawyer if she thinks it becomes necessary; for now, she thinks she can handle this.

"Did you know that your husband was having an affair with
Amanda Pierce?"

"No."

"He's admitted it," the detective says bluntly.

She looks back at him and says, "I didn't know."

"You're familiar with the Sharpes' cabin, aren't you?" Webb asks.

"Yes. The Sharpes are good friends of ours." She pauses. "We were out there in June of this year, and again in July."

"Do you know where the spare key is kept?" the detective asks.

She goes completely still. "Pardon?"

Webb looks at her more intently, and it makes her nervous.

"Do you know where the spare key for the cabin was kept?" he repeats.

"Spare key? I don't know about any spare key," she says.

Webb fixes his eyes on her. "Your husband told us that you knew where the spare key was kept."

She can feel the perspiration start beneath her arms. It's hot in here. Too many bodies close together. She shifts in her seat. "He's mistaken. I'm not sure why he'd tell you that."

"It's an important point," Webb says.

She doesn't say anything. She suddenly feels light-headed. It is an important point. She knows that. They obviously know it, too. What has Keith told them? She realizes now—too late—that she should have told Keith the truth. But she didn't, and now they are in separate rooms being interviewed by the detectives. They should have got their stories straight. They could have protected each other. But that's the thing—she never told Keith the truth because she couldn't be sure he would protect her.

Webb says, "Your husband claims that when he left the cabin at around eight o'clock that night, Amanda was alive, but when he arrived the next morning around ten thirty, her car was gone, and the cabin door was locked. He admits he retrieved the key from the usual hiding place, under the oilcan in the shed." He leans in close to her. "Whoever killed Amanda Friday night cleaned everything up and returned the key to the hiding place. An easy mistake to make," Webb says, "in the stress of the moment."

Glenda can't think of anything to say. It was such a stupid mistake.

"Mrs. Newell?" the detective prods.

But she ignores him, her thoughts falling over one another, remembering flashes from that awful night. Scrubbing the kitchen floor, wiping down the walls, using the cleansers she'd brought from home. Driving Amanda's car down to the bend in the road in the dark and deliberately sinking it. Checking everything over, making sure it was spotless and tidy. She was so exhausted by then that she'd locked up and, without thinking, put the key back in its usual hiding place.

It wasn't until Keith came home the next afternoon, looking so distressed, that she realized her mistake. Realized that he would look for the key and know that someone who knew where the key was kept had been there.

Her best hope then was that the car with the grisly body in the trunk would never be found; that everyone—especially Keith—would think that Amanda had simply taken off. Keith would assume that either Paul—or more likely, Glenda—had been there and had confronted Amanda, and that she'd decided to disappear and leave them all behind for good.

He'd never said a word to her about it; perhaps he was too afraid of what might have really happened. Beneath the confident exterior, he always was a coward. But then they'd found the car. The body. And they've been living with this between them ever since. Her knowledge, his fear.

If only they had never found the car, Glenda thinks hollowly. If only Becky hadn't seen Paul in the car with Amanda that night, they wouldn't have had any reason to look at Paul, to search the cabin, to find the blood. There should have been no way for this to lead back to the cabin—to Paul, or Keith, or her.

"Mrs. Newell?" Webb says again.

"Yes?" She must focus. What is he saying? She can't admit to anything. It must still be possible to turn this around. She'd tried so hard all this time to protect the ones she loves. Adam needs her. He doesn't need his father the way he needs her. Maybe she can still pin this on Keith somehow. It would serve him right, the cheating bastard. She thought of *everything*, except the key. "I don't know about any spare key," she says firmly. "I don't know why my husband would tell you that," she repeats.

Sir."

"Yes, what is it?" Webb asks briskly. He's got his hands full at the moment.

"There's been a report of a homicide."

Webb looks up in surprise. "Where?"

"On Finch Street. Number Thirty-two. Neighbor found her. Called 911. Victim is"—he refers to his notes—"a woman named Carmine Torres. Uniforms are on the scene, sir."

"We'd better get over there. Send Moen to me, would you?"

"Yes, sir."

Webb grabs his jacket and meets Moen on his way out.

"What have we got?" Moen asks.

"We'll know when we get there," Webb says.

They park on the street in front of an attractive gray house with blue shutters and a red door. There's yellow police tape across the front step, and a uniformed officer from Patrol Division standing guard.

"The crime team is on its way, sir," the officer tells him. Webb notices a woman standing off to the side, on the driveway, being comforted by another officer. She's probably the one who found the body.

Webb steps into the house. The victim is sprawled on the floor. The woman is wearing a pink terry-cloth robe and a nightie underneath. It's clear from the obvious bruising around her neck that she's been strangled with some kind of rope or cord. Not something thin enough to cut the skin.

"Do we have what she was strangled with?"

"No, sir."

"Any sign of forced entry?"

"No, sir. We've checked the house and grounds. Looks like she let her killer in the front door, and he did it as soon as she had her back turned."

"She's in her pajamas," Webb observes. "She probably knew her killer."

He bends in closer. She looks like she's been dead awhile—at least a day, maybe more.

"The medical examiner is on his way."

Webb nods. "Who found her—the woman outside?"

The officer nods. "A neighbor."

He catches Moen's eye and the two of them head back outside. They approach the woman standing on the driveway. She's not crying, but she looks like she's in shock.

"I'm Detective Webb," he says. "Can I have your name, please?"

"Zoe Putillo," the woman says.

"You found the body?"

She nods. "She lived alone. I hadn't seen her for a couple of days. I noticed that she hadn't picked up her newspapers. So I knocked on the door. She didn't answer. I tried the door and it wasn't locked, so I went in—and I saw her there." She shudders. "I can't believe it. She was new to the neighborhood, trying to make friends."

"Did you know her very well?" Webb asks.

"Not really. Just to speak to," Zoe says, adding, "She was broken into recently, and she was making herself crazy trying to figure out who it was."

Webb remembers then that Raleigh Sharpe had confessed to breaking into this house. He remembers the address, 32 Finch.

The woman says, "She was making a bit of a nuisance of herself, to be honest, telling people they might have been broken into and not know it. Getting everybody worried." She shakes her head, clearly unnerved. "It's terrible what happened to her. Nothing ever used to happen around here."

"Did you see anyone coming or going from her house in the last few days?"

She looks at him in sudden dismay, as if something has just occurred to her. She says uneasily, "Actually, now that you mention it, I did see someone."

Glenda looks up with a start when Detectives Webb and Moen reenter the interview room. They have been gone a long time, leaving her to stew in her own fear and anxiety.

Webb reads her her rights.

"I don't need a lawyer," she says, frightened.

"Are you sure?" Webb asks.

"I didn't know anything about that key."

"Very well," Webb says equably. Then he says, "Carmine Torres has been murdered."

She feels all the blood drop from her head; she fears she might faint. She grabs the edge of the table.

Webb leans in close. "We think you killed her."

Glenda feels herself blanch, shakes her head. "I didn't kill her."

"You were seen," Webb says bluntly. "Carmine Torres figured out what you'd done—that you'd killed Amanda Pierce." He looks at her for a long moment, his eyes on hers. Finally she looks away.

She lets herself fall apart. There's no way out. Another mistake that she will pay dearly for. She shouldn't have killed Carmine, the prying bitch. She must have been out of her mind to do it, blinded by fear. She'd acted on instinct. She hadn't thought things through. Finally she lifts her head, looks at the detectives, and manages to say, "Yes, I killed her. I was afraid she'd figured it out." She averts her eyes, defeated, and says, "I killed Amanda Pierce. She was having an affair with my husband."

Webb and Moen leave the interview room and consult quietly, down the corridor.

"What do you think?" Webb asks.

"What, you don't believe her?" Moen says.

"I believe she killed Carmine Torres. But I think she was lying when she said she killed Amanda Pierce. Her eyes shifted away at that point. Her body language changed. I think she's protecting someone."

"Her husband?"

"I don't think she'd confess to murder to protect her husband, do you?"

THIRTY-NINE

'm shaking so hard anyone can see it. I feel nauseated, but it's not just from the drinking.

The detectives take me into a room with a camera pointing at me from a corner in the ceiling. I know that my parents are both here somewhere in other rooms like this one. The woman detective brings me a can of soda. They introduce themselves as Detective Webb and Detective Moen; the other woman here is a lawyer.

Detective Webb goes over procedure but I can hardly take anything in; he turns on the tape. He says, "Adam, your mother has confessed to killing Amanda Pierce."

I look back at him, unable to speak, shaking my head. I fight the urge to throw up, swallow the bile back down. She told me never to admit what I'd done. But she never told me she would say that she had done it. I wish she was here beside me, to tell me what to do now. I lick my dry lips.

"She told us that she went to the cabin and beat her to death with a hammer and put the body in the lake."

I start to cry. After a while I manage to say, shaking my head, "No. I killed Amanda Pierce." It's such a relief to say it out loud. It's been like a monster inside my head, screaming to get out. I know my mother has been afraid that I'm going to get drunk and just blurt it out somewhere. I've been afraid of that, too. Well, she won't have to worry anymore.

The detectives look back at me, waiting. I have to tell them everything. "My dad was sleeping with Amanda Pierce."

"How did you know?" Webb asks.

"He keeps all his usernames and passwords written down in a notebook in the back of his desk. I got into his computer and found his private online email account. He'd hidden it. He always deletes his browser history so his email account doesn't show up. I saw their emails. I knew he was seeing someone, but I didn't know who because they used made-up names on their email addresses. She was pregnant. I thought he was going to leave my mom and start a new family with her. My mom didn't know anything about it." I swallow and stop. I wonder how things might have turned out differently if I'd told my mother what I knew instead of going up to the cabin.

"What happened, Adam?" the woman detective, Moen, asks gently.

I blubber out my story. "I knew he was meeting her that night out at the Sharpes' cabin. I overheard him talking to her on his phone. I wanted to see who she was, that's all. I didn't plan to kill her."

It's the truth, and I look at all three of them to see if they believe me, but I can't tell what they're thinking. "I took my mom's car. I don't have my license yet, but I've been learning to drive in her car, and I'd been out to the cabin lots of times with my parents so I knew the way. Dad told us he'd be home that night by around nine. I wanted to get there after my dad left and see her, find out who she was and tell her to fuck off. Tell her that I was going to tell my mother about her." I pause for minute, gathering courage for the next part.

"What time was this, Adam?" Webb asks.

"It was around eight forty-five I think, maybe nine. I'm not sure exactly." I take a deep breath. "I left the car in the road and walked up to the cabin and looked in the front window. I recognized her. I knew who she was. I'd seen her around the neighborhood. I thought about leaving then. I wish I had. But—instead I opened the door. She was standing at the back of the kitchen looking out the windows at the lake. She whirled around—"

I close my eyes for a moment, remembering. I'm shaking again; my eyes fly open. "She was smiling, probably expecting my dad. But then she saw it was me. I don't think she even knew who I was. There was a hammer on the counter. I saw it and I picked it up without even thinking about it. I was so mad—at her, at my dad. It just came over me. This—rage. I just—I lunged at her and hit her in the head with the hammer."

I stop talking and they all stare at me, as if they can't look away. I can feel tears running down my face now and I don't care, I'm sobbing as I talk. "I just hit her and hit her and I didn't even care that I was killing her—"

"How many times did you hit her?" Detective Webb asks after a minute.

"I don't remember." I wipe the snot from my face with my sleeve. "I just kept hitting her until she was dead." I stop talking again. I have no energy left to tell them the rest. I want to go home and sleep. But I know I won't be able to go home. The silence seems to go on for a long time.

Detective Moen asks, "What did you do then, Adam?"

I look up at her in fear. "I sat there on the floor for a while. Once the shock wore off I couldn't believe what I'd done. I was covered in blood. I didn't know what to do." I swallow. "So I called my mother."

Detective Moen looks back at me sympathetically. I decide to look only at her. She seems kind and I'm so scared, but I have to go on. I look only in her eyes, no one else's, as I tell the rest of my story. "I told my mom what I'd done. I asked her to help me." I start to sob again. "She drove up to the cabin in my dad's car. When she got there and saw me—I thought she'd hug me, and tell me it was going to be all right, and call 911. But she didn't." I'm crying so hard now, I have to stop for a minute. After a while I keep going. "She didn't hug me but she said, 'I love you, Adam, no matter what. I'll help you, but you must do exactly as I say.' She was wearing gloves and she handed me some gloves, too. She gave me a big black garbage bag and told me to put it over my head and poke my head through, so I wouldn't get any fibers on the body, and then she told me to pick Amanda up and put her in the trunk of her car. She'd brought me a change of clothes and a lot of plastic bags. Once I had Amanda in the car, she told me to go down to the lake and strip off all my clothes and put them in the bags and wash myself in the lake. The water was freezing." My voice has become monotonous now. "I put on the clothes she brought me. She scrubbed the whole place down until it looked like it did before. While she was cleaning I went out in the rowboat. It was really dark. I dropped the hammer in the middle of the lake and weighed down the bag of my clothes with heavy rocks and knotted it up tight and dropped it in a different part of the lake, just like she told me. Once everything was cleaned up, Mom got in Amanda's car and drove it and I followed in her car. She stopped at a bend in the road. By then it was very late, past midnight. I left her car a little distance away and then I joined her. She lowered all the windows and the two of us pushed the car into the water.

"It sank right away. She told me no one would ever find it. That as long as I kept my nerve and never said anything, no one ever had to know. And then we drove back to the cabin to check everything and to get my dad's car. Then we drove home. I drove her car and she followed me in my dad's car.

"When we got home, Dad had gone to bed. Mom had told him that she was going to her friend Diane's and that I was at a party. He didn't seem to question it, but I don't really know. I don't know if he noticed that both the cars were gone that night. I know he must have gone back to the cabin the next day like he planned. I stayed in my room all day, sick and terrified. He came home and acted as though nothing was wrong, but I could tell he was tense. We all acted as though nothing was wrong. But I'd killed her, and my mom knew, and I think—I think my dad might have guessed."

I look up at Moen and say, "My mom didn't kill her. She just helped clean up my mess. It was my fault. And hers—Amanda's. My parents were perfectly happy until she came along."

"Your mother is an accessory to murder," Detective Webb says.

"No," I protest. "She didn't have anything to do with it." I slump in my chair, exhausted. I look at Detective Moen. I'm too scared to look at Webb, or the lawyer. "What's going to happen to me?" I ask.

She frowns at me, but there's a grim sort of kindness in her frown, and sadness in her eyes. "I don't know." She glances at my lawyer. "But you're only sixteen. It'll get sorted out."

Webb sits back in his chair and watches quietly as Moen consoles Adam, his attorney beside him.

"Do you know Carmine Torres?" he asks.

Adam's face is puffy and blotchy. He looks surprised at the question. Webb is certain Adam has no idea that his mother has killed her.

He sniffs. "Yeah, I know who she is."

"How do you know her?" Moen asks.

"She came to the house, talking about the break-ins. And I've seen her around."

"She's dead," Webb says bluntly.

Adam looks startled. "I saw the police at her house—"

"She's been murdered."

Adam glances at his attorney, obviously confused.

Webb has to tell him. "Your mother killed her. To protect you."

Glenda raises her eyes as the door opens and Webb and Moen walk back into the interview room. She has been sitting here for hours. She now has a lawyer, who has been summoned and is sitting beside her.

Webb and Moen sit down across from her, and she can tell from their demeanor that something has happened. She steels herself for what's coming. Webb takes his time telling her.

"Adam has confessed."

She tries to remain calm, in case he's trying to trick her, but he starts telling her all the details, things that only Adam could have revealed. She begins to cry, silently, tears running down her cheeks, staring at the table in front of her. She'd finally understood, when she arrived at the cabin that night, about Adam's drinking, that he'd started because he'd found out about his father and Amanda.

"He's a juvenile," Webb says. "Amanda's murder was impulsive, not premeditated. He could be out by the time he turns eighteen." She looks at him then, feeling a tentative hope. "But you're going to be in jail for much longer."

Her body sags. She doesn't know now how she withstood it, how she'd borne it without cracking. *How had she ever thought that Adam could handle it?* Of course he confessed. She thinks of the terrible burden of hiding the truth from everyone, hiding what they'd done from her husband, her slow realization that he might have figured it out. Her fear that Adam would get drunk and tell someone what they'd done. Her dawning realization that she had made a terrible mistake.

She looks up at him desperately. "I just wanted to protect my son."

Webb says, "It would have been better for everyone if you'd just called 911."

Olivia looks blankly out the window. The nightmare isn't over, it has simply changed shape. Paul has been completely cleared. Adam has confessed. Olivia can't wrap her head around it—all along, Adam was the one who had killed Amanda, and Glenda had helped him cover it up. And Olivia had had no idea.

The thought of what happened at their cabin makes her shrink in revulsion. She will never go out there again. They will have to sell it. One more piece of her old life—gone.

And Glenda has confessed to murdering Carmine. The shock of it. Olivia imagines Carmine, dead on her floor. They say she was strangled with a cord. She tries not to think of Glenda throttling Carmine from behind; it gives her a feeling of vertigo. Apparently Glenda had seen Carmine as a threat—afraid that Carmine had seen Adam and Glenda driving home in separate cars the night that Amanda was killed, afraid she'd figured it out and would tell the police. Perhaps Glenda had become completely unhinged by then, Olivia thinks.

Glenda thought she was protecting her son. A mother will do almost anything to protect her son.

Olivia wonders if this surreal feeling will ever go away. She wonders how she and Paul will go on. He knows that, for a time, she thought he might be guilty. That lies between them now.

Her eyes well up. How will she cope without Glenda? She can't bear to think of Glenda as a murderer; she will always try to think of her as just Glenda, her best friend. She already misses her more than she can bear. She must manage somehow without her.

Raleigh will plead guilty to three counts of breaking and entering and unauthorized use of a computer; because he's a juvenile, his lawyer thinks he can get him off lightly, with community service. Raleigh has promised them that his hacking days are over. He's said that before. She's not sure she believes him.

Robert Pierce is delighted. As delighted as his cold, dark heart allows.

He hadn't known about Keith Newell. He'd thought, when Paul Sharpe was arrested, that he had been the secret second lover. But it was Keith Newell his wife had been seeing, his son who had killed her. It's good to know, finally, what happened. It's good not to be under a cloud any longer.

Robert recognizes that he's better off without Amanda. Things were becoming impossible between them. He'd considered killing her himself.

Robert watches Becky go out in her car. Now, he pulls on the gardening gloves, grabs the trowel, and goes to the back of the garden to dig up the buried cell phone. Everything has come to a satisfactory close, but still, he must get rid of Amanda's phone once and for all. He hasn't forgotten about that damn teenager, who might have looked in it. There are things on that phone that he really doesn't want anyone else to see. Amanda was smarter than he'd thought.

He's going to retrieve the phone and drive a couple of hours north along the river to a deserted place he knows. He's going to wipe it clean again and toss it into the deep water of the Hudson.

Robert sinks to his knees and digs around in the earth where he buried the phone, but he doesn't immediately find it. He digs deeper, faster, in a widening area, turning over the dirt rapidly, his breath quickening with rage. It's not there.

Becky. She must have seen him in the garden. She was always watching him. She must have dug up the phone.

He rises to his feet, trying to control his fury, and stares across the fence at Becky's empty house. Plotting his next move.